EVERGREEN

A Richard Rogan Novel

KEITH ALLEN

Evergreen (A Richard Rogan Novel)
InnerNinja Media
ISBN: 978-0692500583
First Edition, 2015

Printed in the United States of America

Dedication

For my parents,
who handed me the tools
to follow my dreams

1.

Another sleepless night in Evergreen, she thought as she stared at the slow-turning blades of the ceiling fan. She watched the fake wood wobble and bob as the blades revolved around the gilded housing. She willed her left ear to touch her left shoulder, urging her stiff neck to crack, the sore muscles protesting as she used her hand to deepen the stretch. She rolled on her side and stared out the window, watching the long branch of the cottonwood tree rhythmically slap against the panes of glass. It was the same branch that she had asked her husband to cut down the last time they'd been at the cabin. She wondered why she even bothered coming out here anymore. It used to be a nice retreat from the city, but now it was just a place where she was forced to sit alone and worry about everything.

The cabin had been in her family for years. It was situated on one of the long, narrow bays of Royal Pine Lake in Evergreen, just a short hour from the madness of Queen City. A mere 1200 people called the simple backwoods of Evergreen home. With so few people living on so much land, the cabin felt isolated, which normally was a relief, but not tonight. Tonight it felt lonely—and cold. She thought about her soon-to-be ex-husband off gallivanting halfway across the world with some Polynesian princess. At least he had signed the papers before he'd jetted off for the weekend.

The branch continued to claw at the glass. She had to remind herself that it was simply a branch—and not a giant grizzly bear with blood dripping from its jowls. The fan blades projected shadows across the red and green plaid bedspread with every lightning strike. She pulled the covers up closer to her chin and sighed. It seemed like it stormed every time she stayed at the cabin alone. She closed her eyes again and began to plead for sleep with the churning turmoil in her mind.

A thunderclap tore her from her negotiations; she sat bolt upright, half-expecting the room to be on fire. She rapidly scanned the room. She saw a shadow skip across the open doorway of the bedroom. She jumped out of bed and ran to the door. She looked both ways down the hallway. Nothing. A strike of lightning sent her shadow jutting across the floor. She took a few deep breaths and quick-stepped back into bed. *There is nothing out there—it's just your mind trying to rile you up.* Instead of staring at the ceiling, she now found herself staring at the door. *It had to just be a shadow from the moving branch, or a trick of the eye...right?* She eased herself back down into her collection of pillows and clutched one of them to her chest.

She had been coming out to the cabin since she was a little girl. She and her parents had made the trip out almost every weekend. Her dad had taught her how to fish and how to hunt, but more than anything, he'd taught her how to take care of herself. She smiled, remembering the smell of her father's Brute cologne and the way his hands always smelled like fish. She found the memories comforting. She was her father's daughter—it was going to take more than a couple slithering shadows to bother her.

After fifteen more minutes of lying awake, she reached over and turned on the lamp next to the bed and pulled the romance novel she had been skimming off the nightstand. The rain drummed on as she read about shirtless men riding horses. A chapter later, her head bobbed to her chin as she tried to push through the flowery dialogue. The book fell from her hands; her eyes closed. Finally, she drifted off to sleep, still unaware that she was not alone.

A gust of wind shot across the lake, slamming past the cabin. *Bang. Bang. Bang.* She woke with a start. *The stupid screen door,* she thought, rubbing her eyes. She wondered how long she had managed to sleep. She tried to drift back to sleep, but her eyelids shot open with each bang of the door. The wind seemed to have no intention of letting up, so she sat up, knowing that the only way to make the banging stop would be to go lock the door.

She rested her elbows on her knees, laid her head in her hands, and gently massaged her temples. Why had she come out here again? Something about it being peaceful? She thought about throwing a "For Sale" sign in the lawn in the morning, but her father would come back and haunt her forever if she got rid of the family cabin. *But this place already feels haunted,* she thought.

She lifted her head. She thought she had heard something. Her brow furrowed as she tried to drown out the rain. She focused, listening carefully to the emptiness of the cabin. A few moments later, a soft creak came from down the hall. She knew that creak. The floorboard just outside the kitchen creaked like that.

Someone was in the house.

She swung her legs over the side of the bed. All the weapons were locked up in the den. She eyed the room for a suitable alternative. She picked up the tall lamp and felt the weight in her hand. After removing the shade, she eased out into the hallway, her weapon shouldered. Lightning flashed, sending shadows diving up and down the walls. She jerked back against the wall, expecting any one of them to lunge at her.

She took a serpentine path down the hallway on her tiptoes, just like she had when she used to sneak out of the cabin as a teenager. She had memorized every creaky spot years ago. She felt the cold of the wood floor pressing into her feet with each small step.

She peered around the corner towards the kitchen. She could not see anything in the dim light of the storm outside. She felt a cold chill climbing up the small of her back and a gulp roll down her throat. *Maybe it's nothing,* she thought. *Nothing ever happens in Evergreen. No one even locks their doors.*

She slid against the wall, inching towards the kitchen, glancing back and forth down the hallway. She stopped outside the door, lamp on shoulder. She peeked around the doorjamb into the kitchen. The refrigerator door stood open, the small light from within sending a triangular ray of light across the floor. The package of steaks she had intended on grilling the next evening had been torn open, the contents splayed out in the light. Bite marks edged more than one of the sirloins. She slowly backed away from the kitchen. Her intruder may not be human.

Evergreen was well-known for its bear population. She could see herself taking a shot at a man, but a bear? That was another story entirely. She backed down the hallway past the bedroom and towards the banging screen door. She needed to get out and call the sheriff.

She shuffled her feet along the cold wood floor, intently focused on the hallway. She bumped into something. It wasn't hard like a wall, but soft—soft like flesh. Her eyes grew big, and she drew in a quick breath. She spun around on her heels, raising the lamp above her head. A man stared at her. A man she knew. She stopped her downswing, just managing to avoid cracking open his skull.

"Oh my gosh! You scared the life out of me!" she said, trying to keep her voice low. "I think there's a bear in the house."

He knocked the lamp away and grabbed her around the throat with both hands. She could feel his thick fingers constricting her flesh. The lamp clattered to the floor. She grabbed onto his wrists and pulled; he had the choke set tight. Her vision blurred. She shot her knee up into his groin. He fell backwards, howling.

She ran down the hall to the den, slamming the door closed behind her. Her hands shook as she tried to enter the combination to the gun safe in the corner. On the third attempt, she heard a click. As she pulled open the heavy steel door, the door to the den burst inwards, shards of oak scattering across the floor. She stared at the man standing in the doorway. His eyes glowed, like an animal's at night. He breathed heavily as he stared at her with clenched fists.

She reached for a shotgun in the cabinet. He crossed the room fast—impossibly fast. He smacked the gun from her hands. Then he grabbed the collar of her t-shirt and tossed her across the room. She landed against the far wall, sliding into a tangle on the floor. She could barely see as she sat up. She crawled towards the door, trying to get out of the room, managing to get to her feet. She tottered from wall to wall, trying to make it to an exit. She willed herself forward. She could feel his hot breath on her neck.

His hands found her again. He pushed her down. She fell through the doorway into her bedroom. She scrambled away on her back towards the window. His hands clamped around her throat. He pressed her to the ground. He straddled her. She felt the wood floor against her back. She looked up into his eyes, utterly confused and fearing for her life.

2.

The sun glistened off the crystal-clear water of Royal Pine Lake. Richard Rogan sat staring at a small yellow and red sphere drifting up and down with the nearly unnoticeable waves. The bobber taunted him. It had taunted him all day, bobbing up and down, never ducking under the surface of the calm water. Rogan lounged back into the nose of the boat, laid his head back and watched the big fluffy clouds float across the blue sky. At least the clouds were doing something, he thought. It had been weeks since his team—P.I.T, or the Paranormal Investigation Team— had anything decent to investigate.

After Rogan had driven everyone around him crazy with his listlessness, Troll, the muscle on the team, had suggested that they take a vacation up to Evergreen. Troll had figured that some time away from the city would do Rogan some good. Rogan glanced back towards the rear of the boat, regretting his decision to come along. Troll sat straddling the bench seat of the small aluminum boat they had rented. He looked like a giant mediating monk, perched on the precipice of nirvana. All he needed to do was turn in his cut-off jean shorts and black sleeveless T-shirt for an orange robe. He already had the bald head, which was currently covered with a large straw hat.

Rogan had never been much for the outdoors. He wasn't entirely sure how he'd gotten talked into this little boredom-fest. He glared at Troll, who had been whistling the same annoying song all day. They had talked a little, but mostly they'd stared at their bobbers, waiting for the fish to come. The irony of the whole thing was that Rogan didn't even like fish. In fact, he didn't much care for anything that didn't come between two buns or in the shape of a pancake.

"Troll! Seriously man, stop with the whistling!"

"Sorry, Rogan. Anything over there?"

"Nope. Just more bobbing. You?"

"Nope."

Troll seemed to smile as Rogan pointed out their lack of success. Rogan couldn't figure out why the big oaf was okay with sitting out in the sun all day with nothing but crispy skin to show for it. He could feel his white skin becoming darker and deeper shades of lobster as the day dragged on. He had slathered on sunscreen, but it didn't seem to be helping.

Rogan jerked his head towards the bobber. He could have sworn that it moved, but it just bobbed on. He sighed, and Troll began whistling another fishing shanty. Rogan considered charging the other end of the boat and tackling Troll into the water. Rogan realized that although it might stop Troll's whistling, he would likely just bounce off of the mammoth-sized man. Rogan himself was no slouch. He carried himself at a respectable six foot two and weighed a lean 240 pounds. But even with his considerable stature perched in the far stern, the nose of the boat still lifted slightly out of the water.

Another twenty minutes passed in the real world, which felt like 20 hours in Rogan's mind. He needed some action—a bite on the hook, a zombie lumbering along the beach, a dead mermaid, something to *do*, something to solve.

"Anything?" he asked Troll.

"*Nada.*"

"It's getting close to suppertime. Maybe we should head in and find out if this hole in the wall has a decent diner."

"Probably a good plan, since my famous beer-battered fish seems to be off the menu tonight."

After pulling in their lines, Troll, whose real name was Travis Olsen, started up the mighty six-horse outboard motor. The motor whined and sputtered in the water, but slowly the boat gained momentum. Rogan did like riding around in the boat; he wondered if he could talk Troll into just driving around the lake all day tomorrow. Rogan found relaxation in the gentle slapping of the stern on the water and the briskly moving pine-studded scenery along the shore. The duo pulled up to a wooden dock marked with their cabin number, tied up their craft, and headed the two miles into the small town of Evergreen.

Troll pulled his old blue pickup into a spot outside the Pine Side Diner. There were several cars in the parking lot, which Rogan took as a good sign. Rogan considered himself a bit of a diner connoisseur, mostly because he owned his very own diner back in Queen City, aptly named The Diner. Troll marched into the restaurant with Rogan right behind. They headed towards the booths that ran along the windows. Troll sat down in the furthest spot from the door. Rogan slid into the dark oak booth as Troll glanced out the window and smiled at his blue and white Ford.

"What is with you and that old truck?" asked Rogan.

"First off, it's a pickup, not a truck. Second, she's a classic."

Rogan threw him one of his *you-are-out-of-your-mind* eyebrow raises and grabbed a menu. The first line of the menu read, "Breakfast served all day." This was Rogan's kind of place. Rogan set down the menu and glanced around the diner. The booths along the windows were all made of oak benches with oak tables. The bottom of the bench looked to be a tree trunk sawed in half. The long counter that ran almost the entire length of the building was also made of logs. The stools evenly spaced along one side looked like hunks of tree trunk, many even had bark. A couple of tables crowded the back corner next to Rogan and Troll's booth.

A young woman in jeans and a plaid shirt came to take their order. Rogan went with pancakes, blueberry syrup, and two eggs. Troll went with a hot turkey sandwich, two orders of fries, and a chicken fried steak.

While they waited for their food, Rogan kept an ear open, listening to the local gossip. The small diner had fifteen patrons that evening, including Rogan and Troll. Over the sound of the grills and so many conversations, Rogan could only catch pieces of the conversations while still trying to maintain a coherent conversation with Troll.

"Well, I'm not surprised. Probably ran off with that good-for-nothing from the city," said a woman in her late fifties.

"See the thing about it is they don't make them like that anymore. Now it's all fiberglass and alloys," said Troll.

"Says he took off last night, no one's seen him."

"My baby though? She's made of steel, the way a pickup is intended."

"How long have you had it?" asked Rogan.

"Oh Lord knows, he's a troublemaker, probably ran off into the woods. Mrs. McChesky says she caught him poaching, you know."

"Well, she did just get divorced, you know."

"Wow, I don't know—what's it been? Ten years now at least."

Rogan continued to listen to facts about Ford pickups and conjecture about missing people while he scarfed down his short stack and eggs. By his mental count, a minimum of six people had gone missing in the last few days.

"What's all this talk about missing people?" Rogan asked softly when the waitress returned to fill his milk.

"Oh I know. It's the strangest thing. A bunch of people just up and left."

"And you sure they just left...on their own?"

"I don't know. Not sure what else could have happened, but seems like several of them left in a hurry because they left all their belongings and food lying out. Which up here in bear country, you just do not do."

It seemed highly unlikely that a half-dozen people had decided to leave in a hurry, even more unlikely that they took nothing with them. Rogan swirled a swig of milk around in his mouth, letting the information bounce around in his mind.

Troll put down his fork and stared at Rogan. "We're done fishing, aren't we?"

✳ ✳ ✳

After consuming his pancakes, which Rogan judged to be a respectable 8 out of 10, Rogan and Troll walked out of the diner and down the gravel street towards the sheriff's office. The town was small, including the diner, a general store, a sheriff's office, and a couple of other small buildings. Rogan had to admit that it was peaceful, a stark contrast to the city.

"Wonder why they don't tar this road?" asked Troll.

"Valid question, and also how come it's wet? Didn't rain today."

"True, true. It's almost as confusing as why we are walking to a sheriff's office while we are supposed to be on vacation."

Rogan only smirked a bit as he stepped up on the wooden porch of the sheriff's office. Rogan opened the door and stepped through. Troll sighed and hunched forward; his massive shoulders barely cleared the jambs as he followed Rogan. The office was small, which was unsurprising considering the location and the seemingly infinitesimal amount of crime. There were two cells against the far wall and a set of desks facing the door; the one on the right was slightly larger. To the left of the cells and the desks was a door leading to another room.

The place looked like something straight out of an old western. The floor, ceiling, and walls were all constructed of twelve-inch plank lumber, sturdy, strong, and rustic looking. After a moment, Rogan heard water swooshing. A second later, a tall and slender man walked out of the door to the left of the cells. He wore a light tan cowboy hat with a collar of gold stars circling the lid. His head was down, the brim of the hat covering his face as he adjusted his belt. He wore well-worn blue jeans and a brown shirt. A large gold star affixed to the left pocket clearly indicated that he was the sheriff. On his feet, he wore a pair of cowboy boots that looked to have been through much worse than the jeans. He took another step and looked up at the two men standing in the center of his office.

"Jeez-us. You scared the heck out of me! Shouldn't sneak up on man while he's finishing up his business."

"Clay?"

"Rogan? What the... Why are you up in Evergreen?"

"I could ask you the same. Last time I saw you, you were riding a desk down at central, shoving your nose as far up the captain's ass as possible."

"Yeah, you know, Rogan? That city stuff was never for me. The politics, all the action. Too much for this guy."

Clay Stevens had been a rookie when Rogan left the police force. Rogan had always liked him. He had an easy-going attitude and was never afraid to put in the time. Before Rogan left the service, Rogan's father and twin sister had been gunned down in the line of duty. His mother died of a heart attack shortly after his father's death. He remembered seeing Clay out of the corner of his eye as he walked into the precinct to drop off his badge and gun. After the consecutive deaths of his entire immediate family, he just couldn't do the job anymore.

Clay had been a good cop, reliable and loyal almost to a fault. Rogan wasn't surprised he didn't make it, though—he didn't have the instinct for it, or the stomach. First crime scene Rogan brought him to had been a double homicide, a couple slugs to the chest of both victims. Clay wretched into the nearest dumpster the entire time they were on the scene. Even though he was a good-sized guy, he had a timidity about him. Rogan knew he would never develop the cold-stone face and hardened exterior to deal with the level of criminal that the city produced. After a few months on the job, Clay had transferred to citations and started dealing with paperwork; it had seemed to suit him better.

"Sheriff, eh?"

"Yup, 'bout a year now. I quit down there maybe a month or so after you...you know. Then came out here to stay with my aunt for a spell, and the sheriff here at the time offered me a job as deputy, seeing as he was getting on in age. He retired, and here I am."

"Good for you, Clay. You were a good cop, and don't take this the wrong way, but this place seems to suit you. Better than the city anyway."

"Thanks, Rogan."

"Not to get right down to business, but what's the deal with these missing people?"

"Oh not sure yet, eight missing by my count."

"Up and left...or?"

"That's what the locals seem to think."

"You know better?"

"Something you taught me actually. Coincidences are seldom coincidental."

"Wise words," said Rogan.

"Yeah, I don't have much for answers, though. I went and talked to neighbors, friends...nobody seems to know anything. Some people even seemed to be at a loss for what they did that night. Drunk as skunks, I suppose."

"What's the deal with the road?" asked Troll, staring out the window.

"I'm sorry, big guy. I'm Clay, you are?" asked Clay, extending his hand.

"Troll. Why's the road wet?" said Troll, shaking Clay's hand harder than was necessary.

"Quite a grip there, big guy. Well that's a little invention of one of the locals, actually. His name is Freddie, smart guy, very kind. He installed little sprayers all along the tops of the awnings along Main Street. Each morning, they turn on and spray water down on the road to keep the dust from flying up. Real good idea if you ask me."

"Hmm," was Troll's only response.

"Did you check their houses?"

"What? Oh yeah, I did. Didn't find much useful though. Couple places had their fridges wide open, food all over, others looked like a tornado had torn through. Seemed like they left in a hurry."

"Eight people on the same night? And no one knows why? Doubtful."

"I agree, Rogan. I'll be honest, though; the worst crime I deal with up here is poaching. I haven't had to deal with this kind of thing. Not real sure what to do."

"Well, fortunately for you, Clay, I have been doing some freelance work in this sort of area." Rogan handed Clay his business card.

"Richard Rogan, P.I, P.I.," read Clay. "What's that mean?"

"Private Investigator, Paranormal Investigator. I'm working a niche market."

"Well I don't think we have any para-whatever going on, but I could sure use some help, Rogan."

"Then you've got it," said Rogan as Troll audibly sighed.

3.

Tanya sat up, unsure where she was. She wiped mud off her cheek and spit out bits of dirt. Her head was pounding. She leaned back against a solid dirt wall and ran her hand through her long, golden-brown hair. She could feel something sticky and thick at the back of her skull. She pulled her hand back—blood. She squeezed her eyes shut and pulled them wide open, trying to lift her hazy vision. She could see sunlight above, but it hurt to look. She tried to stand, stumbled backwards, and settled for a crouch. She was in a pit. Branches and leaves were scattered across the dirt floor. She had seen a few of these pits before. It was a bear trap, used by poachers to trap bears. The walls were straight up and down, leaving her fifteen feet down from the surface.

She touched her lip; it had been cracked open, dried blood sticking to the wound. Other than that, she seemed to be in one piece, which was more than she could say for her clothes. Her shirt was torn and tattered. It held together enough to cover the important parts, but not much more. Picking at the shreds of cotton, she wondered if she *had* actually gone toe to toe with a bear instead of a crazy old man.

Tanya wondered how long she had been knocked out. She also questioned how she'd become trapped in a bear pit. She felt her throat, remembering the attack. A man she'd trusted had held her down, forcing the air from her lungs. She remembered his eyes, how odd they looked, how crazed.

Tanya shot to her feet, immediately reaching out a hand to the wall to steady herself. The man himself was lying on the other side of the pit. Presumably, he had been knocked out, just like her. She had known him her entire life. She'd even called him Uncle Vick when she was younger. Vick lived next door to the family cabin. He looked in on it while they were away, which was most of the time. He grew the best tomatoes in his garden. Tanya couldn't think of any reason that Vick, who had always seemed gentle and light-hearted, would suddenly attack her.

She did know how they got into the trap now, though. Vick loved to fish, but he was never much for the woods or hunting. He wouldn't have known how to look for and avoid a bear trap. Tanya's dad had taught her long ago. They used to spend entire weekends in the woods, her dad teaching her everything he knew about nature, hunting, and how to survive in the wilderness. She had no idea why Vick had attacked her or dragged her into the woods, but she did know that she had to do what her dad had taught her—survive, no matter what.

Her head was starting to clear. She picked up a large branch, which she wielded like a club. Tanya slowly paced towards Vick, focused intensely on his unmoving form. She watched for any sign that he might be faking sleep and just lying in wait to attack her again. She kicked at him with her foot. He did not respond. She poked him with her club a few times, but he did not so much as wiggle. Keeping one arm high above her head, branch in hand, she reached out and felt for his pulse; it was weak, but steady.

She backed away and looked around at her dirt enclosure. On the ground, she saw small piles of long prairie grasses. The grasses had most likely been used to camouflage the trap. Tanya picked up a handful and braided several of the long strands together, making a short piece of impromptu rope. She also picked up a long, sturdy-looking stick. Then she went back over to Vick.

Tanya put a knee on Vick's back. She slid the long branch between the crooks of his elbows and his back. She then tied his wrists together in front of him, using the grass rope. It wouldn't hold him for long, but she hoped it would be long enough that she could fight him off if he woke and came at her again.

With her attacker subdued, her next step was escape. She looked up out of the pit. It was hard to tell from her subterranean location, but from what little of the sun she could see she felt it was sometime in the afternoon—which meant she had been unconscious for half a day. She paced around the pit, wondering what she should do. She wanted to be out of the woods before it got dark. She thought about braiding a longer rope from the grasses, but she didn't think there would be enough. She smacked her club against her hand, staring intently at the hole that was standing between her and freedom. She looked down at the club and smiled.

Tanya leaned her weapon against the wall farthest from Vick and began to gather fallen sticks. She broke several over her knee and then used her club to knock them into the wall, creating hand holds. She worked her way up, each rung of her hand-hold ladder requiring her to strike in a couple more pieces of wood.

"Ta...Tanya? Is that you?"

Tanya grabbed on to her newest hand hold and turned her head to look down at Vick, who was now on his knees, staring at her. She gripped the hand hold hard and stared wide eyed at her attacker. She felt her foot slip off the rung she was standing on. She shot her other hand out, losing her club, but she caught a rung in time to stop herself from falling the six feet she had managed to climb thus far.

"Tanya? Why are we in a hole? And why the hell am I all bound up?"

Tanya got her feet planted on two rungs and looked down at Vick, her eyes darting back and forth between him and her dropped club. She was out of sticks. She climbed up, putting all her weight on the top rungs, but with her short five foot four inch frame, she was far from being able to leap for the ledge. She would have to go back down.

"Tanya? Seriously, what is going on?"

Tanya scampered down the makeshift ladder as fast as she could, rolled to the ground, and came up with the club in her hands. She stared at Vick with fire in her eyes. He looked genuinely confused.

"One step this way, and I pound your skull in," said Tanya.

"What? Why? Tanya what's going on?"

"Are you serious? You break into my house, knock me out, and drag me into the woods and you think I'm, what, going to be happy to see you?"

"Honey bear, I have no idea what you are talking about."

"Don't call me that."

"Really, I have no idea what you are talking about. Last thing I remember is going to the diner for some chow, and then I woke up in this hole. Where are we?"

"In a bear trap, smart guy. Nice move by the way."

"Listen, I don't know nothing about any of this. I need you to believe me. I don't know what happened, but it isn't what you think it is."

She looked hard at Vick, sitting there on his knees. His eyes didn't have any of the craziness she had seen in them the night before. He looked confused, and in pain. Tanya wanted to believe him, but she had been there; she knew what had happened. She would suspect that Vick had blacked out from drinking too many cold ones, but she knew that Vick didn't drink, and she hadn't smelled alcohol on his hot breath when he was pressing her throat into the floor.

"Let me get this straight. You want me to believe that you just went out for supper and then blacked out?"

"Yes, that's all I remember. Honey bear, you know me. I wouldn't hurt you. I've known you your whole life."

"Don't call me that! You don't get to call me that after choking me out, ripping my clothes, and dragging me into the woods. What were you going to do, Vic? Rape me? Kill me? Both?"

"What? No, of course not. I love you like a daughter. Please, Tanya. You've got to believe me."

"Only thing I believe is that I have to get out of this pit, and to do that I need to not have to worry that you're going to attack me again. I'm sorry, Vick."

Tanya twisted her upper body, forming the necessary amount of tension in her muscles that her brain calculated she needed to knock Vick out in one blow. He stared at her, shock drawn across his wrinkled face. Tears formed on the edges of the crow's feet by his eyes. She swung full force, but pulled her shot at the last second. The club whooshed, inches from the top of Vick's head.

"Damn it, Vick. I can't do it."

"Thank you, Hon...I mean, Tanya."

Vick had given Tanya the nickname Honey Bear when she was five years old. She used to spend hours running around the edge of the woods. She wasn't allowed to go in, but she was so mesmerized by the looming pines and the grassy root-covered floor that she couldn't help but dart right to the edge and play there. She would stand for hours and stare as deep as she could into the dark woods.

One day, after romping around the edge with one of her many imaginary friends, she'd decided to scare Vick. He was bent over in his garden, tending to his county-fair-winning tomato plants. She crawled through the long grass, quietly moving through the long blades, inching towards her prey. He didn't stand a chance. While he plucked a weed, Tanya leapt onto the short white fence that circled the garden and let out her fiercest five-year-old growl.

"Oh my lord, Tanya, you scared the life out of me. I thought I was being attacked by a bear."

He yanked her off the fence and tickled her until she cried. "You're too sweet to be a big ol' black bear, aren't you? More like, maybe more like a Honey Bear," he said as he scooped her up in his arms and carried her back towards the family cabin.

The name stuck. Vic rarely called her Tanya. Even going through the procession line at her wedding he'd called her Honey Bear, and he'd told the groom that if he knew what was best he would show Honey Bear a good life, otherwise old Vick would come calling. Tanya knew it was an empty threat even at the time; Vick had a hard time smacking a mosquito.

"Vick, I don't know what happened last night, but you did break into my house. You put your hands around my throat, and you choked me out."

"My lord. I'm so sorry, dear. I don't remember doing that. I...I don't remember a thing."

Tanya sighed. His amnesia seemed awfully convenient, but she believed him. She didn't want to, but she did. She looked into his eyes and knew that the man before her now, pleading with her on his knees in his red plaid shirt and faded blue jeans was not the man that had attacked her last night. She decided she would get them both out of the bear pit and back to town. Then maybe she could find him some help. Perhaps living alone had finally gotten to him, maybe he cracked, had some sort of psychotic break. It wouldn't be right for her to leave him here in a hole. She nodded to herself, walked over to Vick, and untied the grass handcuffs she had fashioned.

"Thank you..."

"Welcome. Don't make me regret it. We'll both get out of here, get back to town, then I'll find you some help."

"Some help?"

"Clearly, you weren't in your right mind last night."

Vick just stared at her. He looked like a scolded puppy dog. He looked up at her with sad eyes while he found his way to his feet. Vick was just shy of six feet tall, with thick gray hair. He always walked with a hunch, giving the illusion that he was shorter than he really was. His back seemed most comfortable when it rounded slightly forward, probably from leaning over in his garden and from years bent over a conveyor belt at a factory that made fishing lures. Before Tanya was born, Vick had been injured on the job by a machine on the line. It had left him with a permanent limp, and a hefty payday, since the machine had not been up to safety standards. A permanent limp that Tanya realized he did not have last night during the attack. He had shot across the den without his usual side shuffle. She watched him walk the perimeter of the bear pit now, his right leg trailing slightly behind the left.

"Gosh, your daddy would be proud, girl. This ladder thing you got going here, real smart."

"Thanks. I could use some help, and we need to get moving. The sun is setting."

Tanya climbed back up the rungs with her club, and Vick broke and tossed her sticks. She jammed the sticks in deep, making sure that she used the thicker ends of the branches. She was fine with the smaller pieces, but she felt they might give under Vick's weight. She was one hand hold from freedom as the sun went down completely. Fortunately, it was the time of year when the moon was in the sky by the time the sun set. She looked up at the cool glow of the rising moon that illuminated her escape route.

"We're almost there, Vick. Toss me one more thick one, and we should be good."

Tanya turned on the pegs, reaching her hand out, waiting for the stick to fly into it like it had the last few times. Vick was not standing at the bottom of the ladder. He stood facing the far wall, his hands hanging at his sides. Tanya squinted, trying to see what he was doing in the shadows. She stared, perplexed, as he seemed to be walking into the wall. She watched as he walked forward, bumped into the wall, stepped back, and repeated. She looked up at the lip of the pit; she might be able to make a leap for it at this point, but if she couldn't gain purchase on the grass surrounding the hole, she would have a fifteen-foot drop.

"Vick? You with me?"

Vick bumped into the wall one more time, turned, and stared up at her. He took a few steps towards the ladder, coming fully into the shaft of moonlight that pierced the dark pit. His face looked hard, cold. His brow was furrowed and his jaw set. He looked angry. He pulled in a deep breath of air and screamed as hard as he could up at her. It sounded like a lion trying to put the fear into a gazelle. Vick was gone again, replaced by Tanya's attacker from last night.

She turned towards the lip of the pit, crouched, and prepared to leap for it. She reached out for the lip as her left leg left the foothold. Then she felt herself being tugged downward, a hand grasped tightly around her ankle. The air whooshed out of her as her back smacked against the hard ground.

Immediately he was on top of her, pawing at her shirt. She felt hot saliva drip onto her face and neck. Guttural growls emerged from Vick's throat. Tanya reached out for a nearby branch. Her fingers wrapped around the small stick as Vick ripped her shirt completely off. She could feel him against her. He placed a hand flat on her chest to pin her against the ground and howled up at the moon.

Vick was not a small man. She never knew him to be overly strong, but the hand that was firmly planted against her chest held her stiffly to the ground; she could do little more than wiggle. The stick she managed to grab was small, no bigger than a large pencil. It was solid, though. While his hands were busy trying to keep her held down and tear her shorts off, she jabbed the stick at his eye. The first shot missed, jamming into his check. He growled at her and then smacked her across the face. This was not Vick; this was some sort of animal.

He went back to work on her shorts. He didn't seem to understand how they worked; he just kept yanking at them, which just pulled the elastic waistband away from her abdomen, which would then smack into Tanya's waist when he let go. She drew her stick back again, waiting for the brief moment when he would look down at her shorts at the top of his yank. She focused on his left eye, and then in one rapid motion, slammed the stick into his eye socket. He howled and fell backwards, grabbing at his face. The stick protruded from his skull. He fell backwards, landing hard against the wall. Tanya jumped to her feet, grabbed her lost club, and smacked Vick across the temple as hard as she could. He slumped over in a heap, unmoving.

Tanya crouched under the ladder with her arms crossed over her chest and cried. She had killed a man. He wasn't just a man, though—he was Vick. Uncle Vick, the man who taught her how to catch leeches, the man who loved tomatoes and always knew a good dirty joke. Now there he was, arms and legs twisted, lying on the floor of a bear pit. Blood ran down his temple and across the bridge of his nose. Tanya cried for a few more moments, trying to come to grips with what had happened.

She knew she would not be able to address her grief in the bottom of a pit. She stood up, gathered up what was left of her shirt, and tied it around her chest the best she could. She picked up the last stick she would need to climb out of the pit, clenched it in her teeth, and climbed the rungs of the ladder; the club in her hand making it awkward to climb. She reached up, knocked the last peg in place, and crawled out of the pit. She fell over on her back, exhausted, staring up at the moon.

What had happened to her peaceful sanctuary?

4.

Rogan sat with his feet dangling in the water at the end of the dock. He had barely slept. His mind continued to churn away at the mystery. Where had these people gone, and why? He couldn't help hoping that maybe there would be something paranormal about this case. Rogan had a firm belief in the paranormal, and he had seen many strange things, but he typically found himself debunking the paranormal rather than discovering it. More often than not, it was human influence at work, rather than an otherworldly force, and for some reason, he found that profoundly disappointing.

Rogan had experienced one unexplained phenomena in his life, however. He seemed to have a ghost following him. At first it had appeared only occasionally, but now he was seeing it more often, usually at a distance. Even now it glided across the middle of Royal Pine Lake. Rogan sat and watched the wispy form dance across the glass surface. It looked like an ice skater, gracefully twirling across a sheet of perfect ice. Each time the ghost appeared to him, it looked more human-like. Today, as it glided across the water, he thought he could make out the outline of its body.

Rogan had most recently interacted with his ghost at the infamous Amdahl hotel back in the city. The ghost had led him to a horrific murder scene—which turned out to be the first step to Rogan getting his life back. He had not told anyone on his team about the ghost. He was not convinced it wasn't a figment of his imagination, perhaps a delayed psychosis from the trauma he had suffered in his life.

Rogan wondered, as he watched the foggy form pirouette, if the ghost was the manifestation of his grief. Better than drinking, he supposed as he stood up from the dock. He waved at the ghost and turned, running smack into McKenzie. Her glasses skittered across the dock. Rogan lunged out and grabbed the thick black frames just before they hit the water.

"Smooth," said McKenzie.

"Hey, Mac. You guys got up here fast."

"Angus is a thorn in the side of safe driving. Glasses?"

"Oh yeah, sorry about that. Here you go," said Rogan after wiping the lenses on his shirt.

"Like your shirt is clean. Probably just got fish guts on my specs."

"Fish guts would require us catching fish."

"You guys didn't catch a thing?"

"Just a sweet case."

"Ugh."

Rogan and McKenzie walked back up the dock towards the cabin. Rogan glanced back over his shoulder; his ghost was gone. He listened to McKenzie, who he always called Mac, burble on about all of the ways that Angus had nearly committed vehicular homicide on the drive up. McKenzie was the only family Rogan had left, though they weren't blood related. He patted her on the shoulder as they stepped onto the deck of the cabin. Almost a foot shorter than Rogan, McKenzie was a fireball, and her personality matched the almost unnatural red color of her hair.

"So you seriously cancelled vacation for a case up here?" asked McKenzie.

"Yup. Missing people, vanished, no sign of why. Cars still in the driveways, homes in various states of disarray. Those people either left in a real hurry, or more likely, they were taken."

"Great, kidnappers. You sure do know how to show a girl a good time," said McKenzie as she pushed through the cabin door.

Inside the cabin, Angus was huddled over the coffee table in the living room. He was running wires to various pieces of equipment. Rogan could only guess their purpose. Troll stood leaning against the open entryway to the kitchen, eating a big red apple and watching.

"Hey, Angus. Thanks for driving up," said Rogan.

"Rogs! No problem, bro. You know I'm always down for a sick case."

Angus was a strange enigma. By heritage, he was half Irish and half Japanese, born in middle America, but spent most of his formative years in Maui, where he learned to surf—and talk. As far as Rogan could tell, the guy was a genius. He went to college and graduated with a doctorate in computer science and minors in a bunch of fancy technical things that Rogan didn't understand. All Rogan knew was that Angus was their tech guy, and he was awesome at it. He always seemed to have the latest and greatest equipment, and he always came through in the clutch, no matter what the request. Over the years, he had become a good, reliable friend who Rogan knew very little about. For instance, given that P.I.T did not pay well—or more accurately, at all—it was unclear how Angus came up with the money for all of the equipment he toted around. It was also unclear how he made a living outside of P.I.T. When asked, he had a way of blowing it off or changing the subject.

"Did Troll fill you in?"

"Not really. Mostly he just stood there and ate that apple. Doesn't seem too mellow today."

"Look, buddy. I know you are bummed we aren't out there not catching fish, but you know as well as I do that this is a good case. Whether you want to admit it or not, you want to do this just as much as I do," said Rogan.

Troll took another bite of apple and continued to stare at Rogan. The big man was an imposing figure, even chawing on a bright red apple. At seven foot two and 340 pounds of mostly muscle, he was intimidating, especially with his shaved head, muscled arms, and large yoke of a neck. He'd made all-conference every year he wrestled, and he won a national championship in college. Rogan always joked that Troll was the muscle, which was true, but Troll was also well-versed in forensics and the study of the occult. He recently completed his medical degree as well, which made him Dr. Troll to others.

"Oh, I just hate it when you big girls fight," said McKenzie, plopping down on the couch next to Angus.

"Yeah, you two need to hug it out or something."

Troll turned and walked into the kitchen. Rogan sighed, sat down in the recliner opposite the couch, and filled Angus and McKenzie in on what he knew thus far, which was not much. Earlier that morning, Clay had given him a list of the people who had gone missing. After some deliberation, the team decided to split up and interview the people who knew the missing people.

* * *

Rogan and McKenzie had already talked to several people before walking down Cedar Road. The road was narrow and unpaved, more of a path than anything. Huge tree branches waved over the road, casting the entire surface in shadow. Rogan noted the smell of the cedars that gave the road its namesake. The scent was mild and earthy, but very pleasant. He wondered if he should have spent more time in the great outdoors. Growing up in the city, he only saw small clusters of trees in parks and along boulevards. His dad had been beyond dedicated to the job. Rogan couldn't remember ever taking a family vacation. Once in a while, they would take a long weekend, but usually they did something in town, just in case there was an emergency that only "Big Mike" Rogan could take care of.

"Nice out here."

"Yeah, we should really get out more," said McKenzie.

"Nothing like this back in town," said Rogan, pointing up at the waving branches.

"How many we have left?"

"Two. Both lived alone, so we might be able to snoop a bit."

The pair walked up to the first house, a small brown cabin. Rogan knocked on the pine-colored door. There was no answer. He nodded toward the side of the house. Rogan and McKenzie walked around the house to the backyard. A small, white picket fence surrounded the property. With his long legs, Rogan took an easy step over the short fence. McKenzie opted to use the gate a few fence panels down. The lawn was well-cared for and recently cut. A series of raised garden beds ran along the back fence of the property. Many varieties of garden vegetables grew in the late afternoon sun. Two of the three beds had tomato plants, each with a different type of tomato: cherry, roma, beefsteak—or small, medium, large, as Rogan thought of them. Glancing around, Rogan plucked a small bright red cherry tomato off one of the plants and popped it into his mouth.

"Rogan!"

"Wow, you have got to try these. That is the sweetest tomato I've ever tasted."

"Are you seriously stealing someone's produce?"

"No, of course not. I'm testing them for clues."

McKenzie rolled her eyes at Rogan and headed towards the back door. Rogan snatched three more tomatoes and turned to follow. The back door had a small set of cement steps leading up to it. A screen door hung off its hinges; the back door itself stood wide open. Rogan and McKenzie stood silently next to the steps. The house was silent, so Rogan drew his Smith and Wesson 686+ from his shoulder holster and stepped into the cabin. Since he had gotten his Private Investigator's license, he had the right to carry a weapon again. The city had strict gun laws—not that they helped. Rogan often wondered if it would be better to allow anyone to carry a pistol, strapped to their belts like in the Old West. He liked having a gun again, though; it made him feel like he was back in law enforcement—doing something that made a difference.

He quickly cleared the four rooms of the small building and called McKenzie in. The cabin had a kitchen that led through a wide doorway into a living room. Down a short hallway stood a bedroom and bathroom. The kitchen was torn apart. Food was scattered across the counters, the table, and the floor. Rogan and McKenzie walked through the doorway into the living room. The sofa cushions had been torn open, leaving white fluff covering the carpet. An old television with rabbit ears hummed as static displayed on the screen.

McKenzie asked, "What happened here?"

"Looks like the place was ransacked. If we were in the city, I'd say someone was looking for something and tossed the place."

"Check this out," said McKenzie. She was in the hallway, holding her hand up to the wall. "Blood smear."

The smear started with a human hand print and smeared its way towards the bedroom. Rogan walked down the hall past McKenzie, following the smear. On the bed, two bloody handprints clutched the sides of a large pillow.

"What do you think?"

"It's weird," said Rogan, walking back to the hallway. He held out his hand and followed the smear back into the bedroom, naturally dropping his hand to his side as he entered the room. He looked down and saw drips of blood on the cream-colored carpet. "It's like the guy came home, hands bloody, stumbled down the hallway and then crashed into bed."

"You think the guy that was taken came back?"

"I don't know. If he did, where is he now? Let's check next door."

Rogan and McKenzie left the brown house and walked across the lawn to a slightly larger log cabin. They walked around the house. Rogan peered in a couple of windows; it looked dark inside.

"This person is supposed to be gone too?"

"Yep, Tanya Tucker, according to Clay's list."

All the doors were closed on the cabin. Rogan and McKenzie walked up to the side door that faced the brown house they had just come from. Rogan tried the knob, it was unlocked. He opened the door and listened carefully. He heard glass shatter somewhere within the house.

"Wait here," he whispered to McKenzie.

Rogan crept down the hall, his pistol drawn. He cleared two bedrooms and then came to the kitchen. He turned into the room, weapon whipping left to right across the room. A woman wearing camouflage cargo pants and a tan shirt hunched over a counter between the sink and the refrigerator. Rogan carefully choose his steps, navigating around raw meat and broken glass. Her brown hair was wet and pulled back in a tight ponytail. She had a large knife in her right hand. Rogan pressed the gun to the back of her neck. She spun around, bringing the knife in an arch towards his throat. Almost too late, Rogan blocked her attack with his forearm, sending the knife skittering across the floor. She backed up against the counter, looking like a caged animal.

Rogan asked, "Who are you?"

"None of your business."

"I'm sorry, do you have a gun pointed at me?"

"No."

"Then answer."

She furrowed her brow, staring harshly at him, and then said, "Tanya. What are you doing in my house?"

"Looking for you, actually. Rumor had it you were missing."

"Well, I'm not. How about you put that down, get out of here, and leave me alone."

"What happened to your neighbor?"

"How should I know?" she asked, her eyes slanting towards the floor.

Rogan had a knack for knowing when people were lying. Tanya was clearly lying. Rogan stared at her face. She was hiding something. She knew something about what had happened to the man in the brown house.

"Here's the thing, Tanya. I find you home when you're supposed to be missing, and I find your neighbor's house torn apart, with blood everywhere. You're telling me you don't know anything about that? I'm just trying to figure out what's going on in this town."

"Yeah? Me too, but I didn't have anything to do with the blood over there."

"But you do know something about what happened to Victor, don't you."

Tanya's lip quivered. She darted her eyes away from Rogan, and her right eyebrow twitched. *Guilt*, Rogan thought. Rogan hadn't noticed her hand sliding closer and closer to the sink. In a quick movement, she jerked her arm towards Rogan, sending a pile of silverware and dishwater towards his face. Before he could react, she back kicked him in the chest. He fell straight backwards, tripping over a fallen chair. McKenzie charged into the room in time to see Tanya whip a backpack over her shoulder and run out the back door, grabbing a rifle that had been leaning against the door jamb.

"Rogan? You okay?"

"Damn, Mac, she's good."

McKenzie helped Rogan get his red converse shoes untangled from the chair he had been launched over, and then he got to his feet. He holstered his gun and jogged to the back door. He could just make out the bobbing of Tanya's ponytail as she disappeared into the woods.

"Who was that?"

"Tanya Tucker."

"Thought she was missing?"

"Me too. Let's see if we can catch her."

Mckenzie nodded, and the two took off jogging, hopping over a short fence and then through some tall grasses and into the woods. They started their hunt where Rogan last saw Tanya. Tracking was not on Rogan's list of skills, though. They ran aimlessly into the woods, trying to find a footprint. After fifteen minutes, they gave up and headed back towards the log cabin. They came out of the woods behind Vick's brown house. Rogan sighed and looked around.

"Hey Rogan, check this out," said McKenzie, kneeling in the grass roughly halfway between the two houses.

Rogan knelt down beside McKenzie and looked where she was pointing. The grass was laid flat, the long shoots broken. He looked towards the woods, and the track led right into the underbrush. "What do you think it is?" he asked.

"Looks to me like something, or maybe even someone, was dragged through here. Check out where it starts," said McKenzie, pointing back towards the houses.

Rogan followed the drag marks with his eyes, noticing they led all the way back to the log cabin. "I'll be damned. Let's see where it leads."

Seeming to have more natural tracking ability than Rogan, McKenzie led the way through the woods following the drag marks. They travelled deep into the woods, turning a few times to avoid large rocks and trunks thicker than any Rogan had ever seen. The deeper they went, the darker it got, as the canopy above blocked out more and more light. Rogan pulled a small flashlight out of his pocket and illuminated the area for McKenzie. After turning around one more large boulder, the trail ended at a hole. Rogan flashed his light around the hole. It was roughly eight feet in diameter, and at least twelve feet deep. Rogan and McKenzie knelt at the edge of the hole scanning the pit below. Rogan looked up wishing more of the sun's rays were getting through, but it would be dark soon, and the thick branches overhead were not helping.

"What do you think?"

"I've never seen anything like this," said Rogan.

"Me either. Think maybe it's like a trap or something? Look at all the branches and leaves down there."

"Could be. Wonder what they were trying to trap, and who they are."

"Shine your light over in that corner."

Rogan swung his light to one of the dark corners of the pit below. He ran the light along the outline of a body. It looked to be a man, lying on his side. He did not seem to be moving.

"Dead?"

"I'm thinking so," said Rogan.

"We should find out for sure, or at least ID the guy," said McKenzie, leaning further out over the pit.

The soft moss growing at the edge of the pit proved slippery. McKenzie lost her balance and lurched forward over the lip of the pit. Rogan dropped his flashlight and jerked both arms out towards McKenzie. He caught her by the ankle with his left hand. He dug in with his toes, but he was quickly being dragged into the hole.

"Rogan, Rogan! Let me go."

"No way, hang on, I got you."

"If you don't let me go, we are both going in this hole," said McKenzie, trying to wiggle her ankle free from Rogan's tight grip. "It's not much further, I'll be fine."

Rogan's waist went over the edge. He bent over, using his upper body to lower her further into the hole as gently as he could. She was right, in another couple seconds, they would both be in the bottom. He let go and scrambled backwards, barely shifting his weight in time.

Rogan swung around and peered down into the pit. He could see his flashlight sitting on the ground. "You okay?"

"Peachy, pumpkin," said McKenzie, standing up. "Good thing you have those monkey arms. I only dropped about a foot."

McKenzie picked up the flashlight and looked around the pit. She headed over to the man. She crouched down near him and put her fingers to his throat. His skin felt cold to the touch, and there was no heartbeat.

Rogan shouted down, "Dead?"

"For sure," said McKenzie, looking at the stick poking out from his eye socket.

"Maybe he accidently fell into this trap and the fall killed him?"

"Possibly, but it was a really unlucky landing if that's the case."

"Any ID?"

McKenzie sighed and dug into the dead man's back pocket. She pulled out a wallet, flipped it open, and looked at the photo ID. "Victor Johns, organ donor."

"Well, we found the neighbor. Okay. We need to get you out of there and get back to town. Do trees grow vines? Is that a thing?"

"I don't think so," said McKenzie, turning her back to Rogan.

She opened the wallet to find sixty-five dollars. She slid the bills out and pushed them into the front pocket of her jeans. During high school and for a few years after, McKenzie had been a pickpocket and then a full-fledged thief. She'd always accepted the irony that she more or less lived with a family of police officers, but a girl had to look out for herself. She had picked up a lot of useful skills in those days, most of them learned "on the job," so to speak. She knew that Rogan thought he had ended her thieving ways when he caught her disposing of some wallets she'd pilfered behind the mall, but that wasn't the case. She just got more careful, and if anything, it had sent her after bigger prey. She had given up all of that years ago, but occasionally she still had the compulsion to steal. She couldn't explain it. Plus, the dead guy wouldn't miss it.

"We need some rope or something," said Rogan, getting to his feet.

McKenzie shone the light around the pit, looking for something she could use to boost her up. Her light traveled past what looked like a couple branches sticking out of the side of the pit. She moved the light back, and then up and down. Smiling, she stepped towards what she figured was a homemade ladder. She gripped the light in her teeth and started to climb. The ladder ended short of the top. She would have to make a leap to get to the edge. She had hoped to climb out and find Rogan utterly beside himself trying to figure out how to get her out, but she was going to need help with this one.

"Woogan," she called. "Woogan, over here."

Rogan appeared over the lip of the pit, looking down at her. He looked perplexed—the look suited him. She looked up and attempted to smile; it was hard with the flashlight in her mouth.

"Poow me up."

"How did you get up there?"

"Wadder."

"What was that?"

"Wadder, poow me up!"

Rogan laughed and grabbed her arms. She walked up the side of the pit while he pulled her back. A moment later, she fell over the edge of the pit, landing on his chest. She lingered on top of him for a moment, and then rolled off to the side, ending up in the crook of his arm.

"Well that was fun," said Rogan.

McKenzie stared up at the dim stars that were just starting to appear in the early evening sky. She glanced over at Rogan and sighed.

"Yeah it sure was. Let's get out of here before it's pitch black."

"Agreed, but how did you get out of there so fast?"

"I used the ladder."

"The what?"

"Ladder."

"Don't you mean wadder?"

McKenzie rolled to her side and punched Rogan in the ribs. He laughed and turned on his side to face her. Rogan stared into her eyes. She stared back into his shiny green eyes.

"Mac?"

"Yeah?"

"Can you put the flashlight back in your mouth?"

"You're such an idiot."

Rogan stood up and helped McKenzie to her feet. He took one last look into the hole and then turned and started walking away from the pit. They needed to get out of the woods before it got too dark.

"Where we headed?" asked McKenzie.

"Back to those cabins. We left Angus's van at the end of the road."

"Right, but you aren't going that way."

Rogan looked around. Apparently his directional sense was not good in the woods. He could always find his way in the city, but that was easier because it was logically split into blocks. McKenzie shook her head and pointed in almost the opposite direction from the way Rogan had headed.

After walking for a few minutes, Rogan suddenly stopped and pulled McKenzie down behind a tree. He cocked his ear and listened.

"What is it?" whispered McKenzie.

"I heard something, like a groan almost."

They sat silently for a few minutes. After hearing nothing but silence, they cautiously continued on towards the cabins. Rogan continually scanned their surroundings; he was sure he had heard something. As they rounded a large pine tree, Rogan saw movement. They ducked down by the edge of the tree and watched. About twenty yards off the path, they saw a man walking into a tree. Each time he bumped into the broad trunk, he would back up and try again. Rogan pulled out his gun and approached the man.

"Freeze!" yelled Rogan.

The man continued on bumping into the tree. Rogan got closer and closer. He grabbed the man by the shoulder and whipped him around. Rogan stumbled back. The man's face was covered in blood. Streams of it ran down his cheeks and onto his white t-shirt. His eyes seemed to have no focus, and his head listed slightly to the right. He raised his arms and lumbered towards Rogan.

"I said, freeze!"

The man shuffled towards Rogan, moaning. Rogan sidestepped before the man could make contact with him. The man kept on walking until he ran into another tree and started bumping into it like he had the previous.

"Mac, we need to get out of here, fast," said Rogan.

McKenzie nodded and they took off towards the cabins. As they ran, Rogan saw another half dozen people walking aimlessly around the woods. They could hear groans and moans as the people marched into objects or each other. The people seemed to be completely unaware of their surroundings. Rogan and McKenzie broke from the woods, ran between the two cabins, and down Cedar road, not stopping until they reached the van.

5.

Troll stood in the long, gravel driveway staring longingly at the lake across the street while he waited for Angus to finish questioning a resident. He could see a small boat anchored in the nearest cove. An older man with a tan hat hunched over a fishing pole. A kid wearing a bright yellow life jacket knelt on one of the bench seats, gently rocking the boat back and forth with his constant movement. The scene reminded Troll of the days when he used to come up here with his grandfather. His grandfather always seemed to know where the fish were biting and what type of lure to use. Troll could not remember coming home empty handed a single time.

"Bro, you really need to cheer up," said Angus.

"Huh? What? Yeah..."

"Come on, big guy. One more house, and I'll buy you a frosty one."

Troll nodded as they walked down the driveway and back out onto the gravel road. There was only one more house left on the list that Clay had given them. Troll touched the small bronze star affixed to the pocket of his shirt; he did have to admit it was pretty cool being deputized. He thought that was just something from old Westerns.

"Keep playing with it and you'll get hairy palms."

"You would know. You've been fidgeting with that thing a lot more than I have."

"Yeah, that's true, man. Just weird, never been on this side before," said Angus, tilting the star on his shirt.

"What side?"

"Oh, uhmm, just a figure of speech. There's the house."

Angus had a way of never talking about his past. Troll knew he must be hiding something, but he had no idea what it could be. Troll had not been in favor of putting Angus on the team when he'd sauntered into one of their early P.I.T meetings, but he had a lot of equipment. After a few years of hunting with him, Troll now considered Angus one of his better friends—a secretive friend who didn't share much, but a friend nonetheless.

They walked up the short driveway to the last house. This one was on the lake side, so the house with mint green siding and white shutters blocked the view of the pristine lake beyond. There was light coming from the front window. The team had been out all day talking to witnesses, leaving little natural light left for this last stop. As they walked up the steps onto the front porch, a motion light turned on. Troll threw up a hand to block some of the intense light, while Angus knocked on the door. They waited, but heard nothing from beyond the door. Angus knocked again. This time, shuffling came from the far back of the house. A moment later, the door opened a crack, revealing a short man with long white hair and a stubble grey beard. He eyed Troll and Angus through the narrow opening.

"Help you?"

"Yes, Deputy Rin and Deputy Troll. Here to ask you some questions about the woman that went missing," said Angus.

"She ain't missing any more. Please leave."

"Excuse me?"

"You deaf? She ain't missing. Thank you, but we are good here."

"Sir, there are a lot of people missing. We aren't aware of anyone coming back. Please can we talk to her? It might help us find the others," said Troll.

The door closed. Angus looked up at Troll and went to knock again. Troll grabbed his wrist and gave him a "just wait" nod. Through a reflection in the glass, Troll could see the man leaning against the door. He was chewing on his lip, probably hoping they would leave. They stood in silence until the man's head drooped to his chin. He turned back to the door and undid the chain.

"Well come on in then," he said.

"Thank you. Mr...." led Troll.

"Bart, Bart Jacobs."

"Mr. Jacobs, you reported to the sheriff's office that your wife had disappeared in the night. Now are you saying she's back?"

"Yes."

"Did she say anything about where she'd been?" asked Angus.

"She doesn't remember. She went to bed that night, woke up in the woods. No idea how she got there."

"So she came back this morning?" asked Troll.

"No, she came back yesterday morning," said Bart, looking down at the floor.

"Did she seem...okay?"

"Well, yeah, mostly."

Almost as if in response, a loud clang came from the back section of the house, followed by a high-pitched scream. Troll thought it was human, but could not be sure. Troll looked at Bart, his eyes the size of silver dollars. Angus had already reacted, taking a graceful leaping jump over the lavender-colored sofa.

"Don't," said Bart. "Don't go back there, please." He put his hands out towards Troll. Bart was a good foot and a half shorter and at minimum 150 pounds lighter than Troll. Troll raised his barrel chest and took a single step towards Bart. Troll set his jaw and stared down at the man, but he said nothing. Troll had found that the implication of violence was often more motivating than the actual violence. He could hear Angus stomping down a set of stairs at the back of the small house as he considered Bart.

"Fine, but I warned you," said Bart, stepping out of the way. Troll ran down the hallway and found a door swaying on its hinges across from the back door. The door led downstairs. The stairway was narrow. Troll found himself turning sideways to fit his bulk down the incline. Another clang sounded, louder this time.

"What the friggin' hell," yelled Angus from further in the basement.

"I'm coming!" Troll tried to move faster, but the narrow opening, which was also getting shorter, made it difficult to move. Another clang sounded, followed by a male scream, followed by Angus flying through the air and landing at the base of the steps. Troll squeezed through the final opening of the stairwell to find himself in a small, cement-block basement. The basement looked to be about fifteen feet by twelve feet. A furnace, water softener, and a washer and dryer were lined up along the far end of the space, while a series of pipes ran out along the ceiling and down into a central core. Storage boxes stacked to various heights sat on the floor. The ceiling must have been less than seven feet high, as Troll had to bend forward to avoid scraping his dome against the bare floor joists.

"You okay?" asked Troll, kneeling down next to Angus

"Woah, that was like getting pounded by a full-on Maui-sized wave."

"Is that a yes?"

"Yeah man, I'm kosher as salt. That chick over there though...way strong," said Angus, pointing towards the pipes.

Troll stood up, looking in the direction Angus had pointed. He did not see a woman on his initial scan of the basement. He took a step forward, looking to his right. Searing pain erupted on his left cheek. He grabbed at his face to find blood. A woman crouched low behind a set of boxes, fingers held wide, showing long, fake nails. A broken chain wrapped around her ankle. She stared up at Troll with wild intensity. Troll looked from the red on his hand to the woman and back to his hand a solid look of confusion on his face.

"Now ma'am. I don't know..." Before he could finish his sentence, the woman sprung forward, grabbed Troll by the shirt, and hurled him across the room. He cracked into the vertical column of pipes and landed hard on the floor. He was dazed, partly because of the massive trauma his body had just endured, but also because he had never been thrown before. He got up to his knees to find the woman crouched just out of arm's reach. She drew back her lips, showing her teeth, and growled at Troll.

"What the fu—"

She jumped forward and clawed his chest, leaving a large X of tattered shirt. She leapt back again before he could so much as raise an arm in defense. Troll looked at the wild woman, watching for her next attack. She wore a cream dress with small green flowers. Her hair was mostly brown, but starting to gray. She looked like she didn't weigh more than 120, and she could not have been over five and half feet tall. Her arms and legs were covered in bruises and scratches. It looked like this was not her first fight. Troll stepped forward, hoping to provoke an attack. It worked; the woman leapt at him again. This time he was ready.

He rolled hard to the side, grabbing her wrist as she came towards him, sending her flying over his back and into the washing machine. She bounced to her feet like she hadn't even felt the impact.

Troll crouched low, keeping his knees and elbows flexed. She came towards him. They circled each other, each looking for an opportunity. Troll felt like he was back in college, circling the mat, ready to take down the guy across from him. Though the person he was circling was usually a guy, and usually significantly more than half his weight.

As they circled, Troll used his peripheral vision to glance at the stairway. Angus was gone. Hopefully he had gone to get help. Troll felt confident that he could keep her at bay, but considering she seemed to feel no pain, he wasn't certain how long that would last. He saw an opening and went for it. He shot at her legs for a takedown like he had done thousands of times in his wrestling days. She anticipated the attack and lunged to the side. Troll face planted into the cement floor. He jumped to his feet and nearly knocked his head against a floor joist. She jumped into the air and planted both of her feet into his chest, sending him flying into the nearest brick wall.

She strode towards him, her chest heaving. Her eyes seemed to glow as she growled at Troll. Suddenly, he saw motion out of the corner of his eye. Angus jumped from behind a stack of boxes and landed a flying side kick to the woman's head. She stumbled, caught her ankles, and landed face down on the floor. Before she could get up, Angus was on top of her. He wrapped his arms around her neck and his legs around her waist. She stood up, trying to pry his arms from around her neck, but Troll could see her eyes closing—just a few more second and Angus would choke her out.

She ran backwards towards the wall. Troll lunged to the side and grabbed both the woman and Angus up in his big arms. He squeezed tight as they crashed into the wall. Troll took most of the blow, allowing Angus to keep his hold. After a few more moments of arm flailing, the woman stopped moving.

Angus released his grip, rolled to the side, and sat back against the wall, running his hand through his hair. "Thanks, Troll."

"Right back at you," said Troll, leaning against a cracked depression in the cement bricks. "What was that?"

"Rear naked choke."

"No, I mean this woman. She was way too strong and way too fast."

"I don't know, but we'd better get her good and tied up before she wakes up again."

Angus and Troll tied the woman up as tight as they could with some rope they found in the corner. Troll tied the final knot as Bart walked down the stairs. He seemed shocked to see the woman lying on her side, tied up in layers of rope.

"That isn't going to work," said Bart. "Looks like she broke the chain. She can surely break a rope."

"It's all in how you tie it, chief," said Angus.

"What's going on here? She almost killed us," said Troll, taking a step towards Bart. Bart stumbled backwards and landed on the stairs.

"Look, I, well...she's my wife. I didn't know what else to do," said Bart, putting his face into his hands.

"Keep talking."

"She came home the other morning, like I said. Other than being shaken up, she seemed fine. She had those bruises and scars, but we figured she must have stumbled out in the woods or something." Bart stood up and paced in front of the stairs. "Everything was going fine, and then last night we went to bed, and all of a sudden she got up and started throwing things at me. I asked her what was going on, but she just yelled and screamed. I couldn't understand a word she was saying. I'm not so sure they were words, so I grabbed her and tied her up so she wouldn't hurt herself...or me. This morning, she seemed fine again. Didn't remember a thing."

"How'd she end up down here?" asked Troll.

"It was getting on later in the afternoon. I fell asleep in the hammock outside. Didn't get much sleep the night before. When I came into the house, I couldn't find Harriet. I called for her, but nothing. I worried she ran off again. Finally I checked downstairs, and there she was—chained to the pipe stack, knitting a sweater. Asked her what she was doing, and she said she couldn't risk hurting me. Not too long after, you guys showed up. "

"Bart, we need to find out what is wrong with her. I'd like to take her back to the sheriff's office. We can put her in one of the cells there while we figure out what is going on. That way she won't hurt anyone," said Troll.

Bart nodded and slumped to the stairs again. He put his face in his hands and shook his head from side to side. "This whole thing," he said, "it's just too much."

"We'll figure this out," said Troll, patting Bart on the shoulder. "I'm going to go get the pickup, Angus. You watch her."

"10-4, big guy."

The stairs moaned under Troll's weight. He walked out the back door of the cabin and down the gravel road towards his pickup. He was a couple houses down from the cabin when a smile crossed his lips. Troll knew what this was. It was bad of course, but amazing just the same. Troll walked toward his pickup with a bounce in his step, whistling all the way.

6

Tanya reached into her backpack and pulled out a long strip of venison jerky. She had crisscrossed the straps of her pack over a long branch just above her head and pushed it back to the trunk, just like her dad had taught her. The secret to hunting deer, he always said, was patience. Find a comfortable stand and plan to spend a lot of time there.

Tanya Tucker was not hunting deer, but she did plan on sitting tight in her deer stand. The stand had a small square metal seat with a padded camouflage cover. The seat was connected to a slightly larger platform below, which served as a footrest and also a place to stand if the shot required. The entire apparatus was connected to the tree by thick straps, pulled tight by ratcheting clasps.

She reached over and touched her rifle. It sat butt down on the footrest, leaning against a thick pine branch. She remembered back to when she was younger and couldn't climb up the big pine by herself. Her dad always schlepped a ladder into the woods on those early mornings and boosted her up into her nest. She wished he was here. He always seemed to know what to do. But now, she had no idea what to do, other than hide and wait. People were going crazy. First, Vick had attacked her, and then that man pointed a gun at her. A night in the tree stand seemed the safest bet. The platform was well hidden—no wandering crazy person would be able to spot her.

She stood up and stretched her legs for the fifth time and used her field glasses to look down the long alleyways that stretched out from her tree in all directions. The tree's location at the apex of a number or game trails was the reason her father had put the stand there. She could sit in that one spot and see something coming her way from every direction, but by the time the animal sensed her, it would be too late. Tonight she hoped that the same methodology would serve for people.

The field glasses had been a gift from Vick. He didn't know a thing about hunting, but he was smart enough to ask around for a gift a hunter would want. The glasses were manufactured to work in low-light situations, which allowed her to survey the area during the early morning hours before the sun broke, and they worked equally well this evening, with the moon sending enough light through the thick canopy for her glasses to use to illuminate the area around her.

Tanya stared out at the clearing just to the north of her stand. She had shot many a deer as it walked across that clearing. In fact, she thought as she chewed, she was fairly sure that the jerky she was currently enjoying had come from that clearing. She spotted movement. She dropped her field glasses, causing them to tug slightly on their straps and come to rest around her neck. She sat down and rubbed her hands together, trying to make sense of what she had just seen.

She picked up her rifle and looked down the scope into the clearing. The scope on the rifle was several times more powerful than the field glasses. It was also extremely light sensitive, and it could illuminate an image in almost pitch-black conditions. The scope was actually one of her most expensive possessions. Through the scope, she confirmed what she thought she had seen: a half dozen people walking around in circles, bumping into each other. They stumbled around like they were drunk, most dragging their feet while they walked, arms raised perpendicular to the ground. She recognized all of them from town.

Because she wasn't a permanent resident, she wasn't sure of all of their names, but she did recognize her mailman, Mr. Philler. He still wore his light blue work shirt and navy blue shorts. She took a deep breath and set the rifle down. Why were the townspeople wandering around the woods like drunks? She looked down all the other trails with her glasses. In all directions, she saw people stumbling around, some bumping into trees, a few crawling. She leaned back against the tree and took a sip of water. It was going to be a long night.

She looked up at the few stars that she could see through the tree canopy. She caught herself smiling when she realized that she had been in a situation like this before. She had taken a survival trip to the Serengeti with her now ex-husband. It had not been people wandering around with crazy eyes that night on the African plains, but rather hyenas with menacing, illuminated eyes.

Tanya and her husband had taken one, sometimes two adventure trips a year. Both of them were adventure junkies. Tanya had been through a survival adventure on every continent and in just about every type of environment. While she liked her day job—sitting in a lab testing pharmaceutical samples—she lived for adventure. The couple had been members of a survivalist club. The club had hosted a game annually. The basic idea was that they would drop you and a partner somewhere with little to no gear and then you had a set amount of time to find civilization.

On the trip to Africa, they had been dropped off on the ridge of a wooded crater with nothing but a GPS tracking unit and a single canteen of water. They had five days to find civilization or they would lose the "game." The hyena incident had occurred on the third night. It had rained all day, and neither Tanya nor her husband could get a fire started. That night, as a full moon rose high in the clear sky, the howls began.

Within minutes, they could see eyes surrounding them. Without a fire, there was no way to keep them at bay. Tanya thought that night might be the end of the road. They slowly crawled out of the lean-to shelter they had built earlier. Each of them had fashioned a spear for hunting. They stood back to back, waiting. Both stood as tall and wide as they could and hollered and screamed, trying to make sure that the pack knew that they were a threat. The laughing call of the hyenas grew louder and louder. They estimated that there were a dozen or more looking at them from the darkness. It was clear that the beasts were not going to back down.

As one, they charged the camp. Tanya and her husband climbed the tree that their shelter had been leaning against. They managed to get up into the high branches before the first sets of fangs and claws came crashing in. They spent the night straddling tree branches while they watched the hyenas jump and laugh.

Tanya felt a tickle in her spine and the hairs on the back of her neck rose. She put her hand to the thick bark of the tree; there was a mild vibration coursing through the trunk. Cautiously, she looked down past the footrest of her stand, leaning to the left so she could see around a branch. There, on the ground, a man walked into her tree, backed up, and walked into it again. He didn't seem to know she was up there. It looked like he was trying to walk through the tree. His face and chest smacked hard into the bark with each attempt.

Tanya picked up her rifle, thought better of it, and put it back to rest. She couldn't shoot him. He probably had a family. Plus, the noise might draw the others. She took up her glasses again to check the clearing. The six people were still meandering around, pawing at each other. She was about to drop the glasses and consider a nap when she saw something on the left edge of the clearing. She stood and leaned out for a better angle, the safety strap wrapped around her chest growing taut.

"Two of these are not like the others," Tanya whispered.

Two men were standing at the edge of the clearing. They appeared to be wearing some sort of fatigues. One of the men had a clipboard and was rapidly writing while watching the group of people stumble around. The other held a video camera. What were they doing out here, and why weren't they stumbling around like the others?

"Actually, why am I not stumbling around like the others?"

A groan came from below almost as in response. "I didn't ask you," said Tanya.

Tanya enjoyed the safety of her deer stand, but she had to risk it. Those men didn't look scared. They looked like a research team, which meant they knew what was going on. In fact they were likely the cause, if they were documenting like that. If she could figure out what they'd done, maybe she could find a way to fix it. She had been spared from whatever this was for now, but there was no guarantee that she would stay that way. She needed to know what was going on.

First problem would be getting out of the tree while old thumpy kept banging his head against the bark. She grabbed a large pine cone and dropped it. It landed on the man's head. It didn't seem to faze him. Tanya began to wonder if the midnight wanderers had any idea of what was going on around them. She looked back to the clearing; the two men were heading off into the woods. She jumped to her feet and undid her safety harness, ready to give chase. She saw two red lights and heard the subtle hum of a small engine coming to life. She took a deep breath and sat back down. They were in some sort of vehicle, which would make it easy for an experienced woods-woman such as herself to follow. She did not need to be reckless.

Tanya eased on her backpack and strapped her rifle over her shoulder. She was about to find out just how conscious these people were. Using the natural ladder the thick tree branches formed, Tanya climbed down from the tree, landing as softly as she could on the ground on the opposite side of the tree from the man. He seemed to have no idea she was there. She turned to head towards the clearing and then paused. If that man kept banging away at the old pine, he wouldn't have any face left. She picked up a long branch off the forest floor. While staying on the opposite side of the tree, she poked the man in the shoulder. He didn't respond. She dropped the branch and circled the tree, coming up behind the man. He backed up from the tree. Tanya put one hand on each of his shoulders and gently turned him towards the clearing. He didn't respond to her touch. Instead, the man walked down the game trail towards the other stumbling people.

Tanya stayed behind the man and off the trail. She hoped to use him as an early warning system if anything more dangerous than these bumper people were out tonight. She knew where the red lights had been in relation to the clearing. If she could make it over there, she could find the trail. Staying low, she approached the clearing.

Suddenly, something slapped against her back. Tanya spun around to see a woman wearing a pink nightgown swatting at her. Tanya scrambled back, but the woman kept walking towards her. Tanya turned and ran towards the clearing's edge. She rounded the edge, avoiding two more people. They didn't seem to have the capacity to hurt her; they simply slapped at her with limp hands when she got too close to them—which meant that the people had some awareness but that they could not do much with it.

Tanya reached the other side of the clearing. She could not make out much in the dark—this part of the forest was particularly thick with trees. She decided that she needed to risk turning on her flashlight to find the trail. When she turned on the light, she heard groans and moans from the clearing. The group bumping into each other all turned and began walking towards her. Apparently, they were attracted to light. She worked quickly and found a set of tire tracks, something with four wheels, somewhat wide. *Probably a side by side four-wheeler,* she thought as she followed the trail. She could hear the moans and groans behind her. They were growing closer. She picked up her pace, thinking she could stay ahead of them. Another hundred yards and the woods would open up, which would allow her to follow the tracks by moonlight.

She was so focused on the tracks she didn't notice the man running towards her until it was too late. He tackled her around the waist and slammed her into the ground. Tanya tried to shove him off, but he wouldn't budge. He pawed at her chest, just like Vick had done, trying to tear her clothes. She could hear the groans getting closer. He had her pinned to the ground, his legs kneeling on hers, his hands pressed down on her shoulders. She felt hot saliva drip onto her face as he stared down at her with crazed eyes.

He looked back the way Tanya had come, apparently noticing the stumbling horde. He filled his lungs with breath and let out a deep yell; it barely registered as human in Tanya's ears. While he yelled, his hands loosened from Tanya's shoulders slightly. She took the momentarily relief to reach to her side and pull her buck knife free from the sheath on her belt. She bent her elbow and slashed his chest from left to right, the sharp blade immediately slicing through skin and muscle. He screamed and rolled off her. Tanya jumped to her feet and bolted up the nearest tree.

While she readied her rifle, the man stood sniffing the air. Two of the stumbling men walked into view. The man leapt through the air, landing on the first. He bent over and bit the man's neck. When he pulled away, Tanya could see that a chunk of the stumbling man's neck was gone. She steadied the rifle and took aim on the wild man. She hesitated to pull the trigger; he was a human, or she thought he was. She could not allow him to kill all of the others, though. She put the crosshairs on his back just to the left of his spine, where she knew the heart would be. She let out her breath and held the rifle steady, and then, when the picture within the sight was completely calm, she pulled the trigger. The man threw his arms out wide, his back arched forward, his head jerked skyward. He slumped forward on top of his victim, motionless.

Tanya crumbled into the branches of the tree. She wanted to stay up in that tree and cry; she had taken another human life. More of the stumbling people came into view. *No time for that,* she told herself. She wiped away her forming tears, jumped out of the tree, and continued after the four-wheeler.

Tanya reached the area of forest where she no longer needed her flashlight, and she gladly shut it off. She did not want to attract any more attention this evening. She followed the tracks out of the woods and through some long-grassed prairie land and finally to a highway. The tracks came out of the ditch and turned right onto the highway. Once on the highway, she could not see where the tracks went. She crouched down among the tall grass on the top of a slight rise, took out her field glasses, and looked down the highway. She scanned both sides of the road, looking for some indication of where the vehicle may have gone. At the far reach of her glasses, she could make out a farm. She decided it was her best option. Tanya stuck to the tall grass along the side of the road, ducking down into the grass whenever a vehicle passed. At this point, she didn't know who she could trust; all she knew was that something terrible had happened to one of her favorite places, and she needed to find out what.

She continued on for over a mile until she stood across the road from the farm. Tanya knew the place. Her father had taken her there when she was a girl. It used to be a dairy farm. They also raised chickens. Tanya's father came out to the farm to buy fresh eggs and milk for the cabin. Tanya remembered the family that lived there. They had seven children who were always running wild outside. She never saw them clean, but she remembered that she'd thought a couple of the boys were kind of cute.

Tanya jogged across the highway and crouched beside the long driveway of the farm place. There were lots of tracks in the gravel. Many sizes of tires had gone down the drive recently. That was odd, because she knew the family had moved off the farm years ago. About the time Tanya graduated from high school, the farm went bust. There were a few bad years in a row, and the price of milk and eggs had dropped to next to nothing thanks to the large commercial farms that were popping up all around the countryside. The small family farm couldn't make it. Tanya wondered had happened to them. She also wondered who would be driving around on a farm that had been abandoned almost ten years prior.

Tanya cautiously walked along the side of the driveway. She kept to the tall weeds and grasses as much as she could. The old farm looked nothing like she remembered. The farmhouse had turned a grayish brown color, and many of the windows were broken out. The green-shingled roof bowed in over the porch, which had several cracked boards. There was no light coming from the dilapidated structure.

She crouched down at the side of the house, and slowly worked her way around it, peering in each window. The house was dark. Thick dust covered the floor and walls. Through one of the windows she could see a broken chair with one leg missing, leaning in the middle of the floor. She rounded the entire house, not seeing a single trace that anyone had been in there recently.

A hundred or so yards from the house stood the chicken coop. It was a long, low building with a double-stacked roof. The roof had skylights, or the remnants of skylights, running the length of the building on both sides. A garage leaned over between the house and the coop, leaving the doorway severely slanted. She carefully worked her way around each building looking for signs of the men. Down the path from the coop stood a barn. Tanya remembered the sound of mooing cows coming from the barn from previous visits, but tonight it stood silent. Red chips of paint still clung to the aging lumber; the white trim around the doors and windows had turned tan from the years of sun.

Tanya continued toward the barn, following the copious amount of tire tracks. She stood with her back against the barn door and peered inside. The barn was split into sections. The first section was an open space that used to hold the tractors and other machinery. Barely visible against the far left wall, Tanya could see the four-wheeler. There was also a black Suburban. Tanya walked around the perimeter of the large open space toward the vehicles. She made sure to stick to the shadows. No keys were in the four-wheeler, and the Suburban was locked.

She continued to circle until she got to a smaller set of doors that led into the dairy parlor. The wall between the garage space and the parlor was twenty feet tall, allowing air to pass between the sections since the roof of the barn stood fifty feet up from the ground. The family would bring their cows in through the parlor to milk them. Tanya walked around the milking pit. The cows would walk over the pit on a walkway, while the family would attach a milking device to them. The milk was pumped into large tanks that they either bottled themselves to sell to the people that stopped by, or a truck from a distributor would come to empty the tanks. One of the large, stainless steel tanks still stood on the far side of the pit, though the walkway was gone.

She did not see anyone in the parlor, so she continued to the back part of the barn, which had been a wide open space where the cows could roam and eat. Two large doors opened, leading out to the pasture behind the barn. There was not a door separating the parlor from the cow pen; instead, a tall, metal fence ran from end to end to keep the cows away when it was not milking time. Over the pen was a large loft, where the family had kept hay bales for winter. They baled the hay in the summer and then put it up to store for the colder months.

Tanya climbed up the old staircase leading to the hay loft. She would have a view of the entire barn from there. She found an old pile of hay pitched near the front of the loft, and she nestled down in it, keeping her glasses in hand to help her determine where the drivers of the four-wheeler had gone.

7.

After a hot shower and a cold beer, Rogan was feeling better. He was sitting on the porch of the team's rental cabin, trying to wrap his head around what he and McKenzie had seen out in the woods. McKenzie walked out of the bathroom, toweling off her red hair. She wore a pair of red jersey pajama pants featuring black bats in flight. Over her bright pants, she wore a simple white tank top, which clearly stated in pink block letters that girls rule. She flopped down next to Rogan on the bench; he handed her a beer. McKenzie took a long pull and kicked her feet up on the railing. Neither said a word as they stared out over the water, the moonlight shimmering in the slight waves. McKenzie tilted her head to the side, resting it against Rogan's shoulder. He could feel the dampness from her hair wicking through his shirt. He turned and looked down at her. She clutched her beer in her lap, gently tearing at the label.

"Crazy day," Rogan said.

"Yeah, very confusing. I have no clue what we saw out there...and that woman."

"I have a theory on the man in the woods. The woman, not sure yet."

"The dead one, or the one banging his face into a pine tree?"

"Pine tree face," said Rogan. "I'm going to wait for the guys to get back before I spill, though."

Rogan looked out over the lake again. This really was a beautiful place. He looked at McKenzie again; she seemed deep in thought.

"You okay, Mac?"

McKenzie took another drink and said, "Fine, why?"

"I don't know. You just seem off."

"I'm fine. Just trying to digest the evening I guess," she said.

"That was a close call out there, in that hole."

"I know, but you caught me."

"Barely. Mac, I'm just..."

"Stop."

"What?"

"You're going to say something along the lines of, I'm sorry I got you wrapped up in this, blah, blah, blah. If anything happened to you, etc., and so forth. I've told you this before, Richard. I am not your little sister. I'm a big girl. I can take care of myself."

"I know, but..."

"Do you? You should know better than anyone that no one *makes* me do anything. I choose to be out here with you, even though you are a complete and utter moron most of the time."

Rogan chuckled, took another drink, stared out at the lake, and asked, "Are you done?"

"Only if you are," said McKenzie, glaring up at him. "And stop smirking. I'm serious."

"Oh, I can tell," said Rogan, getting to his feet. In one swift motion, he jerked McKenzie off the bench and threw her over his shoulder. He marched off the porch.

"What the hell are you doing?" screamed McKenzie, pounding on his back.

Rogan set his grip tighter, walked to the end of the dock, and tossed her off the end. She flailed through the air, splashing down in the alleyway of moonlight that cut the lake in half. She quickly broke the surface and sent a huge splash towards the dock. Rogan jumped back, avoiding most of the spray, and then fell back on his rear, laughing.

"You are a terrible human being. Go get me a dry towel, jerk."

McKenzie stood in the water at the end of the dock while Rogan walked back into the cabin, laughing the entire way. She shook her head and waited. She was surprised that the water was not cold, considering the crispness of the evening air. She remembered Troll yammering on about the lake, something about natural springs that kept the lake warm. Apparently it didn't freeze in the winter either.

Rogan came out of the cabin carrying a beach towel. He was still laughing. She smirked and waited, like a crocodile watching a deer approach the swamp. The water at the end of the dock was shallow; even at her five and half feet, she could stand with her shoulders out of the water. She bent her knees as he walked closer so only her face was out of the water. She listened to the creaking dock as Rogan walked across the planks.

"Kind of late for a swim, Mac. Why did you jump in the water?" McKenzie was immediately transported back to her early childhood, when one of Rogan's favorite games was "stop hitting yourself."

"Just give me a hand," said McKenzie, making sure that she was close enough to the dock not to be obvious, but far enough away that Rogan would have to reach. He smiled down at her and reached out one of those big hands of his. She reached for it, not quite grabbing it. He frowned and leaned further out over the water, and as he did, McKenzie burst out of the water. She grabbed his wrist and forearm with both hands and yanked back as hard as she could. Off balance, Rogan flipped feet over head, his back slapping into the water past McKenzie.

Rogan stood up, wiping lake water off his face. "Well played."

"Why thank you," said McKenzie, leaning forward in a mock bow that she immediately regretted. Rogan grabbed her shoulders and dunked her under the water. They continued to play and wrestle in the moonlight, dunking each other, sending torrential splashes, laughing the entire time.

After she dunked him real good, Rogan disappeared under the water. She spun around in circles trying to find him. She knew what was coming, but she didn't know when. She had forgotten that Rogan could hold his breath for a very long time and swim like a fish. He had even competed in swimming in high school.

It happened. She felt his hands clasp around her ankles. She knew it was useless to fight it, so she plugged her nose with her finger and thumb and closed her eyes and mouth. Rogan pulled her under the water, somehow swimming backwards while dragging her along the bottom of the lake. She remembered the maneuver from when they were kids; he called it the shark attack.

She was just about out of breath when she felt his hands slide up her legs and round her back. He pulled her tightly against him, and they broke the surface together almost twenty feet from the dock. She felt down with her feet, realizing she would not be able to touch bottom here. Rogan was standing on the bottom, only his chin up out of the water. He had her in a bear hug. She could feel him breathing, the hard muscles of his chest expanding and contracting against her. She ran her hands down his sides, feeling his thick abdominal muscles. He was smiling. She stared into his green eyes and unconsciously felt her lips part and her head drift to the side.

"What are you two doing out there?"

Damn.

"Oh, hey Angus, we're just cooling off. Long crazy day," said Rogan.

McKenzie sighed as Rogan's grip loosened. She swam in next to him, heading back to the end of the dock.

Rogan pulled himself up on the dock and offered his hand to McKenzie.

"Aren't going to pull me in again are you?"

"You deserve it, but I can't get out yet."

"Why?"

"White shirt. I'm not about to give you boys a free show."

Rogan pulled off his black T-shirt and handed it down to her. She accepted the shirt and looked up at him. She found her eyes following thin streams of water down his chest and across his stomach. The light from the moon made the droplets sparkle as they traversed his thick muscles.

"Good idea. No one wants to see that."

"You could at least pretend you want to," mumbled McKenzie as Rogan walked back towards the cabin.

McKenzie pulled on the wet shirt and walked out of the water alongside the dock. She sat on the shore and squeezed the water from her hair and stared back at the lake gently rippling in the moonlight.

✳ ✳ ✳

Rogan found Troll pacing the length of the cabin when he walked in. Angus was sitting in one of the side chairs, clicking away at his laptop. He walked past the scene and into the bathroom, grabbing a couple dry towels. When he came out, he could see McKenzie glaring at him through the screen door. Her soggy pajama pants stuck tight to her slender legs, his T-shirt hung to her knees. He wasn't sure how she had gone from laughing and having a blast out in the lake to looking like she wanted to stab him. He chalked it up to another mysterious and unexplainable phenomenon in the realm of women. He handed her a towel, which she snatched out of his hands. Then she walked into the bathroom and slammed the door.

"What's her deal?" asked Troll.

"You got me," said Rogan, pulling on a dry shirt, "but I know what's going on in this town. I've been chomping at the bit for you to get back so I could tell you. This case may go down in the epic category."

"Oh, I know. I already figured it out too. "

"Really? So you're over the fishing thing?"

"Mostly, but man, if this is what I think it is, we could have some amazing proof of the paranormal."

McKenzie walked into the living room. She had traded her soggy PJs for a grey sweatshirt and a pair of black shorts. She dropped onto the couch and looked up at Troll and Rogan.

"You two look like giggly schoolgirls," she said.

"I can't help it, this is just...it's amazing. I mean, real suck-fest for the town, but seriously, what a case," said Rogan.

"Okay, okay, let me tell you what I think it is," said Troll.

"No, no, me first."

"How about you ladies go at the same time," said McKenzie.

Troll and Rogan stood across from each other, looking like gunfighters about to draw at high noon. In unison they turned to McKenzie and nodded. McKenzie held up three fingers, and then counted down to zero. At zero, Troll and Rogan turned to each other and spoke.

"Zombies," said Rogan

"Demonic possession. Wait, zombies? Are you serious?"

"Possession? Please..."

The team spent the next hour filling each other in on the happenings of the day. Rogan conceded that demonic possession was a possibility. Troll could get behind the idea of zombies in the woods. Either way, the team was excited about what they had stumbled upon. This could be the case that proved the existence of the paranormal.

Troll said, "Could this place be like ground zero for some demon/zombie scheme?"

"It seems unlikely that these occurrences are happening independently," said Rogan.

"Totally. And what's up with that woman, Tanya, flipping out on you?" asked Angus.

"Right, how is she connected to all this?"

"And let's not forget Mr. Stick in the Eye," said McKenzie.

"Well, either way, what's our next move?" asked Troll.

"I'm thinking we need to work both angles until we figure out what is going on. Troll, Angus: can you get on some research in the morning? Find out if anything bad happened here, and see if there is a priest in the area. Also look into possible contamination points. If it's zombies, we'll need to find patient zero. Mac and I will head in and update Clay. See if anything new happened."

The team all nodded, and then after passing out another round of beers, continued to debate the finer points of zombie and demon lore well into the morning, each of them eventually passing out right where they were. Angus sat in the side chair, his head lying on the top of the backrest, his laptop still softly humming on his lap. Troll curled up on the rug he had been sitting on, his back against the wall under the front window. Rogan sat on the couch, head rolled to the side. McKenzie spread out on the rest of the couch, her head lying on Rogan's thigh, his arm resting on her side.

The next morning, the team split up again. Troll and Angus headed off to find the local historian and a priest. Meanwhile, McKenzie and Rogan went into town. In another scene torn from a western, Clay stood leaning against a post outside the office. His hat was hung low, and the thumb of his left hand looped through his belt, which was circled with pistol shells. He stood with one foot crossed over the other, the tip of his cowboy boot pressed into the wooden deck. The bright morning sun glinted off the gold star affixed to his shirt. He reached up with his right hand and tipped his wide-brimmed hat towards McKenzie as she got out of Troll's pickup.

"Morning ma'am," said Clay.

"Morning, Sheriff..." said McKenzie.

Clay stepped forward and took McKenzie's hand, helping her up onto the deck.

"Thanks," she mumbled as the color of her cheeks was infused with a reddish hue.

Rogan asked, "Any news?"

"Couple more folks missing. Did you turn over anything?"

"Yeah, we have some theories," said Rogan.

Clay nodded and walked into the office. He led them over to a small table by his desk. Rogan walked past over to the two cells. Clay pulled out a chair for McKenzie. In the right cell, a woman lay on her side on one of the bunks; she was facing the wall, her hands handcuffed behind her back, sound asleep.

"That part of your theory, Rogan?"

"It's half of it. I assume this is the woman Troll and Angus brought in last night?"

"Sure is. She was wilder than a tiger last night. This morning calm, normal. Been sleeping for hours."

"Whatever is happening here seems to only manifest at night. We saw some very strange things yesterday."

Rogan pulled up a chair at the table and proceeded to fill the sheriff in on the happenings of the day prior. Clay's eyes went through a cycle of sizes and widths as Rogan mentioned demonic possession and zombies.

"So you think my missing people are in the woods...wandering around?"

"Some of them anyway. Others might be more like the lady in the cell. They go wild at night, and then don't remember a thing in the morning."

"Vick Johns though, you say he's in a hole?"

"Yeah, and I don't think he died in the fall. Someone, or something, killed him, and then built a ladder to climb out.

"Those damn pits are all over the woods. Bear traps. Poachers use them to kill the bears so they don't have to put a bullet through the fur. Terrible things. You, young lady, are very lucky that man had his wits about him, face first into that pit would have been the end, I'm afraid," said Clay, motioning towards Rogan.

McKenzie nodded and ran her hands up and down the arms of the chair. Rogan cocked his eyebrow at her; he hadn't noticed before now that she hadn't said much more than a word. He also noticed that her eyes kept scanning Clay up and down. He made a mental note to tease her about it later.

Rogan whipped around in his chair as the door struck open. A young blonde woman ran in. Her eyes were red and puffy, her hands shaking. She stopped just short of the table, tears streaming down her face.

"Ally? What's wrong dear?" asked Clay, walking over to the obviously distraught woman.

"I, oh my, Sheriff, it's bad. I've never seen a thing like it before."

"Come on now, Ally. Sit down here and tell us what happened."

"Well, I went out to set the bait traps on Little Sully lake, just like I do every morning, and, and..."

McKenzie stood up, walked over to Clay's desk, and brought a box of tissues over to the woman. Clay gripped McKenzie's wrist and smiled up at her as he knelt beside Ally. McKenzie turned an even darker shade of red and went back to her seat.

"Right there at the boat landing, not five feet from my little duck boat, were three bodies," said Ally, wiping her eyes and blowing her nose into a wad of tissues.

"Oh no. I'm sorry, Ally. Did you recognize them?"

She nodded and grabbed out another bunch of tissues. "Mr. Peters, Mrs. Griffith, and old José."

Clay closed his eyes and clenched his jaw. He stood up and placed a hand on Ally's shoulder. He then took his hat off and put it to his chest. Rogan decided he needed to take over the interview. Clay seemed to be on the edge of breaking down.

"Ally, I know this is hard, but do you think you could take us there?" asked Rogan.

"I, I can't. I can't look at them again."

"That's okay, you don't have to. Just get us close and point out where we should look. Then Clay will take you home," said Rogan, looking up at Clay. Clay nodded his agreement.

Rogan and McKenzie followed Clay's brown pickup out of town to the east, down a series of gravel roads, and finally down a single track road to a small clearing at the edge of a narrow lake. Once they stopped, Rogan called Troll and gave him directions to get out to the crime scene. Troll would be their best bet to get an idea of what had happened to the victims if the cause of death was not obvious. Ally pointed down a worn trail in the grass that led to the right edge of the clearing. Rogan and McKenzie walked down the trail while Clay loaded Ally back in his pickup and drove off.

"Kind of squeamish for a sheriff," said McKenzie, turning to watch the pickup pull out of the clearing.

"Clay's a good man, and apparently good-looking too," said Rogan, nudging McKenzie. Later had come sooner than he thought, and he smiled as he watched McKenzie's cheeks flush.

"Shut it, Dick."

Rogan clenched his teeth and turned his head to the side. Of all the ways his name could be split up, he hated that one the worst. Normally he would let whoever'd said it have it, but between throwing Mac in the lake and calling her out on her ogling, he supposed he deserved it.

"You know, maybe you want to start going by Dick, now that you're officially a P.I. Isn't that what they used to call private investigators? Dicks? Like hey, did you know Rogan's a dick? Yep, a big, private dick."

Before he could retort, they exited the grassy path onto a hard sand beach. The boat Ally had mentioned sat pulled up on the shore, an anchor line stretched out and tied around a leaning maple tree. Just beyond the boat, Rogan saw three sets of feet sprawled out at the water's edge. He reached out his arm in front of McKenzie. She knocked into it, not paying attention.

"Ouch... What? You know you deserved all that and more. Wouldn't kill you to be a gentleman once in a while, you know."

"Yeah, yeah, yeah, but look," said Rogan, pointing towards the feet.

"Oh, back to business, then."

Rogan and McKenzie eased around the boat to look at the grisly scene. There, sprawled out roughly five feet apart, lay three bodies. Rogan knelt down by the first body while McKenzie walked around the perimeter of the area. The first body belonged to a man in his late 40s. He had a solid build and a black stubble beard. His clothes had been torn, leaving gashes on his arms and chest. Rogan figured the killing blow was the one he'd taken to the neck. It looked like something had torn out a chunk of his throat.

"Rogan, there are tracks everywhere down here. I think these people were either fighting each other or fighting something. There are many tracks leading here, and then only one set leading off that way," said Mckenzie, pointing east.

"Yeah, and except for this one, it looks like the other two bodies were dragged into place. Something tore out these people's throats."

"That trail out had blood droppings too. Whatever walked off must have been bleeding?"

"If they were, it must have been a minor cut, considering the distance between drops," said Troll from the other side of the boat.

"You made good time," said Rogan.

"Never put me in a situation where he is driving again; the guy is certifiable on the road," said Troll.

"Told you," said McKenzie, walking back to the boat. "Where's Angus?"

"He got a lead on a priest that might be able to check out the demon lady. He dropped me off and then headed over there."

"Okay, do your thing, buddy," said Rogan.

Troll nodded and pulled on a pair of latex gloves. He walked around the bodies, examining their necks and other lacerations. He also walked the perimeter around where most of the footprints were located. He knelt down several times and stuck his finger in the prints. He then stood over the trail leading off to the east and examined the blood droppings. Finally, he returned to the bodies, knelt down, and more closely examined their necks.

"Cause of death, huge bite to the throat?" asked Rogan.

"Most definitely."

"A bear maybe?"

"No, these bites don't resemble an animal bite, and all of the tracks are humanoid."

"Are you saying a person bit their necks like that?" asked McKenzie.

"I would say yes, but the power needed to rip open the throat like this...that person had to have an incredibly strong jaw and sharp canines."

"Canines?"

"The pointy teeth a couple over from your front teeth."

"No way..."

"Yep."

"What are you two talking about?" asked McKenzie.

"Vampires," said Rogan and Troll simultaneously.

"Oh, come on!"

"Here's what I see on the scene. For some reason, four people walked to this location, all coming out of the woods from various locations. Once here, they had one heck of a battle royale. Based on the marks and tracks, one of them finally won out, pulled them all together, and drank their blood. Interestingly, their arteries are torn clean, but the amount of blood in the sand isn't even in the ballpark of how much there should be for a jugular tear like this."

"What is going on in this town? Now we have demons, zombies, and vampires?" said McKenzie, throwing her hands up.

"I know, isn't it awesome?"

"Did I just hear vampires?" asked Clay, walking into view.

"Yep!" yelled Troll.

"Damn it, Rogan, I'm starting to wonder about you, telling me all kinds of crazy things."

"I know, Clay, but we need to investigate from all angles, and strange as it sounds, the clues are adding up where this seems to be something not of this world," said Rogan.

"We should really autopsy these," said Troll, waving his hand towards the bodies.

"They are people, you know. You could show some compassion," said McKenzie.

"Part of the job. Where do you usually process murder victims?" asked Troll.

"Well, that's a good question, actually. Can't say that we've had a murder since I started here."

"Seriously?"

"Nope, other than the last few days, it's normally pretty peaceful around here. I would guess, though, that we would ship them into the city. I would think that would be the closest morgue."

"That's going to take forever," said Troll.

"You would know," said Rogan. Troll worked for the county coroner's office. Until recently, he had been an assistant. After years of apprenticeship, he'd finally earned his full license and was officially a licensed medical examiner.

"Sheriff, I'm a ME for the county. Is there somewhere in town we could take the bodies where I could work on them? It would be useful to get a preliminary look."

"What are you hoping to find? Seems like cause of death is fairly obvious," said Clay.

"I'm wondering if there is anything physical that could explain their erratic behavior."

"Well, we could commandeer the butcher shop, I suppose."

"Perfect, let's load these vamps up," Troll said.

8.

Tanya sat straight up, blowing hay away from her mouth and pulling stems from her hair. She wondered how long she had been asleep. Considering she hadn't slept in a couple days, it was hard to say how much downtime her body had forced her into. From down below, she heard a loud scraping sound, like stone scraping across metal. She dropped back down into the hay. After a few moments, she risked a peek over the edge of the hay loft. She could see two men standing above the pit of the dairy parlor. They were wearing the same gray and black fatigues she had seen in the woods. She craned her ear towards them, trying to make out what they were saying. She could only catch bits of the conversation.

"Going great..."

"...will be pleased..."

"Right on schedule."

"Finally get off these twelve-hour shifts."

While she watched, two more men walked out from the pit, and after exchanging what sounded like pleasantries, the original two men walked down into the pit. Tanya heard the scraping noise again. The two men who came out of the pit walked out of the barn. Tanya chewed her lip as she considered her options.

Tanya wanted to find out what these men had done to the town. She needed to find something that would give her some idea of what had happened, something that would help her fix it. That didn't mean she had to run off half-cocked after the two men. They might be armed, and given their camo attire, they might be trained. She also knew there weren't any answers up in the hay.

She nodded to herself and then cautiously climbed down the ladder. She skirted the edge of the barn staying in the shadows. From her position against the wall she could not see into the bottom of the pit, which she determined meant if anyone was down there they wouldn't see her either.

The door between the parlor and the front of the barn was closed. She had no way of knowing if they were standing on the other side and she wasn't about to find out. She looked around and saw a broken window on the far wall. She made it to the window and climbed out. She looked up at the sun. It was high in the sky. She crouched against the barn and worked her way to the front, keeping her rifle in hand.

She slammed her back into the barn and held her breath as she heard the sound of an engine turning over from inside the barn. A moment later, one of the men drove out in the four-wheeler. He came to a stop by the farmhouse. Tanya steadied her rifle and watched him through the scope of her rifle.

The other man walked out from the farmhouse and handed a clipboard to the driver of the four-wheeler. The driver got out of the small vehicle and turned through the pages on the clipboard nodding. He then tossed the clipboard on the seat of the four-wheeler and followed the other man into the house.

Tanya scanned the grounds between her and the four-wheeler. She wanted that clipboard. If she stuck to the tall grasses and weeds along the driveway she could come out roughly three strides from the vehicle, grab the clipboard and run right back into the weeds before anyone saw her. It was a calculated risk she was willing to make to get the information she was after.

After slowly navigating the brush, Tanya crouched just inside the weed line just a few steps from the four-wheeler. The trek had taken her longer than she would have liked, but she couldn't risk making a noise or being seen. She peered through her field glasses at the house and surroundings looking for movement. It was quiet and she could not see any immediate threats.

Tanya took a couple steadying breathes and the broke from her cover. She grabbed the clipboard just as a surprised man in camouflage opened the door of the farmhouse holding a coffee mug.

Tanya jumped back, pulled her hunting knife clear from its sheath, and slashed the two tires nearest to her. Then she turned and sprinted down the driveway.

"Hey, you stop!"

"What are you doing? Stop now, or I'll have to shoot. Dale, we got an intruder! Come on!"

Tanya kept running; she made it to the road before she felt the first bullet whiz past her. She ran down the embankment on the other side as two more rounds sailed just over her head. She could hear the men behind her, trying to close the distance. She ran through the tall grass and broke through the edge of the woods. Two shells slammed into an old oak just next to her.

Tanya darted and turned through the trees, trying to make the most confusing trail possible. About fifty yards into the thick forest, she nearly ran into a bear trap, this one still set. She skidded to a stop, flailing her arms out to her sides, barely keeping her balance. She could hear the men stomping behind her. They would be upon her soon. She pulled off her outer shirt and threw it into the middle of the trap. Then she ran hard to her right, down a game trail, and scampered up into a giant spruce tree. She straddled a large branch thirty feet off the ground and leaned against the thick trunk, trying to catch her breath.

She picked up the clipboard she had been clutching. There were several sheets of paper clipped to the board. The first one was white, and it simply had a small evergreen sketched on the front, the entire image done in a dark shade of green. She turned through the pages, trying to make sense of what they said. Most of the information was graphs and numbers. One page said stage 1, stage 2, stage 3, with tick marks under each stage. The most ticks were under stage 2. The last two pages were filled with random short notes.

Subject exhibits restlessness. This subject, a male, seems unaware of his surroundings. The transformation seems to happen at different rates, no correlation can be made between weight, height, age, or sex. Regardless of these factors, the stages progress differently for each subject. Believe we have 100% maturation and spread. Entire area seems to be affected. Beginning of Stage 3 seems to be the most violent. The few that have transitioned to end phase are still aggressive, but not nearly as much as those in early stage 3.

Stages, subjects, what was going on? Were the people of Evergreen lab rats for these people? Maybe they were just researchers responding to the strange occurrences? Not likely. Tanya didn't know any trigger-happy researchers. She also wondered if they claimed to have 100% spread in the area why she did not seem to be affected. She certainly didn't have violent outbursts like Vic, and she had ran up a couple trees, but as far as she knew, she hadn't bumped into any. She sat quietly, studying the graphs and data while checking the area for the two men.

On her next scan, the two men walked into view, both holding out their pistols, their eyes scanning the area.

"Hey, over here," said the shorter of the two men.

The man pointed to Tanya's shirt. He walked confidently towards it. As he leaned over to retrieve the shirt, a loud series of cracks filled the air. The man screamed and disappeared. The other man ran over to the hole, flattening to his stomach to look down into the pit.

"Dale, Dale! You okay down there?"

No reply.

"Dale, come on man, you okay?"

Silence.

The man rolled onto his back, sat up, and placed his arms across his knees, his head hung low. Tanya leaned her head back against the tree, tears running down her cheeks. How many more people would she end up killing?

9.

The smell of food carts and fried rice meant he was getting close. The mixture of smells infiltrated the vents of the black van as Angus pulled it up to the curb. He stepped out and sighed. This was about the last place on earth he wanted to be. He parked the van just around the corner from the section of Queen City known as Chinatown. The moniker pissed Angus off. The Chinese were not the only ones that lived in the area, yet the name had stuck. As did the junky tourist shops selling small golden dragons and healing herbs.

Angus pulled the hood of his sweatshirt over his head, covering as much of his face as he could. Many people in the area would recognize him, and none of them would be happy to see him. Angus hadn't stepped foot back in the area in years, but he needed to talk to someone. This situation in Evergreen reminded him of something, something bad. Something that he'd thought was just a myth—or an old man's crazed dream. Angus walked down the narrow, pedestrian-only street. He stuck to the shadows and looked down towards the street. He did his best to blend into the background.

The place bombarded him with memories, some good—most bad. Angus had done a lot of things he was ashamed of on these streets. He checked the walls near each corner as he passed. On most he saw a small chalk circle with two small lines inside. It looked like a face with two closed eyes. It was the symbol of The Black. The syndicate that Angus's father ran.

He turned down an alley. Hanging from an electric line crossing the alley was a black rope, suspended from the rope hung the skeleton of a cat. Angus did not miss this place. After a few more steps down the darkening alley, Angus was surrounded by four men. They all wore black from head to toe. Skintight black masks covered their faces, with only small slits for their eyes. Angus remembered wearing that mask all too often.

"I don't want any trouble, boys. I'm here to see Ken-shin." Angus spoke in fluent Japanese.

Deeper in the alley, Angus heard the click of a lighter. A small ember began to glow in the dimness. He could make out the shadow of a man leaning against the wall.

"You shouldn't have come back," said the man.

"I'm not back. I just need you to answer a question, and then I'm gone," said Angus, switching back to English.

"I feel as though a ghost is talking to me. It sounds like Angus-shin, but that can't be... He died."

"Ken, I don't have time for games. Come over here, five minutes—then I'll be dead again."

"I'd say it'll be less than that."

The four men attacked at once. Angus wasn't surprised. In fact, if they hadn't attacked, he would have been offended. He shot his palms out to the side and connected with the chests of two of the incoming men in black. He then flipped forward, the heel of his foot catching the chin of the man behind and then crushing down on the skull of the man in front of him as he went 360 degrees in the air, landing back on his feet. He quickly threw a series of side and back kicks, dropping all four men to the alley floor.

Ken-shin walked out from the shadows and stood in front of Angus, clapping. The two stared at each other from ten feet away. *He's gotten taller,* thought Angus.

"Still remember some of the old ways, I see," said Ken-shin.

"I didn't come here to fight. And you should know it would take a lot more than four lackeys to take me down."

"The man I used to know maybe, but you, I don't know... You're just a specter that disgraced our family. A half-bastard with a dead mother. A fling my father indulged."

Angus felt his Scottish blood boil. He knew Ken-shin was trying to draw him into a fight. He also knew that he could beat him, but that wasn't why he was here. He didn't want to open old wounds, nor make new ones.

"My father morns the death of his bastard son," said Ken-shin, flicking ashes towards Angus, "but if we see the ghost of him, we are to make sure that he stays dead."

Ken-shin threw his cigarette at Angus and followed its trajectory with a flying kick. Angus stood perfectly still and, at the last moment, deflected the blow with his forearm. Ken-shin landed gracefully, spun, and attacked Angus. Ken-shin was a whirling dervish of kicks and punches. Angus stayed still, moving only his forearms and shins to block the attacks. Eventually Ken-shin backed away, heaving.

"You know that you'll never have the ability to take me on," said Angus. "You may think me a ghost, or a bastard, but never forget that I'm your older brother and that I taught you everything you know."

"What do you want?" wheezed Ken-shin.

"Two things. First, I'd like it if he didn't know I was here. I'm not here to start anything. I'm not crawling my way back. Second, do you know anything about a little town up north called Evergreen?"

"You know I can't tell father. Not killing you would be a great dishonor. And no, I've never heard of this place."

"How far in are you? Is there a chance he would keep certain things from you?"

"What do you think happened after you left, Angus-shin?"

Angus had been his father's right hand. There was nothing of the business that he did not share with Angus. He trusted him implicitly. He also expected him to follow without question. When Angus left, he'd hoped that Ken-shin would be okay, that he wouldn't get sucked into the darkness. It had been false hope. He knew that Ken-shin would have to fill his shoes, even though he was far too young.

"I know, or at least I figured," said Angus, putting his hand on Ken-shin's shoulder. "You've grown up a lot. Too fast, probably. I know that's my fault."

"You left a hole. Father needed someone he could trust. That is all," said Ken-shin, puffing his chest and dropping Angus's hand from his shoulder.

"That isn't all, Ken. When I left, you were young. You weren't ready for all of this. To be part of father's business. There is so much blood on my hands. I hurt so many people. I didn't want this for you. I wish I could have been there, could have stopped him from getting his claws in."

"But you weren't!" blurted Ken-shin. He stumbled a step back, shocked by his outburst.

"I know. At the time I was only thinking of myself. I was selfish. I should have taken you with me."

Ken-shin looked down at the ground. Angus watched the tension fall from his face. Ken-shin slumped against the wall and slid down. He sat and stared at his hands like they were foreign things.

"You left. I was so angry at you. I still am. But...I do understand, Angus-shin. I had no idea what was going on when you left. I didn't even realize what father was...who he was. I get why you ran," he said, his voice barely above a whisper.

"You could too, you know. I could help you, get you out of this life. Do you really want to be lurking around in alleys all your life?" asked Angus, lowering himself to a crouch.

"I would never take the coward's way. Anyway, I can't. I can't leave him. He's my father, and sometimes I hate him. But, he's still my father. That means something to me," said Ken-shin, his glare returning.

It used to mean something to Angus too. There was a time when he would do anything his father asked, without question. It didn't matter how heinous or unnecessary the request, Angus, the good solider, would go get it done. He looked down into Ken-shin's eyes. Ken-shin was not ready to see the truth. He wasn't ready to realize that in a few more years he would be lying in a gutter, bleeding out because of some grudge his father held or some impossible errand he required. Angus loved his brother. He wanted to smack him around until he figured it out, but Angus knew that wouldn't help. It would only steel Ken-shin's resolve.

"How is he?" asked Angus.

"Older, angrier. I wasn't lying earlier. He mourns you. He misses you."

"I miss him too. Not as much as I miss you, but I think about him a lot. It's as you said, he's our father, for better or worse. I also know that by leaving I shamed his higher bullshit honor, so he'd turn a gun on me the moment I stepped foot in the house."

"Yes, that's true. There is a standing kill order on you, with a healthy reward."

Angus opened his mouth to ask how much his life was worth to their father, but thought better of it. It was time to get back to the point—why he had driven all the way back into Queen City.

He couldn't stay down in Chinatown much longer without being spotted.

"Not to get back to business, but are you sure you've never heard of Evergreen?"

"I'm sure. Although I do sometimes think father keeps things from me. His hunger for power has grown since you left. He's much more paranoid now."

"I saw the markings as I came in. The territory has nearly tripled."

"Yes it has. That took a lot of blood and still does."

Angus remembered the constant turf wars. He had lost count of the number of friends and fellow syndicate members he had watched die over a few feet of pavement.

"Ken-shin, do you remember when father used to talk about the Curse of the Madmen?"

"Of course. He talked about it all the time. He said our ancestors used it back in Japan to destroy their enemies with no bloodshed on our side."

"Right. I remember him talking about how the Curse would make the enemy dumb during the night. That they would walk aimlessly while our ancestors slaughtered them like cattle."

"Yes, and if they were attacking a defended place, like a city with high walls, they would drop the Curse into the water supply and wait. After the dumb ones stopped bumping into each other, they would turn into madmen and kill one another. I used to love that story. He always seemed so happy when he told it, so proud of our ancestors."

"What if I told you I think it's real?"

"Ridiculous, Angus-shin... It's a story."

"I've been up in Evergreen. There are people there wandering around, bumping into each other. Then this morning, they found a couple dead by a lake—killed. It sounded just like the story to me."

"It can't be, Angus-shin. There were dragons in father's story. It cannot possibly be real."

"Please, Ken-shin, think. Has father said anything about the Curse lately, anything at all? Smallest mention."

"No, nothing. But I can't imagine father wanting anything to do with a small town. I really know nothing about it. He hasn't even told the story in...years."

That in itself was odd. Angus's father loved the Curse of the Madmen story. He told it at minimum once a month while Angus and Ken-shin were growing up. He also told it anytime he entertained guests. It was his favorite story. Angus couldn't imagine his father not telling it any longer. Unless he was hoping people would forget about it. Ken-shin tapped another cigarette out of his pack and lit it.

"You'd better get going," he said, letting out a puff of smoke. "Not many down here would let you go."

Angus nodded. A big part of him wanted to stay. To look after his little brother, stand up to their father. He wasn't ready for that confrontation yet, though. He wondered if it would happen sooner than he thought. Angus believed even more strongly now that his father was involved in whatever was happening to Evergreen. He remembered his father talking at length about the Curse being real. He said that one day he would prove it. Maybe today was that day.

He also needed to come up with a plan about what he would tell Rogan and the others. When Rogan had called Troll and told him that a couple bodies had shown up, Angus had seen the perfect opportunity to sneak away and follow up on his hunch. Angus trusted Rogan and the team, but he couldn't tell them about his past. He wasn't sure how they would react. He worried that they would reject him once they figured out that while they hunted monsters, one had been standing right next to them the whole time.

Angus got to his feet and helped Ken-shin up.

"I'd like to say it was nice seeing you...but it wasn't," said Ken-shin, smirking.

"Screw you, little punk," said Angus, lightly punching Ken-shin in the shoulder. He turned to walk away and then stopped. He looked over his shoulder at his brother and smiled. There was still a little piece of the real Ken-shin in there, a little chunk of morality that their father hadn't yet stripped away. Angus would be patient. His brother could still be saved. He would wait for his moment.

* * *

It was late afternoon by the time Troll had his impromptu lab setup. Clay had talked the owner of the butcher shop into letting them examine the bodies there. Troll picked the back room because it was chilled and there were long stainless steel tables that would work well enough for examination tables. The smell of curing bacon and aging steak hung in the air. It was a nice contrast to the sterile formaldehyde smell Troll was used to. Along the far wall were large band saws and a machine that he assumed was for slicing cuts of meat into thinner pieces. Thick plastic hung over all the doors, keeping the cool air from escaping.

The place was not ideal, but it would work well enough. Troll crossed his arms, trying to decide which of the three victims to start on. He wished he had his tools. He had spent a mint on his custom-made scalpel set. He had the maker build the handles longer and thicker so they would be easier to handle with his big hands. Troll figured that fancy chefs always had their own knives; he should have his own scalpels. He hadn't been a certified medical examiner for long, and he had worked long and hard to earn the title. The residency with the county had been the highlight of the journey. It took almost no time at all for him to accept a full-time job with the coroner's office once he'd passed his board exams. As a medical examiner, he had to take the same canon of courses as medical doctors, but Troll never had any interest in being a healer. He was intrigued by death— and by the why and how of murder.

Using a clipboard and a yellow legal pad he had procured from the sheriff's office, Troll walked around the bodies, jotting notes. He had also hung his digital voice recorder from a hook that was suspended from a track, which was likely used to move large animal carcasses from the back into the prep area. He reached up and turned on the recorder so he could make audio observations as well. The recorder would be useful because soon enough his hands would be covered in blood and sinew, making it difficult to work a pen.

"First victim. Mid-forties male, Caucasian, bald. No ID. Apparent cause of death laceration to the throat. Second victim, roughly thirty-year-old female. Caucasian, blonde, No ID. Same cause of death. Third victim, late fifties male, Hispanic, black hair, No ID. Cause of death conflicted at this time."

Troll looked down at the Hispanic man. He was slender, with a muscled upper body. He had the same bite mark as the other two victims, but unlike them, he also had taken a massive blow to the back of the head. Looking at the bite marks, Troll felt it was likely that he'd died of the blunt force trauma and was then bitten post mortem.

Troll walked over to the bench where he had thrown a bunch of the butcher's knives into a pot of boiling water. He was surprised by how close the butcher's tools looked to the tools at the coroner's office. Troll found it fascinating that while humans did everything they could to pretend they weren't animals, the distinction wasn't all that different under the skin. The fact that Troll would be able to easily use the same tools used to butcher a cow to open up the murder victims gave credence to that thought. He took out a long, straight-edge knife that would serve as his main scalpel.

Troll walked back to John Doe number two. He assumed this was Old Jose, but without a formal ID, he stuck with John Doe. He took blood samples, cultures, and photographs. Luckily, Troll always kept a field kit in his pickup, just in case he was called out to an emergency. He just wished that he also had the equipment to actually test the samples. He wanted to get the samples tested quickly. The information would likely provide a lot of clues about what was going on with the residents of Evergreen. He quickly took a round of samples from the other two victims, carefully labeled them, and put them into a small box.

Rogan had taken off to go connect with Angus, McKenzie stayed back, supposedly to help with the examination. She had started the pot of boiling water, but other than that, Troll hadn't seen her. He knew she was not a big fan of bodies and blood.

"McKenzie, are you out there?" shouted Troll.

He heard some movement, and a moment later, Clay stuck his head through the thick vertical slats of plastic leading to the front. He appeared to be looking anywhere but at the bodies. Troll could not comprehend how this guy had become a sheriff.

"Where's McKenzie?"

"Oh, poor thing looked white as a sheet after all this. I sent her on over to my office to rest for a spell."

"You don't look much better yourself."

"Yeah, well, this is my job. I figured I'd just sit up front here in case you needed anything."

"I do. I need you to take these samples and get them to the city lab right away." Troll scribbled on his legal pad, tore off a page, and handed it to Clay with the small box containing the samples. "Here, I wrote down the directions. Send it to the address and put the note inside."

"Will do," said Clay, quickly backing out of the room. "We have a courier that heads in every day. I'll send them out with him," added Clay, shouting through the plastic barrier.

Troll shook his head, picked up the knife, and began cutting into John Doe number two. He followed standard autopsy procedure, making sure he didn't skip anything.

"Observation on second John Doe. His muscles are thick and full of fluid. It is almost as if they were flooded with ATP. "

Adenosine triphosphate, more commonly called ATP, is the energy source for muscles and cells. Muscles use ATP to contract. Generally, muscles store a very small amount of ATP and must refresh the supply after contraction. Troll could not conclude why this man would have what seemed to be an inhuman amount of ATP. *Maybe this is what gives vampires their super strength,* he mused. He continued on through the examination, eventually getting to the brain. He found a suitable electric cutting tool and cut around the crown of the man's skull. After removing and weighing the brain, he examined the different regions of tissue.

"Now this is odd. His amygdala and hypothalamus are both greatly enlarged. The amygdala is nearly double normal human size. Make note to check these regions on the other two victims."

Troll placed the brain back on the tray he had sterilized and finished the examination. He then went on and repeated the exact same procedures on the other two victims. He had to admit that he was a little sad to see that all three of the victims had normal canine teeth, and none appeared to have any sort of rotting flesh. He did find that all three of the victims had longer fingernails than was normal. The nails extended almost three quarters of an inch past the end of the finger and were very hard. Troll cleaned up and sat on a stool, jotting notes on the legal pad.

He wished he could get those test results back; he would need to know about the victims' blood before he could completely form his hypothesis.

10.

Rogan sat with his back to the far wall of the diner. He had located a large, round table in the corner that would allow the team to sit together. Like everything else in the diner, the table was made of solid chunks of wood. Rogan ran his finger across the dark and light streaks of the lacquered top. He was the first to arrive back in town after his unsuccessful attempt to locate Angus. He'd checked both of the small churches in town; Angus had not been at either.

After downing his second glass of water, no ice, he leaned back against the wall and thought about the case. There were so many puzzle pieces, and none of them seemed to fit together. He wanted to believe that it really was zombies or vampires, but he wondered if those types of ghouls only existed with cinematic magic. The thing he couldn't figure out was why these people were acting so strangely. He had hoped it would end with the aimless wandering around, but whatever was going on here had escalated to violence. It also seemed odd to him that it only occurred at night—which gave credence to the vampire hypothesis, he had to admit—but if the woman locked up across the street was any indication, this crazy ordeal not only happened at night, but those affected had no recollection of it during the day.

Rogan lowered his eyes towards the door as McKenzie and Clay walked through. Ever the gentleman, Clay held open the door, allowing McKenzie to enter first. They walked to the table. Clay pulled out a chair for McKenzie and then slid into one of the white oak chairs next to Rogan.

"Evening, Rogan."

"Hey, Clay. Mac."

McKenzie nodded and grabbed a menu. Rogan wondered what her deal was. She had been cranky all day, even by McKenzie standards.

"You guys find anything?"

"No. I waited in the butcher shop for Troll, took a couple samples, and sent them off to the city with our courier. He said 'interesting' a lot, though. Not sure if that's helpful."

"Could go either way, Troll's definition of interesting is not always in line with a normal person's."

"I spent the afternoon in Clay's office, trying not to be sick. I talked to that woman, though, the one that threw Angus and Troll a beat down."

"And?"

"She seemed completely normal. Her name is Harriet, so even a normal name. She was worried that she had hurt someone."

McKenzie paused as the waitress came to the table. Rogan noticed that it was the same waitress from a couple days ago. He smiled up at her; she glared back. She didn't seem to have the easygoing pep she had the last time he had been in the diner. Nor did she seem chatty. McKenzie and Clay placed their drink orders, and the waitress walked away without any sort of acknowledgement.

"Anyway, she asked me about her husband, and if he was all right. I told her he was. I asked her about what she'd been through. She said that it started a few days ago. The first night, she woke up in the morning lying under a tree in the backyard. She figured she must have been sleepwalking, even though she had never done it before. The next night, she woke up in the woods. She had scratches up and down her arms, and no idea where she was or how she got there."

"Interesting. So she either found her way home the first night, or got more adventurous the second," said Rogan.

"Right. And then the third night, she didn't leave home. Instead, she beat the tar out of her husband, and he tied her up. Then we kind of know where it went from there...Angus and Troll got tossed around by a housewife—threw her in the pokey, the end."

"And she doesn't remember any of it?" asked Clay.

"Not a thing. She said she remembers eating supper each night and then nothing until the next day."

Rogan rolled his empty water glass between his hands. He looked over at Clay, who was rubbing the bridge of his nose. McKenzie passed the time by chewing on her thumbnail.

"We're going to figure this out, Clay."

"I know, Rogan. It's just, I feel like this is the city all over again, Ol' Clay in over his head. I'm supposed to just be writing up tickets for speeding and telling underage kids to be more careful next time. Not dealing with Lord knows what this is."

"Clay, you're a good cop. Don't sell yourself short," said Rogan, patting Clay on the shoulder. "We'll get your boring little town all boring again. No worries."

Clay smiled and nodded. The door to the diner swung open, and Angus and Troll walked through. They joined the group at the round table. The waitress returned with fresh drinks and slapped a couple more menus down.

"Know what you want?"

"We'll probably need another minute, honey," said Clay. The waitress sighed and stomped away.

"What's her deal?" asked Troll. "She was all kinds of nice the last time we were in here."

"No idea. Seems like everyone's in a bad mood though," said Rogan while looking directly at McKenzie, who rolled her eyes at him and went back to researching the menu.

"Angus, where were you? I checked both churches."

"Churches?"

"Yeah, you were going to find a priest to talk about the whole demon angle."

"Oh yeah, right. No, I did a video conference with a priest over in Rome. Cool guy, awesome Italian accent," said Angus, trying to mimic an Italian accent with negligible success. "He said it could be possession, but that it's unusual that the vessel would be allowed to function normally during the day. It would be more likely that the demon would try its best to act like the vessel."

"Vessel?" asked Clay.

"There is a school of thought that all our bodies are is vessels for a soul, so when a demon crosses over and possesses someone, they pour themselves into a vessel. Or in other words, your body, then they take over and repress or reject your soul," said Troll.

"Damn."

"I know, right? So anyway, priest dude thinks it is unlikely that this is demonic, though he did suggest we look to see if there were ever any massacres here or any sort of mass death. Could be angry spirits rising from the beyond during the twilight hours."

"We didn't see anything like that in the city history; this place has always been about as quaint as it is now," said McKenzie.

The waitress stomped back over and stared at the group. Rogan noticed that the volume of all the conversations in the diner had raised a level. It seemed like everyone was arguing.

The waitress crossed her arms and began tapping her pen on her green notepad.

"Well, I guess I'll start," said Rogan. He ordered a cheeseburger basket. The group went around, each placing their order, ending with Troll, who ordered three cheeseburger baskets and a twelve-ounce sirloin.

"How can you be hungry after being elbow deep in dead people all afternoon?" asked McKenzie.

"How could I not be hungry? That was a lot of work."

"And was it worth it?" asked Rogan.

"It was...interesting."

The group stared at Troll while he slowly sucked down his soda. It was all Rogan could do to not reach over and yank the glass from his hand and yell at him to get on with it. Most people assumed Troll was a big dumb jock type because of his yoke-like shoulder girdle and beer keg-sized neck, but in reality, Troll was well above the average mark for intelligence. He scored in the top 5% on the MCAT for entry into medical school, but unlike a lot of people with that level of book smarts, he was observant and wise as well.

Rogan had grown to trust Troll's instincts as much as his intelligence over the years, though he would never understand why Troll went after the lower-paying job of medical examiner when he could have easily have been a top dollar specialty medical doctor. Troll finally set down his glass, keeping it in hand, the condensation running trickles down his dry knuckles.

"Three victims, as you guys know. Not to disappoint, but none of them had particularly pointy teeth, nor was any of their flesh rotting. Their fingernails were all longer than one would expect them to be, and sharpened. I took samples from under the nails and found blood and skin tissue. They all had lots of scratches and bruises, all inflicted in the last forty-eight hours, I would say. Given the evidence under the nails, I would say they were fighting each other using their nails to strike and slash. Other than that, everything was fairly normal, except for two things," said Troll, taking another agonizingly long pull of his soda.

"The muscles of all three victims were engorged with fluid. It was almost like they had grown in size overnight and were suddenly able to take in a lot more energy. I would say that they were all to the point, or just beyond the point, of human capacity," Troll continued.

"That might explain the hundred and twenty pound woman locked up across the street tossing you across the room like a leaf," said McKenzie.

"Assuming she has the same thing going on as the three victims, it certainly would. Based on the measurements I took from the female victim and some rough calculations, her power output would be in the ballpark of six times her normal strength."

"Duh-amn," said Angus.

"Why doesn't she have that kind of strength now? I mean with that you'd think she could just yank those bars right out of the wall," asked Clay.

"Either because she doesn't want to—she's worried about hurting someone—or because something triggers the muscles at night. I have no idea what that reason is yet. I'm hoping the blood samples I sent to the city might help. I put a rush on it, so with any luck, I'll get a call back tonight."

"Trigger it, you think someone or something might be controlling these people?" asked Rogan.

"No, I don't think so. I think it's more likely that they have something biological going on. Like I said, maybe we'll know more after the lab runs the samples, or if I would have had a microscope, maybe, but I'm just speculating at this point. Now to give some back to the vampire theory, the bites to their necks were definitely human. The skin was torn too much to tell if it was the same set of teeth, but this was without a doubt not an attack from a bear."

"So three people, more likely four people, since we saw a set walking away. They fight—which the first question is why?—and three of them are killed—leading to the second question, why?" said Rogan.

"I have a loose theory on that based on the abnormalities I found in their brains."

"Dude, you ripped their brains out? Maybe *you're* a zombie."

"If I was, you'd be safe. Nothing up there worth eating," said Troll, tapping Angus on the head. "But, you'd be amazed at what you can learn about someone by poking around in their gray matter."

The waitress returned with a large tray full of food, which she simply dropped in the middle of the table before walking away. Rogan watched her walk away; her fists were clenched tightly as she walked with her arms pinned to her sides. He took another glance around the diner; two men sitting at the counter were fiercely arguing about something he could not hear, but both men's faces were bright red. The bigger of the two men kept slamming his fist on the countertop. To his right, in a booth, a couple sat on opposite benches, staring intently at one another. Each had a fork in their hand, and a single piece of apple pie sat in the direct center of the table.

"Wow, this place has really changed," said Troll, watching the waitress walk away. "Anyway, to varying degrees, they all had enlarged amygdala and hypothalamus glands. The older man's amygdala was nearly twice as big as it should have been."

"Meaning?"

"Those two glands do a lot, but I think most apropos to our situation is that both have been linked to aggression and sex drive."

"Which might explain the violence," said Rogan.

"Correct. There was also evidence of some sort of trauma to the basal ganglia, though I have no ideas about what caused it. Now, in the case of our three dead non-zombie, non-vampire friends, I believe this is what happened, keeping in mind I'm speculating on some of this: I believe the woman was down by the lake, getting some water. If I'm right, those glands being enlarged and the basal ganglia being damaged would devolve someone back to their basic animal needs. So she's down there scooping up some water, the older man comes along, his amygdala is taking over his thinking, and his basic need to reproduce takes over."

"In other words, he tried to rape her," said McKenzie.

"'Mate' might be more accurate given the circumstances, but yes. He attacked her from the back and pushed her to the ground, which would explain many of the bruises, but I don't believe he got a chance to finish the job, so to speak.

He got her pinned down, but then another man came out of the woods and pulled him off. They fought, bare knuckles, claws out. They were probably screaming and sending off war cries, which drew in the last man, the one that lived.

Based on the footprint depressions we saw leaving the scene, he was much heavier than the rest of the group. I believe he ignored the two fighting men and went for the woman. The two fighters decided to team up against the bigger enemy and attacked the big guy while he was trying to mate with the woman. Then the three of them fought, and the big guy got behind the younger man and tore out his throat. His jaw muscles would need to be strengthened a great deal to pull it off. While the neck chomping was going on, the older man's fight or flight kicked in, and he tried to run. The big guy chucked a rock at him and cracked the back of his skull open. He then drug him back to where the other man was and tore his throat out."

"And the woman, why didn't she run off while all this was going on?" asked Clay.

"Her need to mate would be just as great as the others, but she would only want to mate with the strongest—the alpha male if you will—so that her progeny would be strong. I believe she gave herself willingly to the big man, who then thanked her by ripping her throat out. There was evidence of recent sexual activity in the autopsy."

"Gory," said Angus.

"Why would he kill her though, if he wanted to reproduce?" asked McKenzie.

"That has me puzzled. Maybe he decided she was inferior, or the enlarged and damaged glands in his brain prompted him to kill. I don't know..."

"I can't argue with your findings, Dr. Troll, but the question remains...why?" asked Rogan.

"I have no idea. I'm hoping the blood will show something."

"I sent the samples in with Rick, the courier, soon as you handed them to me, so your people should have gotten them a few hours back," said Clay.

"Thanks," nodded Troll.

One of the men at the counter got to his feet. He grabbed the other man by the collar and yanked him back off his stool and onto the floor. Rogan jumped to his feet. The man on the floor got up and the two men started exchanging blows. The rest of the diner seemed content to watch. Rogan ran over and pulled the two men apart, taking a shot to the chin in the process.

Using his long arms, he held the two men back the best he could. The staring contest between the couple in the booth ended. The man reached under the table and flipped it upside down in one motion and then attacked the woman. He tore at her shirt and pressed her into the bench. Clay charged over and pulled the man off her, keeping him at bay. An older man who had been sitting by himself in the corner of the diner stood up and simply walked out, bumping into tables and stools on his way. The waitress jumped over the bar, landing on Rogan. She scratched at his face. He held up his arms in time to block most of the slashes. It took both Angus and McKenzie to pull her off.

Troll, as the biggest man in the diner, found himself surrounded by six men. They circled him like he was prey, each one grunting at him. Clay lost control of his man. The man tackled him into the nearest table and then went back to trying to tear the woman's clothes off.

Rogan got to his feet. The diner was complete chaos. People were fighting everywhere. Those that weren't fighting were wandering around aimlessly, heading towards the door. Clay pulled himself off the floor, pulled his six-shooter, and fired a round into the ceiling. The only people to react to the gunshot were Rogan and his team. The rest of the diner seemed to have no concept of what the noise was, and they weren't at all scared by it.

A man in a trucker hat that read, *I only drink beer on days that end in Y*, grabbed an older woman who was part of the aimless wandering group from behind. He pulled her head to the side and bit down hard on her jugular. Blood sprayed everywhere. He seemed to be drinking her blood and then let her slump to the floor. Rogan charged in. The man in the trucker hat grabbed him around the throat before Rogan could even react. The man tossed him across the diner.

He flew over three sets of tables and landed in a pile on top of three men that were wrestling on the floor. Rogan was able to fight his way out of the dog pile and get to his feet again. He took a moment to refocus his suddenly blurry vision. The six men surrounding Troll attacked at once. The big man defended himself the best he could, sending knock out shots to two of the men before they even touched him. The other four grabbed on, and as a unit, pulled him to the ground. It was like a pack of coyotes taking down a bull. Clay and Angus were tussling with a couple guys who were trying to get to the waitress. Rogan rapidly scanned the room, trying to find McKenzie. He jumped up on a table, frantically trying to find her, his heart pounding out a faster and faster beat.

"Mac?" yelled Rogan. "Where are you?"

"Help!"

Rogan swung his head towards the call. It was her. She was in the corner, holding onto the coat rack. Three men had her surrounded. She jabbed at them with the coat rack to keep them away, but it wasn't working. The man on the left grabbed her arm, forcing her to drop her weapon.

Rogan's vision cleared; he felt rage flowing through his veins. He leapt table to table through the chaos until he came down behind the three men. He threw a vicious right jab to the first man's kidney. The man went to the ground instantly, groaning.

He grabbed the other man by the neck and using his momentum and shoulder sent him flying over his back, slamming the man into the nearest table. The man who had grabbed McKenzie's arm was on top of her. She was struggling, snarling, kicking, scratching the man's face.

The man grabbed each of McKenzie's wrists. She spit in his face. He yelled. It sounded like an imitation of a lion's roar. He moved his hands to her throat. Rogan grabbed the coast rack and swung it up. Before he could connect the shot, the first man slashed his back. He could feel sharp, strong nails driving into his back, leaving torn flesh from his right shoulder down to his left hip. He dropped the coat rack and fell to his knees. The man jumped on top of him, forcing his back to the floor.

Rogan looked over at McKenzie; she wouldn't be able to hold on much longer. He had no choice. He grabbed the man by the back of the head with his left hand and his chin with his right. With one rapid motion, he twisted his hands, breaking the man's neck. The man fell on top of Rogan. Rogan rolled him off and jumped to his feet. He kicked the man holding down McKenzie on the bridge of the nose. The man fell backwards, grabbing at his suddenly bloody face.

"Ok?"

"Barely."

Rogan nodded, turning back towards the man with the bloody nose. The man screamed again and charged at Rogan, arms held wide, ready to slash. Rogan threw out one leg, crouching low as the man came in. He grabbed him around the bicep, twisted, rolled and sent the man flying through the air into the counter. Rogan couldn't tell if he had killed the man or if he was simply unconscious, and he wasn't sure he cared either way.

"We need to get the hell out of here," yelled McKenzie.

"Agreed. Guys, we need to make a break for it," yelled Rogan as loud as he could.

"No shit," said Angus, dropping an elbow on the back of a guy's head.

"Ain't going to make that door," said Clay.

"Angus, make us an exit. Clay, get over there and help Troll."

Angus jumped onto a table. He had one of the big hunks of wood from the counter in his hands. He hurled it at one of the big glass windows over the booths. The glass shattered, making a very large, but very sharp, hole. He jumped from the table and pushed off a wall, landing a side kick to a man's chest. He landed, rolled, and came up with the leg from one of the chairs. A man dove at his legs. Angus did a standing backflip onto the top of the table nearest the broken window and broke out the rest of the glass. Meanwhile, Clay got to the dog pile that Troll was at the bottom of. He started pulling off the men, but it was not going well.

"I need to help," said Rogan to McKenzie. "Angus!"

"10-4 boss," said Angus. He dropped the chair leg, jumped from the table, dropped a hammer kick to the top of one of the crazed diner's skulls, spun and kicked another man in the face, leapt onto the counter, rolled, and landed next to Rogan. Rogan gave a quick eyebrow raise towards Angus and then nodded.

"You stay behind him, Mac. Angus, you know what to do."

Rogan charged into the fray, knocking out three more men before he got to the pile. He could see Troll's legs sticking out, but the rest of him was covered by crazed people. In all there were five men keeping him down. Working together, Clay and Rogan pulled each of the men off. They made sure that each man they pulled off was unconscious before moving onto the next. More than once another crazy would come up from behind and start in on the attack, it meant slow going getting Troll from under the pile.

With just two men left punching and scratching at him, Rogan was pulled backwards by the man in the trucker hat. The man pinned him to a table. Rogan could feel his hot breath against his face. The man had a vise-like grip on Rogan's throat with his left hand. His mouth was covered in thick red, the blood dripping from his chin onto his white shirt. He punched down hard at Rogan's face with his right fist. Rogan managed to deflect the first blow.

Out of the corner of his eye, he saw Clay flying backwards, and the two men that had been on top of Troll flew almost straight up. Troll got to his feet. Rogan grabbed the trucker hat man's fist with both of his hands as it came driving again for his face. It was all he could do to hold the fist back. A large arm wrapped around the man's neck. After a moment, the grip on Rogan's neck lessened.

Rogan scrambled to his feet. Troll had a deep choke hold on the man. The trucker hat fell to the ground, Troll released his grip, and the man followed. Troll's face was puffy red and black. Blood streamed out of his nose, and from under both his eyes.

"Hey Rogan," said Troll. He tried to smile, wobbled, and fell face first to the ground, landing on top of the trucker hat guy.

"Shit. Angus, get Mac out of here. Clay."

Clay got to his feet and ran over. Rogan and Clay each put their heads under one of Troll's arms and lifted him up the best they could. Angus worked his way along the wall with McKenzie in tow. She had a hunk of wood in her hands. Rogan managed a smile as she cracked a guy across the face.

Straining under the load, Clay and Rogan worked towards the broken window. They reached the booth where Angus and McKenzie were waiting. Angus dropped down behind Troll's limp body and started fighting off the group that was moving towards them. He was a blur of arms and legs. Rogan knew that Angus had a martial arts background, but he had no idea he could fight like that—it was just another part of the enigma.

With McKenzie's help, the three heaved Troll's body on top of the tabletop. Then, with McKenzie outside the diner and Clay and Rogan on each arm, they inched him through the broken window, being careful not to add any new cuts to his already beaten body. Once he was clear, Clay jumped out the window. Rogan turned and took care of a guy that had gotten a grip on Angus with a side kick to the ear. Angus jumped backwards onto the tabletop.

"Thanks."

"Don't mention it," said Rogan, hopping out the window.

The scene outside wasn't much better than inside. Groups of people wandered the streets, bumping into one another, lampposts, garbage cans, and just about everything else. Mingled in with the seemingly harmless people were men and women that moved with purpose. They stayed low, their arms outstretched as they moved through the crowd. It looked like wolves working their way through a pasture of sheep.

"What the hell are we going to do!?" said McKenzie.

"We need to find some place to ride this out," said Angus.

"Agreed. Clay, I'm thinking we make our stand at your office."

"Sounds mighty good to me, Rogan."

Clay, Rogan, and McKenzie worked together to drag Troll across the street to the sheriff's office. Angus stayed out front to clear a path. The human wolves didn't seem to be interested in them. It looked like they were after something; the way they moved, it was almost like they were stalking prey. Rogan couldn't get a gauge on what they might be tracking, considering that they were surrounded by prey in the way of the slow-moving zombies.

The group made it to the door. Clay unlocked it and they pulled Troll inside. Rogan closed and locked the door. Angus and Clay pushed the large oak desk in front of it. Rogan looked around the building. Two doors to deal with, two windows on the front, one on the side, and a hatch in the ceiling. While doing his scan, he also noticed that the woman that had been locked up in one of the cells was gone, as was the door to that cell.

"Looks like we had a prison break."

"Wow, how did she rip those hinges off?" asked McKenzie, running her hand up and down the iron rods.

"No clue. Okay plan. Clay, we need something to board up those windows."

"There's a wood pile out back."

"Great. Angus, you and Clay get some boards, nails, and something to use as a hammer. Mac, let's pull these mattresses out of these cells and get Troll on them."

Angus and Clay went out the back door. McKenzie and Rogan arranged the mattresses in the cell without the door. They pulled Troll over and on top of the beds. Rogan reached down and checked his pulse; it was pumping. His face was unrecognizable. It was swelling by the second, red, black, and blue puffs of skin. His eyes were circled by deep purple. McKenzie found a towel, ran it under the faucet, and started wiping the blood away from Troll's eyes, lips, and nose. His shirt was shredded, slash marks crisscrossing his barrel chest. Bruises were forming on his sides.

Clay and Angus came running back through the door, slamming it shut behind them. Each had an armful of boards. Someone was banging on the door from the outside. Clay locked the door and Angus held up a board while Clay drove home nails with the butt of his revolver. An arm smashed through the small side window, swinging wildly, gripping at the air. Rogan jumped up, grabbed a board and beat at the arm until it retracted. Clay and Angus ran over and started in on the now-broken window. All around the building, he could hear moans and screams. Rogan cracked open the gun case, and pulled out a combat shotgun.

"Nonlethal?" he called over to Clay.

"Bottom shelf, yellow shells."

Rogan pulled out a box of shotgun shells; they were yellow and crowd control was printed on the box flap. He dumped the box of twenty-five shells into his pocket and loaded eight up in the shotgun. The front windows broke at the same time, a shirtless man in each. Rogan cocked the shotgun and blasted a sandbag round into the chest of the man in the left window. He cocked again, the casing flying backwards over his shoulder and fired again on the second man. Rogan looked out the window, and could see that a crowd was forming outside, maybe ten men, all shirtless, covered in blood. The first two men were lying on their backs, clutching their chests.

"Hurry up guys," yelled Rogan, reloading the two spent rounds.

Rogan jumped into the window and started pumping rounds into the crowd. He had to keep them back long enough for Clay and Angus to get the windows secured. The men snarled at him and clawed at the air towards him, but they stayed back after Rogan had dropped half of them. He could hear Clay pounding in nails next to him. It wouldn't be long now.

A cold breeze went past as Rogan perched in the window. The scene on the street was like nothing he had seen. He felt like he was in the middle of a B-rated zombie movie, holding a boom-stick. He wondered if he and his team were the only non-zombies left as he scanned the crowd mulling around the building.

It seemed like there were three types of behavior going on. The first was exhibited by the wandering masses. They seemed to have no idea what was going on around them; they just walked around aimlessly. The second group he could see was ultra-violent. Like most of the people in the diner. They wanted to kill or rape everything in sight, but they didn't seem to have the wherewithal to do it effectively. Then there were those wolves Rogan saw earlier—and this group in front of the office. They also were violent, but they seemed to have intelligence. They stalked their prey, they knew that the sheep would be there whenever they wanted, and they worked in teams.

Rogan fired another round into one of the men that got too close. He looked out, trying to find the group that had been stalking through the wanderers. He saw them off to his right, running towards a small bed and breakfast that sat at the edge of the main street. Just out in front of them, a girl was running as fast as she could. She ran up onto the deck of the building and ran through the door.

"Rogan, Rogan, come on. Squeeze in here, and I'll put the last board up."

"Put it up, I'll be back in a minute," said Rogan, hopping out and then running towards the bed and breakfast.

The group of shirtless men followed. Rogan fired over his shoulder as he ran, dropping three of the men. He ran behind the grocery store and charged to the back of the bed and breakfast, hoping to avoid the wolves out front. He came up on the rear porch and fired down a full load of bean bags onto his pursuers. He opened the door, slammed it closed and locked it. Then he reloaded.

By his count there were six people chasing the girl: four men, and two women. He ran towards the front of the house and waited in the front room, gun steadied towards the door. It was oddly quiet. He held his breath and listened. At the end of his ability to hold in air, he heard a small squeak upstairs. It was the kind of squeak that an old house like this makes when someone steps in a weakened spot of a wood floor. *The girl must be upstairs,* he thought.

Amazingly, the wolves must have heard it too. All at once, they came crashing into the house. Rogan heard glass shattering in all directions. Two men came in through the front windows, a woman came in to his left, a man to his right. He heard two more crashes from the back of the house. He laid a round into the nearest man and ran backwards up the stairs. The woman tore off after him. He popped a round off into her chest that sent her rolling head over heels backwards down the stairs. The rest of the group stopped at the bottom of the stairs.

Rogan stood at the top of the flight and pointed his shotgun down at them. They were all looking back at a large man who had walked in through the front door. He had a scar across his forehead. His arms were covered in scratches. His hands and mouth were covered in blood, some of it dry. Rogan figured most of it was not his. The man stepped forward and stared up at Rogan. He was taller and broader than all the rest of the group, and if they had a leader, he was most certainly it. What had Troll said? *The alpha male,* thought Rogan.

The alpha sent out a thunderous roar. The others jumped up and down, beating their chests. Then, at once, all six charged up the stairs. Rogan managed to drop two of them. A hand grasped around his ankle as he clambered backwards, trying to get up the second flight of stairs. He put the shotgun barrel right on the man's shoulder and pulled the trigger. He howled and fell backwards, blood pouring down his dangling arm. Rogan reached the top before a woman and a man grabbed him, yanking him to the ground. The shotgun clattered away.

He managed to roll to his back and sit up in time for the woman to tackle him to the ground. She straddled his chest, reaching both hands back and out as wide as she could, showing her sharp claws. Before she could slash down, Rogan threw a punch to her solar plexus, expelling the air from her lungs. She rolled off, gripped her chest, and wheezed while she tried to catch her breath.

The other man still had a grip on his ankle. Rogan pulled his free leg back and kicked the man in the face. It took three stomps to get him to let go. Rogan got to his feet as the final two charged up the stairs. He had already shot both of them once. The man made it first. Rogan grabbed him by the wrist, spun in a full circle and sent him barreling back down the stairs. The flying man rammed into the second woman and took her down the flight of stairs with him. Rogan grabbed the gun and ran down the hall towards the origin of the squeak.

He got to the last door on the left; it was locked.

"Anyone in there?" he asked, knocking on the door. "I'm here to help."

He could hear a heavy stomp coming up the stairs. Rogan needed to get this girl and get out of here before that big monster found them. He knocked again. No answer. The alpha reached the top of the stairs. He turned towards Rogan and glared. His big arms were held out, ready to charge. Rogan raised the shotgun, and the alpha charged like a raging bull. Rogan fired off a round into the man's chest. It barely slowed him down. The alpha crashed into Rogan, and together they slammed through the doorway at the end of the hall.

The room was a bathroom. Rogan found himself pinned against the bathtub. Water sprayed everywhere from the remnants of the sink. The shotgun was just out of reach. Rogan felt around with his hands, and he found a broken pipe under the sink. He yanked it free while the alpha reared back to strike down on Rogan. Rogan twisted his torso and smacked the alpha across the face with the metal pipe. The alpha staggered back.

Rogan reached for the shotgun, but the alpha stomped down on his arm. He had a piece of splintered wood from the door in his hand. He thrust it down at Rogan's chest. Rogan used the pipe to deflect the blow, but he did not deflect it enough; the wood found flesh and penetrated deep into Rogan's right thigh. Rogan tried the pipe attack again, but this time the alpha grabbed the pipe and ripped it out of his hand.

The alpha stood up and tore what was left of the sink off the wall. He held it over head and sent it flying down at Rogan. Rogan managed to roll out of the way just in time, feeling chunks of porcelain smacking into his back. His leg was throbbing. The wood shard embedded itself more deeply with every movement. Fortunately, he had rolled towards the shotgun. He rolled back, bringing the shotgun up, and fired. The shot connected with the alpha's shoulder. He roared and slammed his fist down into Rogan's chest. Rogan felt the air driving out of his lungs. He fought the blackout and scrambled to his feet. He could barely put weight on his injured leg. He gulped in deep breaths while the alpha clutched his shoulder. Rogan eyed the door.

The door was only one step away, and he tried to make a break for it, his leg complaining. He managed to get out of the bathroom. He stumbled backwards, falling to the ground at the top of the stairs. The alpha came charging out of the bathroom. Rogan sent a shot into his leg. The alpha's legs went flying out from under him, and he slammed face first into the hardwood floor. The alpha was shaken and struggling to get up. Rogan took advantage of the opportunity. Using the railing as a brace, he kicked the alpha repeatedly in the side of the head until he stopped moving.

Rogan hobbled back to the locked door. He tried knocking again, but got no response. He wasn't sure the alpha was down for good. He needed to get the girl and get out. He stepped back and slammed his shoulder into the door. The old door swung open. He stepped inside and closed it the best he could. There was a heavy wooden dresser next to the door. It took all he had to push it in front of the door of the small bedroom.

The room had a double-sized bed in the center, with pink floral wallpaper. Other than the dresser, there was a small desk and a closet. Rogan walked around the end of the bed. Cowering in the corner, with her knees pulled in tight to her chest and her face buried in her knees, Rogan found the girl. She had wispy blonde hair that was hanging around her legs. She wore jeans and white tennis shoes.

"Hi, are you okay?" asked Rogan. "I want to help you, get you somewhere safe. Can you talk?"

"Stay away. Everyone here wants to hurt me. Please just stay away."

"I don't want to hurt you. I want to keep you safe. Please, my name is Richard, what's yours?" said Rogan, kneeling down in front of the girl, his leg screaming in the process.

The girl glanced up from her knees. Blue eyes considered Rogan through her blonde hair. She leaned back further. Her eyes were red and puffy. Rogan figured she couldn't be more than ten. She had on a pink t-shirt with the face of a cartoon cat on the front. Rogan heard pounding on the door. The girl started to cry again.

"No, no, no..."

Rogan stood up, looking for an escape option. Though he wouldn't chastise her about it, the young girl had not picked the best hiding spot. They were two floors off the ground and in the corner of the building. The only exit would be through the now-blocked door or a jump out the window, which would likely result in a broken bone or two. On the upside, there was also only one entry for the alpha to use.

"Okay. I know this is scary, but I need you to hang in there, okay?"

The girl sniffled and looked up at him again and nodded. "I'm Lizzy."

"Hi, Lizzy. I think we are going to be okay. I put that huge dresser in front of the door, and we are way off the ground. So I think if we just hunker down here until morning, we'll be okay."

Lizzy nodded and laid her head back against the wall. Rogan knelt beside her, the shotgun trained on the door. The pounding and banging continued for another couple minutes. Then it stopped suddenly. Rogan listened carefully, hoping to hear the heavy feet walking back down the stairs, but he heard nothing. It was deadly quiet.

Another minute passed with no sound. Suddenly, just to the right of the door where the dresser had been, a large fist came crashing through the plaster and lathe wall of the bedroom. Rogan nearly dropped the shotgun, but he managed to hang onto it as he got to his feet. He jumped to the other side of the bed as the first fist retracted and a second came in right next to the first hole.

Rogan skidded to a stop before the wall. Another fist shot through the wall like it was paper. Rogan raised the shotgun at the hole, which was about the size of a basketball now. Rogan inched forward, making sure he would be out of punching range, and waited. For a moment, nothing happened, and then, as he hoped, the alpha put his head in the hole. The only thing he would be able to see was a shotgun barrel, and if his vision had been enhanced too, maybe the bean bag flying out of the end of the barrel before it nailed him in the forehead. The alpha crashed backwards with a sickening crunch of plaster.

Rogan risked a look out the hole. The alpha was slumped against the far wall, his head hanging backwards beyond the functional limit. Two of the other men knelt beside him, poking at him with their fingers. Rogan put the barrel through the opening and sent a shot into each. Then he reloaded the shotgun while he weighed the options. He didn't like where they were, but it was pretty bad out there. He wasn't sure he had enough rounds to get them back to the sheriff's office, and even if he'd made it there, he couldn't be sure there would be a way in. He sat on the edge of the bed with the shotgun across his knees. Lizzy came out from the corner and sat next to him.

"What are you thinking about?"

"I'm trying to decide if we make a stand here for the night, or if I risk us trying to get back to my friends."

"You're bleeding."

Rogan looked down at his thigh; a circle of red had formed around the wood hunk in his leg. He knew better than to pull it out—that would just be like pulling the cork off a champagne bottle. Lizzy stood up and walked to the head of the bed, she came back with a pillow. She pulled off the case and put the pillow under Rogan's knee.

"To keep it elevated," she said and then tightly wrapped the pillow case around Rogan's wound. She pulled it tight. Rogan fought back the urge to whimper, but he felt water forming in his eyes. "That should slow it down some, but not much. You really need some bandages, probably stitches."

"How do you know that?"

"I'm a girl scout. I have a badge in first aid."

"Huh, I thought girl scouts was just cookies. Lizzy, why did you come up here?"

"It's my room. My parents are across the hall, or well...they should be," said Lizzy, starting to sob.

"Can you tell me what happened, Lizzy?" asked Rogan, putting a reassuring hand on her shoulder.

"My dad brought us up here for vacation. He used to come up here with his dad when he was kid," said Lizzy, wiping tears off on the quilt on the end of the bed. "We were going to go fishing, I guess, and just, you know, do family stuff. We got here and had some supper downstairs with the owners. Then Dad took us down by the lake to see the sunset over the water. It was beautiful. Then it got bad."

"People started attacking you?"

"Yeah, it was like they came out of nowhere. We were walking back, and then all of sudden there were these people all around us. We ran. I think they killed my parents," said Lizzy, crying hard again. Rogan rubbed his hand across her upper shoulders and looked towards the hole. He needed to keep her safe.

"I'm sorry, Lizzy. I'm so sorry."

She turned and buried her face into Rogan's side and cried. He held her. He didn't know what else to do. He hadn't heard any commotion outside the room for a while, so he wondered if maybe, with their alpha gone, the others would wander off to find a new group.

"What's that?" asked Lizzy. "It tickles."

"Huh? Oh, my phone. I have a phone!"

Rogan pulled his cellphone of his pocket and answered it.

"Hello?"

"Rogan?"

"Mac?"

"Yeah, oh my god, I thought you were dead. You weren't answering your phone."

"I've been a little busy. Is everything okay there?"

"We're good. The entrances are all boarded up. Where are you?"

"Remember that B&B on the end of main?"

"The one with all the pink flamingos and lawn gnomes?"

"Yep, that's the one. I'm upstairs, barricaded in a room. I found a girl who isn't crazy."

"Really? I was starting to think we were the only ones not affected by whatever is going on. What's the plan?"

"Well, I'd like to get back there to the first aid kit, as it occurs to me that I'm losing some blood, and while this sheet is slowing it down, I really need something better."

"You're bleeding? Crap, Rogan. Okay, we'll come get you."

"No, no, too dangerous."

Click.

"Well, Lizzy, I guess my friends are coming to get us."

"We better get you patched up for the trip then," said Lizzy.

Lizzy bunched up a piece of the quilt that she and Rogan had torn. She pressed it against Rogan's leg and then tightly wound another pillow case over the wound. Rogan got to his feet and tested the bandage, it was solid. He could move, but every step sent razors of pain up his nervous system. He hoped he would get some mobility back once the hunk of door was out of his thigh.

Rogan checked the hallway through the hole in the wall. The path looked clear. He and Lizzy pushed the dresser aside just enough to get out of the room. Lizzy kicked the downed alpha in the thigh as they went by. Rogan smiled; he liked this girl. One stair at a time, Lizzy helped Rogan down the stairs. Putting weight on his leg was nearly unbearable. The more they moved, the worse it got. Rogan sat at the top of the first flight of stairs to rest.

"When do you think your friends will get here?"

"Soon, I hope. I haven't heard any gunfire, though. I'm not sure if that is a good or bad sign."

"Maybe they're being all ninja about it, and the bad guys can't see them."

Rogan laughed and tousled Lizzy's hair. "I hope you're right."

"Come on, Richard, let's get the rest of the way down."

"You can call me Rogan. Everyone else does."

"I like Richard," she said, pulling Rogan to his feet.

"Stubborn, I see."

Lizzy just smiled and helped him down the next step. Rogan had one hand on the railing. He leaned hard into it, keeping the weight off his bad leg. Lizzy stood next to him, holding him around the waist, helping to ease him down each stair. She held the shotgun in her other hand. The house was quiet. Rogan listened hard, but he couldn't hear any movement. He felt sure the house was empty. A house has a certain soundlessness when it is completely empty. Rogan could always sense it. The air just felt...empty.

Rogan and Lizzy made it to the bottom of the steps. They set up camp in the corner of the front parlor. It meant having their back to the outer wall, but they also had a full view of all entrances into the room. Lizzy dragged over a plush red velvet chair for Rogan. He sat down without argument.

"Red. You know, that way if you bleed all over it no one will be able to tell."

"So wise for a child."

"I'll have you know I am not a child," said Lizzy, staring at him with her hands jutted sharply into her hips.

"My mistake, kid."

Lizzy scowled at him and stomped off. She came back dragging a wood bench with a high back. She was surprisingly strong for a young girl. She turned the bench so that the seat faced Rogan's fancy chair. Then she sat on the floor next to Rogan.

"Cover?"

"Of course."

"Is there a badge for that?"

"No, I don't think so," said Lizzy seriously.

In the distance, Rogan heard an engine. It sounded like the motor of a larger vehicle, maybe a truck. Rogan looked around the parlor; there were two men and a woman laid out there, all part of the wolf pack that had come with the alpha. He hoped that they weren't all dead. He hated that he had to take lives tonight, even if it was to protect Lizzy and his friends. He knew that what was happening to these people was not happening by choice. They could not be held responsible for their actions, but he felt like he could be held responsible for his. He still had conscious thought, after all. He'd chosen to kill those people, even if it was in self-defense.

Rogan had prided himself on the fact that during his years as a cop he'd taken only a couple lives; he always shot to maim, never to kill, partially because he treasured life but also because he subscribed to his late father's philosophy of crime and punishment. "Big" Mike Rogan used to say that killing a criminal was giving them the easy way out. If they were dead, they wouldn't have to think about how their actions affected their life and others'. Capture a criminal alive, he said, and he suffers through court and then through jail.

The engine noise grew closer. Based on what he had seen so far, he didn't figure even the alphas would be capable of mastering a vehicle, so the vehicle coming towards them was either his friends or someone else that hadn't joined club crazy yet.

Rogan's eyes were growing heavy. It felt like the weight of the shotgun laying across his lap was increasing with every ticking second. He and Lizzy sat in silence, listening to the house and the engine. It grew louder and louder. Then, blinding light came blazing through the front windows. Rogan covered his eyes. The engine roared. The light bounced off the walls. Then the front door exploded inward, followed by the front end of a black conversion van. The front doors swung open. McKenzie jumped out of one side, shotgun to her shoulder. Angus rolled out of the driver's side, scanning the room with his shotgun.

"Over here," said Rogan.

"Where's the bad guys?" asked McKenzie.

"Me and Lizzy took care of them. Lizzy, this is Mac and Angus."

"Huh, that makes the whole crashing through the front of the house thing feel unnecessary," said Angus.

McKenzie ran over and helped Rogan to his feet. Angus stayed by the van and watched out the window for company.

With his arms over McKenzie and Lizzy, Rogan hobbled to the van. The group got in the black van, and Angus gunned the motor, flying backwards down the steps, across the lawn, and back out into the street. Fallen pink flamingo parts littered the lawn. Deep tire tracks made a clear path up and into the bed and breakfast.

"That might have been overkill," said Rogan, leaning against the desk in the back of the van. Angus's van looked like the back of a sting vehicle from a police show. Banks of computers and monitors hung on the walls or were strapped under the dual desks that ran the length of the back of the van. Lizzy sat in the rolling chair that was locked into place by two straps to one of the desks.

Angus laughed and tore around the edge of the building to the alley that ran along the back of the main street. He came to a stop behind the sheriff's office. Angus stood up, hunched into the back, and threw open a small door in the ceiling. He pulled himself up onto the roof of the van and reached his hand down. Rogan nodded towards Lizzy. She got up and took Angus's hand. Rogan watched her white shoes disappear through the ceiling. Next, McKenzie went up with the help of Angus and Lizzy, and finally all three of them reached to pull Rogan's bulk through the ceiling. He had to turn so that his shoulders went out diagonally. Once he got his shoulders out, he was able to pull himself up the rest of the way, with help from the gang. Rogan looked up and saw Clay standing on the roof, only a couple feet above the roof of the van. The group all got up onto the roof, except for Angus. He dropped back down into the van and pulled it away from the building. When he came back Clay, threw him down a rope.

"How did you get on the roof?" asked Rogan.

"Oh, the last sheriff had a trap door installed. You pull it down and it makes a stairway up to a flat part on the roof on the front of the building. He used to sit up there and 'patrol' the town from his rocking chair," said Clay.

"Convenient."

The group went over the crest of the roof to the flat spot. There sat an old rocking chair, and next to it a set of stairs led down to the floor of the station. Clay and Angus helped Rogan down the steps and over to one of the office chairs. McKenzie grabbed the first aid kit.

"How's Troll?" asked Rogan looking over at Troll, who looked to still be unconscious.

"He's still breathing," said McKenzie. "But that's about all I can say."

McKenzie pulled out rolls of gauze and bandages. She did not have a look of confidence in her eyes as she stared down at the wood shard extruding from Rogan's thigh. He waved Lizzy over, who was leaning on the bars of Troll's impromptu recovery room, staring at the big man.

"Mac, Lizzy here is a girl scout. She even has a badge in first aid. Maybe she can help you."

"It's true. I almost have my advanced first aid, even."

McKenzie smiled up at Rogan and handed Lizzy a roll of bandages. Together they cut away a hunk of Rogan's jeans around the wood and cleaned up the wound with alcohol. Rogan winced more than once.

"Okay, Richard. I think we need to pull the wood out."

"Richard?" said McKenzie, eyebrow raised.

Rogan shrugged. "Well, let's just get it over with."

Using a pair of pliers from Clay's pocket tool, McKenzie took a grip on the wood. Lizzy stood by with a wad of cloth.

"Okay, on three," said Rogan.

"Fine, you count," said McKenzie.

"One...son of a bitch!"

"Oh, sorry, did I go too soon?" asked McKenzie, holding up the wood stake; it was much smaller than Rogan had thought, especially considering the pain it had caused. He looked at the wood and at his thigh, confused. He would have sworn he had a massive wooden spike jabbed into his leg, but what McKenzie held in her hand was barely more than a splinter.

"What?" asked McKenzie.

"I thought it was a lot bigger," said Rogan.

"Why do men always think that?"

The girls went back to pouring alcohol and cleaning the small hole in Rogan's leg. Lizzy surprised everyone by stitching the wound up. She smiled at her handiwork and then McKenzie covered it with gauze and adhesive bandage.

"You learn to stich wounds in first aid class?" asked Rogan.

"Oh no, but I do also have a badge in sewing. I sew up my teddy bear all the time, I figured, how different could it be?"

"How diff...? How...ugh," said Rogan. He stood up, testing his leg. Much to his surprise, it felt significantly better. He hoped to not have to run for a while, but he could tolerate walking.

"So we figure we can keep watch up on the roof, and then in the morning, sort this out. Not sure there is much else we can do," said Clay.

"Watch is a good idea, but I think we need to take the big guy into the city for some medical attention," said Rogan motioning towards Troll.

"Think we can risk it?" asked Clay.

"He might have internal bleeding or something. We can't just leave him lay," said Rogan.

"I can't just leave my town like this Rogan," said Clay.

"I know. I'm thinking you and I stay here, perhaps muster up a distraction while Angus, Mac and Lizzy make a run for it with Troll in the back of the van."

Angus nodded and stood up, heading for the door. Clay chewed his lip considering the plan. Troll sat bolt upright.

"Troll!" yelled McKenzie.

Troll looked around, confused, taking in the scene. The group all huddled around the entrance to the cell.

"You okay, big guy?" asked Rogan.

"I don't know yet," said Troll, "give me a minute."

Troll ran his hands up and down his arms and legs. He pressed his fists into his chest, sides, back and stomach. He grimaced more than once.

"Yep, I'm fine," proclaimed Troll.

"Are you sure, man? You look pretty rough. We were just making a plan to run you into Queen."

"Well, I mean I'm no doctor but, oh wait, that's right, I am. I'm fine."

"And in a chipper mood," said Angus.

"I could use some variety of pain medication," said Troll.

McKenzie brought Troll some water and a couple aspirin. Then with Lizzy's help she began cleaning and bandaging Trolls bumps, bruises and scrapes.

"Okay, so we stay here?" asked Clay.

"Yes, I don't think we have a reason to risk leaving at this point," said Rogan listening to the constant moaning and banging outside, "but we do need to call out for help."

"The little lady took care of that while you were out being a hero," said Clay nodding towards McKenzie.

"Yeah, I called the Queen City dispatch, and also the state police while Clay and Angus finished fortifying our hideout," said McKenzie.

"Nice work, are they sending help?"

"After I convinced them I wasn't coo-coo, the State Police said they are going to set up roadblocks to stop people from accidently stumbling into this mess. They said they'd reach out to the National Guard too and get them in here to try to get this under control. I just hope they don't come in here guns blazing. I don't think these people are lost."

"I would agree. From what I saw, whatever has happened to these people has reduced them to less than human, but I don't think it's permanent. They seem to only be reacting, not thinking. Though some seem to be smarter and stronger than the others, it's almost like there are packs forming," said Rogan.

"Humans are by nature a social animal," said McKenzie.

"So what happened out there?" asked Angus.

Rogan sat down against Troll's cell and told the group what he and Lizzy had gone through. Then Angus went up the staircase to take the first watch. Rogan did not argue one bit; he could barely keep his eyes open. He slid over and propped his head against the corner of the cell and the outer wall. McKenzie walked over and sat down beside him, leaning into his arm. He lifted it and her head fell to his chest as he put his arm around her shoulders.

"I thought we lost you," she whispered.

"You wish."

"Not one bit."

Rogan smiled, leaned his head back, and took one last look around the room. Clay sat in his chair, cowboy hat slung over his eyes, shotgun across his lap. Troll was once more passed out on the mattresses on the floor of the prison cell. Lizzy sat on the stairs, looking around the room. She met his eyes. He smiled and waved her over. She half-ran, looking much younger than she claimed to be. Rogan scooted away from the wall, pushing McKenzie with him. Lizzy snuggled in between him and the wall.

For a moment, everything felt okay.

11.

Even with the wandering horde below, the sun coming up over the tall conifer trees that backdropped the main street of Evergreen was a sight to see. Rogan sat in the old rocking chair on the flat part of the sheriff's office roof. His leg felt stiff, but surprisingly, it didn't hurt much. He would have to remember to commend Lizzy on her fine patch job when she woke up.

Rogan had slept hard after the rough night battling the wild people of Evergreen. He woke up just before sunrise with an ache in his back from leaning against the steel bars of a prison cell. Both his arms were asleep, since he had a young woman sleeping on each one. He had always dreamed of waking up in just that position, but considering that one of the women was barely old enough to claim the categorization and the other could just as well be his sister, it was not all he had hoped for. He rolled a shotgun in his hands, watching an old man wearing a blue robe and flip-flips bump repeatedly into a stop sign. Rogan clutched his guts as they rumbled. He hoped that with the rise of the sun, the mob would dissipate; he was in need of some flapjacks.

The triangular ray of light from the rising sun slowly expanded down Main Street and towards the sheriff's office. As the light hit the wandering people, they seemed to snap out of their trance. Some looked shocked to be out in the street, others simply stopped bumping into things and walked off, presumably towards their homes. Throughout the night, Angus and then Clay had taken shots at the wilder Evergreen residents, hoping to protect the wandering sheep from the roaming wolves. Clay had reported that he hadn't seen a wolf in over an hour when he handed watch duties off to Rogan.

Rogan heard the stairs complaining loudly as heavy footfalls headed up his way. He glanced down the opening to see Troll emerging out of the roof access hatch. His face was heavily bruised, but not nearly as puffy as the previous evening. His arms and legs were bandaged and large circles of bandages wrapped around his big chest under what was left of his shirt.

"Morning," said Troll, gingerly sitting down next to Rogan with a groan.

"Well, good morning. I thought we might have lost you there for a minute, big guy."

"Shit, a couple yokels hopped up on god-knows-what? No contest."

"You clearly remember the evening differently than I do."

"To be honest, I don't remember much after the brawl broke out. McKenzie gave me the highlights."

"Feeling okay though, considering?"

"Pretty hungry. Other than that, just kind of numb. I think I'm so bruised up that my body doesn't know what to tell my mind. What's the plan?"

"Well, odd as it seems, the sun seems to be breaking everyone out. Hoping the way gets cleared and we can make a charge for the diner and get some food, then come back here and hole up. Figure out what the heck we are going to do."

"I'm going to call into the lab in a bit, see if they found anything in the blood work I sent in."

"That would be good. Other than that, buddy, you need to take it easy. I mean this in the nicest possible way, but you look like an abused punching bag."

"Yeah, yeah, real funny."

Rogan chuckled and lightly patted Troll on the shoulder. Together they watched the crowd of people slowly start to separate. Troll began to whistle. Rogan was glad his friend was okay. His team was his family—it was hard to see one of them injured. Soon the road would be cleared and they would be able to head out to get supplies. After that, he didn't know what they were going to do.

Rogan sighed and scanned the street. He ran his eyes across the rooflines of the Main Street buildings, trying to get a better sense of the town. Each awning had sprayers attached to it as part of the solution to keep the dust down on the packed dirt main drag. Rogan raised an eyebrow as he noticed that each building also had one and sometimes up to three cameras mounted flush to the roof. From the ground, the small round cameras wouldn't even be visible. For such a small town, it seemed odd that there was so much security. He made a mental note to ask Clay about it when he headed downstairs.

"Feels good up here. I can see why that old sheriff sat up here all the time," said Troll.

"No doubt. Plus it's an amazing vantage point; you can literally see the entire town from here."

Troll got to his feet, putting a hand to the roof to steady himself on the way up. He stretched out his arms and pulled his shoulder blades together. He looked very much like a bandaged bear stretching out his paws in the morning.

"Sure you're okay?"

"Yep. Stiff as heck, but once I was awake, I was able to use the medical supplies Clay had to mix up a nice cocktail. The girl, what's-her-name, down there and McKenzie did a nice job on the bandages."

"Lizzy?"

"Yeah. She's surprisingly bright for a kid. Should probably consider the medical field. I can sit in the chair for a bit if you want to stretch your legs."

"You sure you're up to it?"

"Yeah, I think I can manage sitting in a chair. Come on, make me feel useful."

Rogan nodded and headed down the stairs. He heard Troll exhale loudly and plop down in the rocker. The runners creaked and cracked as he rocked it back and forth over the landing.

Angus and Clay were both asleep in the cells. McKenzie and Lizzy were sitting at Clay's desk, playing cards. They both looked in Rogan's direction and smiled as he stepped off the last step.

"Morning, ladies."

"Morning," they said in unison.

"How long have you been up?"

"I don't know, maybe an hour," said McKenzie.

"Yeah the big guy woke up, and that kind of woke all of us up," said Lizzy.

"Troll," said Rogan.

"Where?"

"His name."

"Whose?"

"Troll's."

"What?"

"Lizzy, the big guy's name is Troll," said McKenzie.

"Ahh, why didn't you just say that?" said Lizzy, staring at Rogan.

"I—never mind. How long has Clay been down?"

"No clue. He woke up when Troll began banging around like a caged Sasquatch, but fell right back asleep."

Rogan nodded and walked into the cell. He needed to talk to Clay, so as much as he would have liked to let the man in the wide-brimmed hat sleep, he rocked his shoulder. Clay sat bolt upright, hands scrambling on the floor around him.

"Rogan, damn. You scared the ghost right out of me."

"Sorry, Clay. I just have a question, something odd I saw while up top."

"Sure, what's doing?" asked Clay, rubbing his eyes.

"Why in a town like Evergreen are there so many security cameras?"

"Cameras? What are you talking about? I don't think the bank even has one."

"From on the roof, I could see at minimum two cameras on each roof running along the main street, all pointing in different angles."

"No, that can't be. No one has need of anything like that up here."

"Well get up, Tex, I'll show you."

Rogan helped Clay to his feet. The two of them walked up the staircase and onto to the roof. Troll was leaned back in the rocking chair, arms hanging, mouth wide open, sound asleep, with the shotgun perched between his legs, barrel pointing straight at his face.

Rogan shook his head and gently took the shotgun. He leaned it against the roof's edge, barrel pointed in a safe direction, while Clay looked out over the town.

"I'll be damned."

"Told you."

"Rogan, I have no inkling as to why there are cameras pointed all over heck in my town."

"Well that might be a good place to start, then. Let's wake up Angus."

✳ ✳ ✳

The team split up shortly after Rogan and Clay came down the stairs. There were two immediate issues: First, after a night of fighting off a horde of crazy townies, the team was hungry, and the best Clay could do was a couple expired granola bars and a bottle of orange soda. The other issue was the cameras. After waking up Angus and filling him in on the cameras, issue two fell squarely to an oddly excited Angus. Angus dashed up to the roof while Rogan was still explaining that Clay didn't know where the cameras had come from. Less than a minute later, he came leaping back down the stairs with a black laptop in his hands.

"On it... You guys get us some food," said Angus, plopping down at Clay's desk.

"Okay then. I guess we're on food," said Rogan to Clay.

The team carefully removed the boards covering the rear door of the sheriff's office, making sure to leave the nails in so that they could be put back up quickly.

"Okay. Clay, you and I will head over to the diner and get some supplies. Once we head out, Mac, lock this door."

"Oh, like hell you're leaving me here," said McKenzie.

"Mac, come on, I need you to stay here and hold down the fort."

"Clay can hold down the fort."

Clay looked sheepishly back and forth between Rogan and McKenzie, pulled his hat low, and took a step away. McKenzie shoved her fists into her hips and stared up at Rogan. "I'm going."

Rogan rubbed the bridge of his nose and said, "We don't know if it's safe out there."

"All the more reason for me to go, so I can watch your back."

"Mac, please just stay here...watch Lizzy for me...and lock the door."

"Not happening," said McKenzie, shouldering past Rogan and out the back door of the office.

"Wow, stubborn as a mule," said Clay.

"You have no idea," said Rogan. He looked over at Lizzy, who was curled up in the corner staring at the wall. He wished he could think of something brilliant to say to her, but when his folks died, he just drank until he couldn't think. He didn't figure that would work for a child—not that it had worked that great for him, either.

"I'll look after her, Rogan. Go catch your girlfriend."

"Mac? Oh no, she's not my girlfriend."

"Is that so...?" said Clay, closing the door.

There was a thump as the deadbolt dropped into place. Rogan stood staring at the door and thinking up a retort, but nothing came, so instead he rounded the corner of the building and found McKenzie marching across the street to the diner. Her fists were tightly clenched as her feet pounded the dirt road. When she got moving, she was a force to be reckoned with.

McKenzie got to the door first, turned, and tapped her foot while Rogan did his best attempt at a jog to catch her. His leg felt okay, but a not-so-subtle shot of nerve pain coursed up his body with every ambling step. He opened the door, and she sauntered in. The diner was empty...except for the bodies of several fallen Evergreen residents. Broken bits of chair and table scattered the floor. Broken glass covered the few booth tops that were still intact.

"Hello?" yelled Rogan.

No answer. Rogan kicked over the counter and walked into the kitchen. He found an empty onion box and went to the fridge. He loaded the onion box up with lunch meat, bread, cheese, and assorted fruit. He walked out of the kitchen to find McKenzie loading up a box with bottled water and beef jerky.

"So, is it stealing if the entire town is trying to kill you?"

"Maybe we should leave an IOU," said Rogan.

"I wonder where the rest went," said McKenzie, looking around the diner.

"I'm just glad there aren't more littering the floor."

"That whole thing was crazy. More than once, I thought one of us was going to be a goner."

"We got lucky. That was too close."

"We have to figure out what is going on before this whole town kills itself."

"I know...I've never seen anything like this."

"I feel terrible for Lizzy; her family comes in for a trip, and they drive right into carnage central."

Rogan nodded. "I just don't know what to say to her."

"Me either. She started staring into the corner after you and Clay went up top, just sitting there like a statue."

"She was so brave last night. I was wondering when it would hit."

"You should talk to her, since you've been through it. I mean...you know, losing loved ones to violence."

After he'd lost his family, Rogan fell deep into depression. He gave up shaving, showering, eating, or drinking anything that didn't contain alcohol. He felt confident that if it weren't for McKenzie that he would have died in some gutter with whiskey rolling off his cold lips. Using her gift of extreme stubbornness, she snapped Rogan out of his stupor and dragged him kicking and screaming back to the world of the living and hygiene conscious.

"To be honest, I wouldn't know what to say, because really, there is nothing to say," said Rogan, picking up his onion box. "Plus we both know I wouldn't be here if it weren't for you."

McKenzie smiled and picked up her box of water and jerky. "Let's get out of here. This place is kind of creeping me out. I feel like I walked onto the set of some post-apocalyptic TV show."

"And off we go with our scavenged supplies for the end of the world."

Rogan and Mckenzie carried their finds across the street and to the rear door. After knocking and confirming they were not looking to eat anyone, Clay unlatched the door and let them in. McKenzie played server, dishing out food and water to everyone while Rogan went to look over Angus's shoulder.

"Find anything?"

"Oh dude, these guys are pretty good."

"Huh?"

"Masking their IP, dodging networks, even shot a loop out through Malaysia. Sneaky bastards, I'm telling you."

"So does that mean you did or didn't find anything?"

"Oh, yeah man. Those cameras are all basically webcams, and they are all feeding back to a central server. Just a little bit longer, and I'll be able to track the packets back to the end point."

"Sure, endpoint, packets, yeah, good work," said Rogan, shaking his head and walking away. He grabbed an orange, a ham sandwich, and a bottle of water. Lizzy was still staring off into the corner. There was a plate of food sitting next to her.

Rogan walked over and sat down right next to her, close enough that her back touched his shoulder.

"Not hungry?" asked Rogan. Lizzy did not answer. "Here, maybe just try to eat this orange. You don't want to be getting the scurvy, arr," said Rogan in his best pirate voice.

Lizzy didn't respond.

Rogan sighed. He knew from experience that jokes wouldn't do it, but it had been worth a shot. The only thing that would heal her wounds would be time, and even then it would just be a bandage.

"I know you don't want to talk, and I know you don't want to eat, or do anything. In fact you probably feel like you can't do anything. Tell you what. I'm just going to sit here, so take your time."

Rogan ate his lunch. Then he leaned back against the wall and waited. Angus was feverishly typing at his laptop, a corner of a sandwich hanging out of his mouth. Clay stood by the front of the building, staring out a crack between a couple of the boards over the window. McKenzie busied herself sorting the food and drinks. Lizzy stared at the wall.

Rogan could hear the roof creaking as the runners under the rocking chair rolled back and forth. Rogan set his mind working on the puzzle. He had to figure out what was going on with these people. A part of him wanted to just jump into their cars and head out, cut and run, chalk Evergreen up as a loss. He couldn't do that, though. He was and would always be a member of the storied Rogan family. The family that could always be counted on to keep law and order. Helping people was a hereditary trait passed down through the generations—a trait that always ended in death.

Putting his head back against the concrete wall, Rogan closed his eyes. He needed to come up with a plan. He had hopes that Angus was on to something; maybe the cameras would lead them somewhere, but it was just as likely that they were following a herring. He felt himself nodding off. He fought his bobbing eyelids, but eventually he failed.

Rogan wasn't sure how much time had passed since he'd put his head against the wall to rest his eyes, but he did feel refreshed. Angus was still pounding away at his laptop. McKenzie was asleep, curled up on a bench by the desk. Troll was eating what looked like a sandwich straight out of a Scooby Doo cartoon—six slices of bread, meat, cheese, and a lettuce leaf between each slice, making a tower of sandwich. That meant the slight creaking from above was Clay. Rogan turned to Lizzy. She was no longer staring at the wall. Instead, her bright blue eyes were staring straight at him. He could see water welling up around her crystal lenses.

"Richard? Is everything going to be okay?"

"Yeah, Lizzy, everything's going to fine."

"You don't know that."

"Sure I do. Look around. See those people over there? I believe in each one of them, everyone on my team. We're all going to figure this out together."

"Richard?"

"Yes?"

"My parents died."

"I know, honey." Rogan put his hand on her shoulder. Her lip quivered. Then her eyes, her brow, and finally, her entire body started to shake. When she couldn't hold it any longer, she cried out, the dammed up water spilling out of her river-blue eyes. Lizzy jumped into Rogan's arms. She caught him a bit off guard, and he wheezed out as she crashed into him. She balled up pieces of his t-shirt in her hands and plunged her face into his chest, and she cried. Rogan held her tight. He didn't say anything. He just held her and let her cry.

After nearly ten minutes, Rogan felt Lizzy's grip on his shirt loosen. He ran his hand through her blonde hair as she turned her head to the side and fell asleep. It reminded Rogan of all the times he had held McKenzie in the same way when they were much younger. Sometimes it was because of something her mother had said, other times she had fallen or hurt herself, but usually it was because of some boy that had picked on her. He would wait for her to cry it out and fall asleep. Then he would get up, find the boy, and beat him to within an inch of his life.

Rogan didn't consider himself a violent man, but he had learned early on that he would do just about anything to protect his family. He wished now, sitting there in that old jail cell holding Lizzy in his arms, that he could put her aside and go find whoever killed her parents, even if they would have no recollection of what they had done. He looked over at McKenzie. She was still curled up on the bench, her hooded sweatshirt balled up under her head, serving as a pillow. She was staring at him. They locked eyes for a moment. McKenzie smiled and drifted back to sleep. Rogan smiled and leaned his head back against the wall.

Rogan's eyes shot to the barred window across the cell. There, floating just outside the bars, was his ghost. He had a strange feeling that it was happy. He also wondered if he was really losing his mind. Rogan smiled up at the foggy, star-like apparition in the window. He looked down at Lizzy and then back, but the ghost was gone.

Very carefully, he laid Lizzy down on one of the mattresses in the cell and quietly walked out into the main office. He looked down to see almost a perfect circle of tears in the center of his t-shirt.

"Rogs, buddy, just in time. I totally cracked this puppy."

"And anything useful, Angus?" asked Rogan.

"Yeah, all those cameras? After whipping all over the net, they eventually find their way back to the same place—took a while to smoke out the physical locale, but it's not far from here."

"Nice work. Where exactly?"

"I cross-referenced it with a government satellite that I...never mind. Anyway, it looks like an old farm north of town."

"Why would a farm have camera feeds running back to it?" asked McKenzie, stirring from her nap.

"I'm guessing it isn't a farm anymore," said Rogan. "Mac, can you go relieve Clay? I want to see if he knows anything about this place."

After stretching, and exaggerating a yawn, McKenzie disappeared up the stairs. A moment later, Clay came down. "What did you find?" he asked.

"All those cameras are hooked up to the same place, a farm north of here."

"That doesn't make any sense."

"You know anything about this place?" asked Rogan, pointing to the satellite image Angus had gotten.

Clay stared at the image. Angus zoomed it in and out, showing Clay the surrounding area. Clay nodded. "Sure, that's an old dairy. Severson's or something like that. Closed up about the time I got to town. Family went south, I think."

"Who owns it now?" asked Rogan.

"No one, far as I know. I think they just abandoned it."

"Best I could find is that the land and buildings are owned by some big bank back in the city," said Angus.

"Think it's worth checking out?" asked Clay.

"Absolutely," said Rogan.

12.

After a great deal of debate, the team decided to send Rogan, Angus, and Clay to check out the farm. Troll, McKenzie, and Lizzy would stay back and keep the office protected. It was after noon by the time the three men had loaded up into Angus's van and headed out towards the farm. Rogan drove while Angus gave him directions based on the map on his laptop. They drove on gravel roads north of town, eventually coming out on an asphalt two-lane road that ran from east to west.

Rogan turned the van onto the road and headed east. He looked to the south to see the thick forest that stretched out from Evergreen. He figured the forest must be nearly three miles of thick trees and brush, which meant that he and McKenzie had barely made a dent looking around the first day when they found the dead man in the bottom of the dirt pit. There could be any number of people wandering around in the woods, lost, confused, or worse. Those that had gotten violent might be hiding out in the deep woods as well.

After another mile, the old farmstead came up on the left. It had a long gravel driveway that had almost been overtaken by prairie grasses and weeds. As they pulled into the driveway, Rogan noticed a large number of wheel marks in the dirt. Odd, considering the place was supposed to be abandoned.

"What's the plan?" asked Clay.

"I think we block the driveway with the van. Then go see if anyone is home," said Rogan, pulling the van to a stop on the narrowest part of the driveway. He looked out at the farmstead, noting the farm house, an old chicken coop, a garage that had nearly fallen in, and a large barn. "Angus, any way to know which building the signal is coming from?" asked Rogan.

"Yup, one second." Angus clicked away on his laptop. "Okay, looks like the traffic is all ending at that big-ass barn."

"Okay, I vote we just go straight there then. Those other buildings all look pretty rough."

"I agree. Let's sweep that barn," said Clay.

The three men got out of the van. Rogan carried a pistol grip assault shotgun. Clay unstrapped his colt six shooter, while Angus popped a clip into a Mac-10 submachine gun.

"Where the hell did you get that?" whispered Rogan as the trio ducked down in the weeds beside the driveway.

"This old thing? Just a little something I picked up along the way," said Angus, laying a kiss on the top of his machine gun.

"Just...questions first, shoot later, okay?"

Angus nodded and pulled the strap over his shoulder. They maneuvered the best they could through the long grasses and weeds along the driveway, eventually coming out at the side of the barn. Rogan burst out of the weeds and came to a stop outside the big door of the barn. Angus and Clay followed shortly after. Rogan glanced around the corner of the barn, and seeing nothing, he turned into the building and knelt down in the shadows next to the door.

Shotgun drawn, he scanned the open area. It was clearly meant for parking equipment. There was a black Suburban parked against one wall. It had a trailer hooked to it that held a side by side four wheeler. Other than that, the large, open space was empty. Keeping to the outer wall, Rogan made his way around the open space, sticking to the shadows, keeping his eyes and weapon scanning for movement. He reached the Suburban. It was empty.

Rogan could make out Clay on the far wall, clearing the opposite end of the open space. They met at a double door. Rogan nodded toward Angus, who had stayed at the entry door to watch for anyone coming from behind. Angus ran into the open space, froze for a second, and dove behind the Suburban. Clay and Rogan exchanged looks, while Angus belly crawled over to them.

"What the hell was that?" asked Rogan.

"We're on candid camera," said Angus pointing up.

About ten feet up from the double door, a camera was mounted. "Shit," said Rogan. "I guess they probably know we're here."

Almost in response the camera started to scan the floor of the open space. "Guess there's no point in being quiet anymore," said Rogan, stepping in front of the doors. Angus took his place along the left side of the door. Clay stood ready on the right. Rogan raised his red Converse shoe and smashed it into the door just above the knobs. The doors exploded inward. Rogan ran through, scanning the room with the shotgun. He made a note to commend Lizzy on her patch job; his leg felt great. Angus took the left, Clay took the right. Much to their surprise, they stood in an empty milking parlor.

"What the heck?" asked Clay.

"Split up. Eyes up, ears open," said Rogan.

The three men fanned out across the milking parlor. The room was completely empty except for an old milk tank and a bunch of debris. They walked through to the open stall area, looking for signs of life. After concluding the search, they returned to the milk parlor.

"Well, looks like we're bust," said Clay. "Maybe we should head back, make sure we're back in the office before dark."

Rogan sighed. There had to be something here. He looked over at Angus, who was typing away at a tablet computer. Rogan stood at the edge of the pit, looking down to where the dairy farmer would have stood to hook up the milking machine.

"I'm telling you, bro, the signal is coming from this barn."

Rogan nodded and continued to stare at the floor, trying to figure out their next move. His eyes walked along the edges of the narrow pit, taking note of the many cracks and the layers of dust. The dust abruptly stopped about halfway along the length of the pit, making a straight line across the floor, connecting wall to wall. There were also a number of boot prints in the dust. A trail went from the far side of the pit leading to the dust-free crack in the floor, and not a single print went past the line. Rogan jumped down into the pit and walked to the line. There were a large number of prints in the center and heading toward the left wall. Rogan walked to where the collection of prints massed.

"What is it?" asked Clay.

"There are a ton of prints down here—all of them stop in this area."

"Dude, maybe like a secret door or something."

Clay and Angus walked around the pit to stand behind Rogan. Rogan ran his hand along the wall nearest the prints. The wall felt smooth and cold. He ran his hand along cracks and small crevices that had formed, but for the most part, the concrete wall was smooth and solid. Finally, his fingers fell into a large crack. Under his fingers, he felt something metallic. Rogan pressed down and heard a hiss. He leapt back and brought up the shotgun as the dustless crack in the floor began to lift upwards. The concrete slab tilted away from Rogan, supported by two large pistons. The pistons reached their limit, and with a flicker, a series of lights came on. They were evenly spaced, leading down a concrete stairway.

"Well I'll be cow kicked," said Clay.

Angus and Clay jumped down into the pit, as Rogan, shotgun first, started down the stairwell. He went down ten steps to reach the bottom. The stairs led down into a small room that looked like a kitchen. A small electric stove sat along one wall, next to a stainless steel sink and small refrigerator. A table with four chairs sat at the other side of the room. The remnants of a card game covered the top of the table. Rogan walked through the doorway straight ahead to find a room slightly larger than the kitchen. Along one wall hung two bunk beds. On the opposite wall, and making the turn along the far wall, was a desk with four swivel chairs. Above the desk hung twelve monitors, while on the desk sat four keyboards and computer mice.

"Nice setup," said Angus, walking into the room.

"Quiet. We don't know if someone is down here with us," whispered Rogan.

Next to the bunk beds, there was a closed door. Rogan went to the door and swung it open. The room was small, with shelves running down both walls. The shelves contained boxed and canned foods as well as medical supplies, paper, and blank CDs.

Angus and Rogan both jerked their heads towards the kitchen. A sound like breaking glass echoed through the small underground rooms. They ran to the door to see Clay lying flat on his back at the bottom of the stairs. He got to his feet and charged up the stairs.

"You! Freeze! Sheriff!" called Clay, taking the stairs two at a time. The door above hissed as Rogan and Angus got to the bottom of the steps. They raced up the stairs, but it was too late. The trap door had closed tightly.

"Clay, Clay, you up there?" called Rogan, banging his fist on the bottom of the concrete slab. "Angus, there must be a button or something on this side too, help me look for it."

Angus and Rogan frantically ran their hands along the walls of the stairway, but they found nothing. While searching the kitchen, they heard a loud boom from above. Dust rolled down from around the concrete slab.

"What the hell was that?" asked Angus.

"Let's find out," said Rogan, smiling. "I found the button. Ready?"

Angus nodded and stood at the bottom of the stairs, pointing his machine gun up the steps. Rogan was standing in the doorway between the kitchen and the computer area, where he had found a small sliding panel with a button marked "exit" inside. He nodded at Angus and pressed the button. Instead of a hiss, the door groaned. It rose less than an inch before stalling and returning to its starting position.

"Great. Something must be blocking it."

"Maybe we can see on one of those monitors in there," said Angus.

They went into the computer room. Angus slid into one of the swivel chairs behind a keyboard. Rogan looked up at the monitors—they were all flashing line after line of zeros and ones. The sequence continued to run down each monitor.

"What's the deal with the monitors?" asked Rogan.

"Shit, shit, shit..."

"What?"

"They're deleting the hard drives--trying to cover their tracks."

"Can you stop it? There might be evidence on those computers."

"I'd say there is definitely something if they are blazing the computers."

"Speaking of...do you smell smoke?"

✳ ✳ ✳

Tanya looked up from the clipboard she had been studying to see a van driving down the road near the farmstead. The more she read of the notes and data she had recovered, the more questions her mind created. She was missing far too many pieces of the puzzle to see the whole picture.

She had managed to fall asleep in the old deer stand she was currently hiding out in. It wasn't the first time she'd slept in a tree, but her neck was paying for it. She rubbed the aches as she watched the van come to a stop in the driveway of the farmstead. She hadn't seen anyone come or go from the farm since taking up her post.

Tanya pulled out her field glasses and watched the sheriff and two other guys get out of the van. She could have told them it was a trap. The place was still crawling with those yahoos in camouflage. She liked the sheriff. He was a nice man, helped her grab up her groceries once when she'd sprawled them across the parking lot outside the small corner store in town. She wished she could warn him. Maybe she could at least watch his back.

Tanya jumped out of her tree and stalked in to the compound through the tall grass prairie. In her time surveying the property from the safety of the forest, she'd discovered the location of the many cameras stationed around the property. She knew her best approach would not be to go near the driveway; rather, she needed to cross the street to the west of the property and come through the corn field that butted up to the back of the old barn.

She crawled in through a broken-out window in the barn and scrambled up the ladder to the hay loft. Her dad had always told her to take the high ground. She lay down at the edge of the loft, her rifle barrel sticking out through two hay bales. She was just in time to see a man in camouflage charging out of the milking parlor and out towards the front of the barn. If she would have been in position even a couple seconds earlier she could have considered a shot. Right on the man's heels ran Sheriff/eligible bachelor Clay Stevens. She couldn't risk the long shot on the running man with the sheriff so close to the target.

While she was considering if she should run out after them to help Clay, the first man came riding back into the milking area on the four-wheeler. She scanned through the open space but could not see Clay anywhere. Had they already gotten the jump on him?

The man on the four-wheeler rammed the front end of the vehicle into the center of the large milk tank that had been sitting on the edge of the parlor. The tank started to rock back and forth. The man backed up, got up to ramming speed again, and sent the tank teetering back and forth. With one more push, it finally fell into the parlor pit below. Had the other two men been down there? Did he just crush them?

The man stood up and spun the four-wheeler around. Before he could hit the accelerator, Tanya pulled the trigger, shooting a .270 caliber bullet right into his rear. The man howled in pain and rolled off the side of the four-wheeler. Tanya slid down the ladder, landing hard on the ground below. She got to her feet and charged the man. He didn't see her coming as she slammed her boot into his temple. One shot was all it took to knock him out; his arms and legs fell limp.

Tanya ran to the double doors. She pointed the rifle out the opening, scanning the area. No one was in the barn. She ran to the outside door. She could see no one outside. She wondered where the sheriff had run off to. She scanned the tracks, but there were too many boot prints outside the big doors to make any determination.

After scanning one last time, she ran back to the parlor. She found some rope and tied the four-wheeler man to a post. Then, after confirming that she was alone and in no immediate danger, she risked a look down into the pit. She envisioned seeing a pool of blood growing out from the tank bottom, and perhaps a hand sticking out twitching—thankfully, she saw neither. They must have been inside whatever hidden room was down there.

Moving cautiously and being sure not to get caught on a camera, Tanya scouted the farm grounds in the hopes of finding out what had happened to Clay Stevens. She thought that maybe he had been hurt and had flung himself into the tall weeds to hide, but there was no blood. In fact, there were no signs of struggle at all; it was as if he had run out of the barn and just disappeared.

* * *

"Shit! Fire, Fire, Fire!" yelled Rogan from the storage room.

"Oh hell, they must be destroying the servers," called Angus, running over to the storage room.

Rogan came running out, almost smashing head on into Angus before continuing to the kitchen. Angus ran into the storage room. A locked server rack stood against the back wall, stacked top to bottom with computer servers and a multi-array storage rack. The fire had been ignited near the battery backup system, which meant lots of fuel and a short distance to the hard drives in the storage array.

Angus grabbed the handle and immediately pulled his hand back. The metal was already too hot. He took two steps back, crouched, and sent a flying back kick into the handle. The door popped out of the locking mechanism and rebounded off the wall. Angus brought it to a stop with the bottom of his sneaker. Working quickly, he reached around flames and yanked out hard drives from the top shelf of the storage array. He knew Rogan was after a fire extinguisher, but he also knew that these drives were magnetic disks and that once the extinguisher liquid hit them, it would be almost impossible to retrieve data from them. He managed to pull five of the twelve hard drives before the flames engulfed the entire array.

"Duck!"

Angus ducked, covering the recovered hard drives with his body while a spray of white foam went over his head and into the server rack. The fire fought back as long as it could, but it was soon snuffed out by the fire-extinguishing foam. Angus sat back on his heels, surveying the damage. The battery backups were completely fried, and the storage array was a melted ball of gray plastic and thin aluminum. The bottom set of servers was likely done for, which left three untouched. Angus jumped up, reached around the rack, and pulled all the cables out of the back of the three servers.

"What are you doing?"

"I want whoever owns these to think they burned up, so I pulled the network connections."

"Oh, good idea. What are those?" asked Rogan, pointing at the small pile of drives.

"Hard drives. Hoping maybe we can get some data off them, figure out what the heck they were up to down here."

"Wow, you can do that?"

Angus wondered how Rogan had gotten by so long with such a small understanding of technology. The way Rogan stared at Angus when he did something with a computer made him feel like some sort of wizard. He wondered how he would look with a long thoughtful beard and tall staff. Truth was that Angus didn't think what he did was all that magical; it was all just zeros and ones. Angus picked up the drives and walked back out to the main area of their subterranean prison. He shoved the hard drives into his laptop bag; they would have to wait until later.

"Okay. Next problem, we have got to get this smoke vented out," coughed Rogan.

"Should be a ventilation system right? These guys couldn't survive down here without air coming and going."

Rogan nodded. The two looked around the room for a vent. Angus found one in the ceiling above the desk. The grate was closed. He reached in his pocket for his always-handy multi-tool and extracted the screwdriver. After a few turns, the two screws holding the small grate in place gave way. Angus pulled off the grate and stared into the vent. The opening was small, barely larger than Angus's arm. He couldn't feel any air.

"Flashlight?"

Rogan ran into the kitchen, and returned a second later with a small flashlight. He tossed it up to Angus. Angus peered into the hole with the flashlight. Just past the opening a piece of metal blocked the metal tube. Angus tapped it with his screwdriver and sighed.

"Well?" asked Rogan.

"I think these punks mean to suffocate us. Air vent is blocked with a solid metal plate."

"Not sure how much longer I'm going to be able to make it, breathing in this smoke," said Rogan.

"For sure, dude. Plan B?"

"Look around for something metal. I'm thinking maybe we can open the trap door again. It went up, what, maybe an inch last time? If we can jam something in there before it slams down, that would give us an air hole."

Angus nodded and ran into the storage room, crouching low to stay under the rising smoke. He considered the parts of the server rack, but it was all aluminum. The shelves were the same situation, all lightweight metal. Attached to the wall next to the rack he noticed hundreds of twisted blue and white wires dropping into a case. He assumed it was a phone switch and made a mental note to check it out later.

"Any luck out there?" asked Angus?

"Not yet. Wait, maybe these pipes, but I have no idea what's in them."

Angus ran out of the storage room to see Rogan staring at a set of iron pipes that were attached to the ceiling of the main room by hangers. The pipe ran through the wall and into the storage room, one way and over to the bank of computer monitors the other way.

"Conduit. It's conduit, man. We can use that."

Using their body weight, Rogan and Angus each grabbed onto the end of an eight foot section of the pipe and yanked down while hanging from the bar. It took three hard yanks before the iron bar broke free from the metal hangers. The section clanged to the floor, exposing long orange and blue cables stretching from each end. Angus knew they were fiber optic and cat 6 cables for the computer network. He pulled out his multi-tool and cut through the jumble of lines.

The room was full of haze by the time Rogan and Angus had their pry bar completely freed. Coughing and holding a hand over his mouth and nose, Rogan carried the bar into the kitchen and angled it up the steps. He jammed the end right into the corner where the door's edge met the top step. Angus pushed the button to open the door. The mechanisms groaned and squealed as they tried to lift up whatever had fallen on top of the door.

"Come on baby, a little more now," yelled Rogan. The door was open about a half of an inch. The conduit was one inch in diameter. "No, no, no, come on now!"

The door stopped its upward trajectory. The bar would not fit into the opening. It would be only a moment or two before the door came crashing back down. Angus charged up the stairs past Rogan. They just needed a little more before the machinery gave in.

Angus planted his feet on one of the higher steps, his back flat against the stalled door. He bent his knees slightly. He only needed to lift the weight a little to help the mechanism lift the door the last half inch—or so he hoped. He pressed into the stairs with his feet as hard as he could. His legs shook. He felt blood vessels popping out on his forehead. The door would not budge. Rogan turned on the steps. While keeping his long arms out and his hands wrapped around the bar, he pressed his back against the door as well. Being a good six inches taller than Angus, Rogan was able to press from two steps down. Both men yelled with effort, pressing with everything they had. The door would not relent.

"Okay," huffed Rogan, "one more try. On three we go at the same time. Give it everything you got left."

Angus just nodded; he was completely out of breath.

"One..."

Angus and Rogan set their feet. Angus felt the cement steps under his heels. He knew he would get the best leverage if he pressed through his heels and not his toes. He focused on the thought of pushing the floor away with his heels.

"Two..."

Angus sat back as far as he could, forcing more tension into his legs. He grabbed Rogan by the belt and pulled him back as well. With his long legs, he needed to sit back so his big leg muscles would do the work. Too far forward, and he would be relying on the smaller muscles of his legs and putting most of the load on his lower back and knees.

"Three!"

Angus pressed the floor away. He screamed out, putting everything left in the tank into this one effort. He stared at the floor as drops of blood splashed on the cement step below. He felt like his eyes were going to pop out of skull; his ears rung, and his body quaked under the immense effort. His vision blurred, first at the edges and then inward until finally he could take no more.

13.

Dead anything made McKenzie squeamish. The entire town of Evergreen made her downright nauseous. She had made a half dozen emergency runs to the nearest garbage can since she and Troll had decided they should help the people aimlessly wandering around the street. By early afternoon, they had managed to assist everyone they had found wandering around main street find their way home.

Then they turned to the even worse task of caring for the dead bodies. It turned out that one of the first bodies they came across was Barry, of Barry's Butchery and Fine Meats. Troll had recognized him from the previous day when Clay had commandeered Barry's meat shop to become an impromptu examination area. The long, narrow white building would now become cold storage for the fallen of Evergreen until they could identify and properly bury them.

McKenzie leaned against a bench and waved up at Lizzy, who was standing watch on the roof of the sheriff's office. She waved back. McKenzie wondered what would become of the girl. She hoped that she had some family that would take her in. If she did not, McKenzie would pull whatever strings she could to find her a good home. McKenzie worked as a social worker with the city. She specialized in helping the families of drug and alcohol abusers, but she had plenty of friends and contacts in the child protection arena. McKenzie grew up in a bad home, one filled not with love, but with crack pipes, bongs, and empty bottles of whiskey. She sometimes wondered what her life would have been like without the Rogans. She wondered if she would even be alive. They more or less adopted her at a young age. They were her refuge and her salvation from the dark haze that hung around her mother. She missed them every day.

Troll whistled. Break time was over. McKenzie grabbed onto the legs of an older woman wearing a blue floral shirt and beige pants. She remembered the woman from the diner. She had been sitting at a table with an older man when the chaos broke out. McKenzie wondered if the man had made it.

After several more trips into and out of the Butcher's shop, they had cleared the area between the sheriff's office and the diner. Troll threw McKenzie a bottle of water and they both slumped down against the front entrance of the Butcher's shop. McKenzie took a big gulp and checked her cell phone for the hundredth time. She couldn't believe that Rogan hadn't called in--well, that wasn't true, she could completely see him getting lost on some trail of clues and forgetting about the carnage left behind in town.

"Still nothing?"

"Nope. Didn't call you?"

Troll pulled out his phone and shook his head. "Getting late. Hope everything is all right."

"Yeah, I'm starting to get worried. We have what, maybe an hour of daylight left?"

"Looks about right, and I don't think we have any reason to believe that there won't be an encore of last night."

"I know. I wish there was something we could do to stop this. I mean all those people we just carried in, died for what?"

"Pretty much nothing in my book," said Troll, slugging back some water.

"Well, we told people to try to lock themselves in, but if they get that super-strength thing going on, that is going to do little good. Isn't it weird that some of them zombie out, while others seem to go werewolf/vampire violent?"

"Yeah, I have a bit of a theory on that. I think the disease or whatever this is, has stages. My guess is that everyone is different, or maybe it depends on your exposure level to whatever is causing this. I'm thinking though you start in the wandering around bumping into stuff phase and progress to the raging monster phase over a period of time."

"Great, so if that's true, we would expect to see more limb rippers tonight."

"Afraid so. I wish the lab would call back. It'd be nice to know what we are actually dealing with."

McKenzie leaned her head back against the wall and looked up at the sky. Under different circumstances, it would have been a beautiful day. Big fluffy clouds floated by in the gentle breeze. The sun was warm, but not so warm as to be hot. *Today would have been a perfect day to sit on the shore of the lake with my feet in the water, maybe an iced tea in one hand, a steamy romance in the other,* thought McKenzie, staring up at a long cloud that looked like a train to her.

"Ugh, Rogan, where the hell are you?" grumbled McKenzie.

"You tried to call them yet?"

"Yeah a bunch of times. Neither one of the morons can be bothered to pick up, apparently."

"Ta-Rooollll! Maa-Kennn-zeeee!"

Troll and McKenzie both snapped their eyes towards the top of the office, where Lizzy stood holding a bull horn. "Come here quick!"

They jumped to their feet and ran to the office. Lizzy met them at the back door, opening the deadbolt.

"What is it, Lizzy? Are you okay?" asked McKenzie.

Troll charged into the station, fists clenched, scanning the single room, and then turned to look at Lizzy with a face of confusion.

"Yeah, I'm fine. Some lady is on the phone."

"You answered the phone?"

"I thought maybe it would be Richard."

"Who? Oh...yeah, okay good idea."

"So no intruders?" asked Troll, unclenching his fists and jaw.

"No, Mr. Troll. Just a lady. I think she might know where the guys are."

With that, McKenzie grabbed the handset off of Clay's desk and held it to her ear. Her mind whirled with the possibilities: This woman somehow captured them and wants something or she'll kill them. They got themselves killed and this woman found their bodies. The lady is the mastermind behind this whole thing and is going to present McKenzie with a puzzle she must solve or Rogan, Angus, Clay, and the entire town will die at midnight.

"Hello? Is someone there? I hear breathing."

"Sorry, sorry, yes, I am here, who is this?" asked McKenzie.

"My name is Tanya Tucker. I'm looking for Clay Stevens."

"Tanya of Cedar Road?"

"Yes, how did you know that?"

"We came to your house the other day; you knocked down my friend and bolted into the woods."

"Oh, that's why that guy looked familiar. I'm sorry about that, seems it was a misunderstanding. Is the sheriff around?"

"No, he's out with that guy."

"Well, not exactly, at least not anymore."

"What do you mean? What happened, are they okay? Did you do something to them?" McKenzie yelled into the phone. She felt her body shaking with a mixture of fear and rage. "I swear, if you hurt them..."

"No, no, nothing like that. I swear, I didn't do anything to them. Look, I'm hiding out on an old farm north of town. Sheriff Stevens and the two other guys came here, but it was a trap. Sheriff Steven's made it out, I think. The other two are trapped in some sort of bunker or something. They dumped a big tank on top of the door. I tried to move it, but it's too heavy. We need something big to pull it out."

McKenzie let out a sigh of relief. Rogan had merely gotten himself trapped again...that was pretty normal.

"Okay, Tanya, can you give us directions? We'll find a big truck and head out there."

Tanya gave them the best directions she could from the office to the farm. She told McKenzie she would disable the cameras before they got there. She also mentioned that she had managed to capture one of the men who had dropped the tank on the door. McKenzie relayed the information to Troll and Lizzy. McKenzie loaded up a couple of shotguns with non-lethal ammo, while Troll went to find a vehicle. A few minutes later, she heard a loud engine idling behind the office.

"Lizzy, I'm tempted to have you stay here."

"By myself? No, McKenzie. Please take me with you. I can't be alone when the dark comes again."

McKenzie nodded. She knew it would be best to bring her; she just didn't know what they would be bringing her into. McKenzie reached into the gun closet and found a double barrel twenty-gauge shotgun.

"Lizzy, you ever shot a gun?"

"No."

"Tonight might be your night," said McKenzie, handing the small shotgun to Lizzy. Big Mike, Rogan's dad, had insisted that McKenzie learn how to shoot a variety of guns. He'd said that she needed to be prepared to protect herself, reminding her that it was hard to know what kind of situation might require some solid self-defense. McKenzie wondered if he had ever considered a zombie apocalypse.

Lizzy rolled the gun around in her hands like it was some mysterious artifact. McKenzie found a box of beanbag rounds for the twenty gauge. Troll came in through the back door, smiling.

"Ladies, your chariot is out back."

"Are those flashing lights I'm seeing through the door?" asked McKenzie.

"Yep. Seems like old Clay was holding out on us. He had a huge diesel truck in the garage back there."

"Weird. So that crappy brown one he was driving around earlier was just a decoy truck?"

"Apparently."

"Awesome. Let's roll."

✳ ✳ ✳

Angus's head pounded worse than the morning after his twenty-first birthday. It was hard to breathe; in fact, he couldn't breathe through his nose at all. Angus willed his eyes open and stared up at a wooden slab. He wondered what had happened. The last thing he remembered was trying to squat up a thousand pound slab of concrete with Rogan. He ran his hand through his hair and down his face, trying to get the grog out. He felt wads of tissue in his nose; he looked down to see dried blood streaks running down his t-shirt. He wiggled his toes, just to make sure he wasn't paralyzed. He wished he could say this was the first time he had woken up like this, but that would be far from the truth.

He managed to roll to his side. He could see the bank of computer monitors across the way, which meant they were still trapped in the bunker and he was laid up in one of the bunks. Out of the corner of his eye, he saw something blue flying towards the wall of monitors, it bounced off and returned, then again, and again, and again. Angus managed to pull himself up into a half sitting position on the bunk bed. His body ached; his head throbbed. With all the tissues up his nose, he felt like he had gone twelve rounds in the ring. The feeling reminded him a lot of his younger days, back before he'd learned to mellow. If it hadn't been for weed and surfing, who knows what kind of monster he would be today.

Angus looked past the bunk to see Rogan sitting on the floor, leaning against the door to the storage room. He had a Twinkie hanging out of his mouth. It looked like a giant fluffy cigar. He threw a blue ball against the far wall with his left hand and caught it with his right. Angus owed Rogan a lot, a lot more than Rogan knew. Whether he knew it or not, Rogan had changed Angus's life. He was the reason Angus wasn't dead or in jail.

Back when Rogan was still a cop and Angus was an employee of his father, Rogan gave Angus some advice that changed his life. Angus had been sent out to enforce a contract that his father had put out on a rival group. Angus and two of his men went down to a casino called the Lucky Rabbit, which was really a front for a gang of the same name. A fight broke out, and the two men Angus brought with him were shot early on. Angus ran for it, but he was surrounded in the alley by six well-trained men. He managed to take down two of them before they got the upper hand.

Then, as if the neon rabbit shining down on him was bringing Angus luck, a tall man in red shoes came whistling down the alley. He pulled a revolver out of his hip holster and flashed a gold badge. The rabbits scurried off, leaving Angus lying in a pool of pain and blood. Angus could remember the words of their conversation word for word as they sat by a dumpster waiting for an ambulance.

"Here, take a look at your face," said Rogan, holding up a broken piece of mirror. "Is this what you want? Fighting all the time, getting your face pounded black and blue? Not a good way to pick up the ladies."

Angus tried to laugh, grabbing his ribs and spitting up blood.

"Look. You're young. I know you think you need to do this, probably a family thing, right?"

Angus nodded.

"I get that. My dad's a cop, my granddad was a cop, his dad was a cop, you get the picture, so guess what...I'm a cop." Rogan leaned back and looked up at the few stars that were visible in the slice of sky above the alleyway.

"Thing is, kid, that's all I've ever wanted to be. Not because of my family, but because I believe in what I do. Can you say that? Do you believe in what you do? Sent out like a raging bulldog to settle some score just because your dad or uncle or whoever pulls your strings says so?"

He wanted to say yes, that he did believe in the syndicate, in the business, but he knew he would only say that because it's what his father would have wanted to hear. Instead he looked up at the stars.

"Kid, we're going to get you patched up. Then you have a couple choices. You can go live your life, the life you want to live. Or, you can go back to the family business, and next time I might not be walking past the alley when you're getting the snot kicked out of you. I want you to think real hard about your life, about what you really want. It can't be this."

Wailing sirens and flashing lights bounced off the alley wall. Two paramedics and a set of police officers in blue ran down the long, narrow alley towards them. Rogan chuckled, shaking his head at the sky.

"Funny thing is, kid, I don't even know if you understand a word I'm saying. Do you even speak English? I hope you do, and I hope I don't find you lying dead behind one of these dumpsters someday."

Rogan stood up and waved towards the group running in their direction. He pulled a business card from his pocket and put it in Angus's breast pocket.

"You need help finding your way, you call me, okay? You deserve a better life than this."

Angus tried to say thank you, but his throat was too messed up. On a normal day, he would have told a slice of pork like Rogan to eff off, to mind his own business; he might have even threatened him and his family, but that night he didn't. Maybe because he couldn't talk, or maybe because he was ready to listen. Either way, after getting out of the hospital, Angus Rin, his father's top enforcer, retired.

He emptied his bank accounts and all the hidden stashes of cash he'd kept. He put it all in a metal briefcase, and he went to the airport. He saw a man and a woman walking towards him from the baggage claim area. The man wore a red shirt with large white flowers that was way too big for him, and the woman had on a blue dress with green flowers. She had a white flower sticking out from her black hair. They looked extremely happy. Angus would settle for not angry.

He asked the couple where they had been, and they answered, in unison, "Hawaii!" Then, for the next couple of minutes, they rambled on about how beautiful it was and how peaceful. Angus thanked them and then bought a one-way ticket to Hawaii, where he learned to surf and smoke weed while going to college for computer science. He never talked about life before Hawaii. In fact, he'd told people he was raised on the island.

Angus wondered if Rogan had any idea that he was that punk kid, beaten bloody in the alley. One day, after surfing one of the biggest waves he had ever seen, Angus sat in his small beachside bungalow, listening to Marley. He reached into the drawer of his side table, looking for some matches to light the joint he'd fished out of his pocket. His hand found a crumpled up piece of paper. It was Rogan's business card. Angus decided he would head back to Queen City and thank him. It was something he still meant to do.

Angus swung his legs to the floor, testing them for stability. He gingerly got up, leaning on the top bunk. Rogan caught the ball and looked over at him.

"Hey buddy, I was starting to wonder if you were going to wake up."

"What happened?"

"We tried to lift a little more than we could handle. You blacked out, went head over ass down the steps. Sorry about the tissues in the nose. I couldn't get them to stop bleeding."

"Oh, yeah no problem, thanks," said Angus, pulling out the wads. It felt good to pull in fresh air through his nose. Angus noticed the air did not smell of smoke. "I take it we succeeded, though?"

"Barely. You had that last Herculean effort, and I managed to jam that rod in there. We couldn't have had more than a millimeter to spare. Twinkie?"

"Huh? Oh, yeah, I'm starving, actually." Rogan tossed Angus a snack cake. Angus walked over and sunk down to the floor next to the door. Rogan bounced the ball off the wall, Angus caught it. Angus threw the ball, Rogan caught it.

"How long have we been down here, you think?" asked Angus.

"Feels somewhere around forever. It's definitely dark out, though. There is no light coming in from the crack, so six to eight hours, maybe?"

"What's the plan?"

"I've been thinking about that. I came up with a good one," said Rogan, throwing the ball.

"Cool, what is it?" asked Angus, catching the ball.

"Simple. My plan was to wait until you woke up and then ask you what that plan is."

Angus looked over at Rogan, who had the smirk on his face that he always had when he said something funny or sarcastic. Angus broke out laughing, followed by Rogan. They laughed for a few minutes and then began passing the ball again.

"To be honest, I don't have a plan. I think we might be kind of screwed on this one," said Rogan.

"Richard Rogan, giving up? Come on now."

"Oh, we both know I'm not too shabby at giving up."

"Not anymore. Not since we started the crime-solving side of the business."

"I guess that's true. I feel a lot more like the old me, you know?"

"I get that. Though I'm pretty happy in the now," said Angus.

"With your nostrils coated in dried blood and your body bruised up from taking a header down the stairs?"

"I meant more like metaphorically or whatever, you smartass. Though bruised up and beaten does feel a little too familiar."

"I know...we've been taking a beating lately. Sorry I dragged you into this."

"Eh... Who wants a boring, broken-nose-less life?"

Rogan laughed and said, "I figure we're probably stuck down here until Mac and Troll come looking for us. Hopefully Clay got away."

"I'd say that isn't looking like too solid of a bet, considering we're still trapped down here."

"True enough," said Rogan, bouncing the ball again.

The two men sat in silence, passing the ball back and forth. Angus's mind drifted to Chinatown. He still couldn't figure out why his father would be involved in this. From the glance he got of the man who ran out of the bunker, he was white. Angus's father would never do business with white people. Briefly marrying one with fire-red hair and producing a child, on the other hand...

"Angus, can I ask you something?"

"Shoot."

"I don't pay you much. Okay, let's be honest. I don't pay you anything. What do you do for a living?"

Angus leaned his head back against the wall and caught the ball. He wasn't ready to have this discussion with Rogan. He wasn't sure how he'd take it. Even though Angus no longer beat people up for money, the apple didn't fall that far from the tree.

"To be honest, I have a big inheritance I live off of. I just invest it, and that's about it."

"Really, stock market stuff?"

"Yeah, you can make some pretty good money if you pay attention."

That was only a half lie. Angus did mess around with the stock market, and he considered the large amount of cash he'd taken with him to Hawaii an inheritance of sorts. Rogan stared over at him, his eyes a sea of concentration. Angus held his best poker face.

"I'll let you get away with that for now. Someday though, I want to know the real story," said Rogan, bouncing the ball back off the wall.

Angus had always been impressed with the way Rogan seemed to have a built in BS detector. It was nearly impossible to lie to Rogan. Someday he would come clean with him; he just wasn't sure when that would be.

"On a different subject, did you come up with that plan yet?" asked Rogan.

"No. I mean we obviously aren't going to be able to lift that door any more," said Angus, touching the rims of his nostrils. "The computer equipment is all shot; our phones don't work down here. I'm not sure how to call for help at this point."

Angus was thankful that Rogan let him get away with his half-truth. Rogan was a good guy, a man that Angus could respect and follow. He didn't know where this journey would end, but as long as Rogan was leading the way, Angus planned on following along. They ate the rest of the box of Twinkies and continued to play catch, neither of them saying a word. Rogan got up, walked into the kitchen, and returned with a six pack of beer.

"Where are you finding all this?"

"This place is stocked. I mean, if you're going to get stuck in a bunker, so far, this is the one. There is a ton of food and drinks. Now if we could get cable, maybe watch a couple cheesy horror flicks, this place would be all right."

Angus laughed and cracked a beer. "Bro, how the heck do we get into this stuff?"

"I want to say stupidity," said Rogan, clinking his bottle off of Angus's.

Angus laughed and took a long pull of his beer. He wasn't much of a beer guy, but it tasted amazing at that moment. He spun the bottle around in circles on the floor, staring at the sweat rings forming on the concrete floor. Then he remembered the phone switch.

"There was a phone switch!" said Angus.

"A who what?"

Angus stood up and jogged into the storage room. There, mounted next to the server rack, was a phone switch. Angus pulled the cover off as Rogan came up behind him. Hundreds of blue and white wires twisted around, ending up in pairs of small ports that ran up and down both sides of the casing. There was also a thick black cable that went into the side of the casing, terminating into eight separate pairs of ports. Angus looked up to see that the black cable exited through the ceiling. He had a bad feeling that he knew what it was.

"That's a lot of wires."

"Yeah..."

Angus began mentally routing the paths through the switch in his head, trying to determine if he could use it to call out. It wasn't looking good. All of the lines were incoming and terminated within the switch. Angus double-checked everything to be sure, but he knew immediately that this was going to be bad news. He followed the only wire leaving the switch out to the main room. It ended in the bank of computers. Angus sighed, picked up his beer and took a long pull.

"Well?" asked Rogan.

"You want the bad news or the badder news?"

"Dealer's choice," said Rogan slumping against the wall.

"So all of the wires in that switch are incoming. Which means we have no way to make an outgoing call."

"Okay, was that bad or badder?"

"Depends on your perspective I suppose. The other news is, I don't think any help is coming."

"What do you mean?"

"It looks to me like every phone in Evergreen was routed to this switch. That means that every call made in Evergreen was caught by this switch and answered by the people in the bunker."

"Oh shit. So those calls Mac made...they came here?"

"Yep, we won't be seeing any tanks roll in."

"For the record, that is the badder news. What about cell phones?"

"There is a black cable running into the switch back there. I'd bet a fair amount of dinero that it routes all the way to wherever the cellular towers are for this area, and that on that tower they placed a capture tool to grab all outgoing traffic before it makes its way out."

"Wow...who the hell are these guys? Wait...Mac called me when I was over in that bed and breakfast."

"Right, it's only outbound traffic that is getting captured. We can call all we want within whatever boundary around Evergreen these guys set."

"Great. So basically we are back where we were, a bunker full of snack cakes and beer and not an escape plan to show for it."

"I don't know...that cell cable has me thinking. I might be able to build some sort of transmitter out of those servers that weren't totally toasted, but it's going to take some time and at best we'll be able to send some Morse code."

"I'd say we're made of time," said Rogan.

Angus nodded. He went to the storage room and removed one of the servers. He carried it back to the main room and began to dismantle it. Then he perked his ears towards the kitchen. He could swear that he heard a voice.

"You hear that?" asked Angus.

"No?"

Angus got up and jogged into the kitchen with Rogan on his heels. The sound was muffled, but he could hear voices coming through the crack. Angus pointed up towards the crack and at his ear, looking at Rogan.

"I hear them too," whispered Rogan.

"Good guys or bad guys?"

Rogan shook his head. "Not sure."

Rogan ran back into the main part of the bunker. Angus carefully crawled up a few steps towards the crack, listening. There were several different voices, maybe three of four. Rogan returned and handed Angus his Mac-10. Angus gripped the handle tight and took aim at the crack. The shadows shifted; someone was standing right at the edge of the crack. Angus saw thin, white fingers come through the crack and then disappear. More muffled discussion.

The sound of metal clanging against metal sounded from above. Angus looked down at Rogan, who only shrugged. Angus then heard what he thought was the rumble of a big engine. The engine noise grew louder, strained. A loud scraping sound thundered overhead. Angus stumbled down a few steps, Rogan stopping his descent with a hand to the back. The engine noise grew louder, but it could barely be heard over the scraping.

"Someone's pulling off whatever is on the door," shouted Rogan. "Be ready."

Angus nodded. They took up positions near the stairway. Angus crouched back from the end of the stairs. He would be able to send up a spray of bullets before whoever was up there got down more than a step. Rogan crouched low next to the steps, giving him a visual angle on whoever might appear.

"Wait for my signal before unleashing with that thing," yelled Rogan over the scraping noise. "Might be our friends up there, come to save our butts."

Or it might be the people who locked us in here coming to finish the job, thought Angus. Then the scraping stopped. The hum of the engine died off. Rogan nodded to Angus, a silent *be ready*. The voices returned. Angus tightened his grip on the stalk and leaned against the wall for support. Suddenly, the concrete slab began to move upward. The metal bar they'd used to get an air crack clanged down the steps. Rogan pointed his gun up the stairs, staying in the shadows the best he could.

A pair of black shoes with white skulls on the side appeared on the top step. Angus followed them up to a pair or light-colored jeans with rips over the knees. He'd seen those knees before. He let out a sigh of relief and stood up. He looked over at Rogan, who was smiling.

"About damn time," Rogan yelled up the steps while holstering his pistol.

"If you'd stop getting your dumb ass trapped, you wouldn't have to wait for us to rescue you."

Rogan ran up the steps two at a time and threw his arms around McKenzie, carrying her back out of the bunker. Angus ran back into the main area and grabbed his backpack and the remaining beer. Then he charged up the stairs. There stood Rogan, McKenzie, Troll, Lizzy, and a brown-haired woman that he didn't recognize.

"Wow, you look like crap," said Troll.

"You should talk," replied Angus, tossing him a beer.

"Where's Clay?" asked Rogan.

"No idea. Tanya here called the sheriff's office to let us know you had managed to get yourself trapped yet again. No sign of Clay."

"Tanya. You're the woman that throttled me and ran off the other day," Rogan said, rejoining the conversation after he'd released McKenzie.

"Sorry about that. I didn't know who the bad guys were at the time," said Tanya.

Tanya gave them the highlights of what she had seen since running away from her house, ending with Clay and the other man running out of the barn.

"And no sign of him?" asked Rogan.

"No. It was like he vanished."

"You said you captured one of these guys in black fatigues?" asked Rogan.

"Yeah, over here," said Tanya.

Tanya led Rogan over to the column where she had tied up the man. Angus could tell from a distance that the man was dead. He guessed poison. He didn't miss his old life at all, but at times he found himself thankful for the skills and knowledge that he had acquired.

"He's dead," said Troll.

"Poison," said Angus. "Look under his tongue."

Troll opened the man's mouth and looked under the tongue. He pulled out a small white capsule.

"Damn," said Rogan.

"Who the hell are these guys?" asked McKenzie.

"I don't know, but we need to find out," said Rogan.

"What about the sheriff?" asked Tanya.

"Okay. It's pitch black out there, which means that the wolves and zombies are probably out strolling by now. I say we double time it back to the office. Clay would likely head back to town if he managed to get away. We'll regroup and figure out what to do. Tanya, I think you should come with us. It isn't safe out here," said Rogan.

Troll unhooked the heavy chain from the pickup and then got behind the wheel. McKenzie and Lizzy piled in beside him. Angus, Rogan, and Tanya, each carrying a shotgun with beanbag rounds, sat in the pickup bed. Troll started up the rumbling engine and they tore off out of the farm. Angus waved at his van as they drove by, easing the truck into the bushes to clear their own impromptu roadblock. He loved that van.

"We'll come get her tomorrow, buddy," said Rogan.

The sky was starless, thick clouds stretched across the black sky. Occasionally a flash of light shot across the sky far to the west, followed by the rumbling boom of thunder. With no natural light, it was hard to see if anyone was hiding out in the thick grasses along the side of the road. Rogan continually scanned the ditches and trees hoping to get some glimpse of movement in time to do something about it.

Angus sat on one of the wheel wells and scanned the right side of the road, Tanya stood leaning against the cab of the pickup, staring through a set of binoculars and scanning 180 degrees from the left to right of the pickup. Rogan jerked his gun to his shoulder as something broke from prairie grasses and onto the road. He eased the gun back down when he noticed the animal had four legs and antlers. He wondered what they would find when they got back to town. The situation was getting worse by the day.

The pickup turned onto the gravel road towards town. Although their route had been clear so far, Rogan thought he saw some people wandering in and out of the woods a few times along the way. It was starting to seem like the entire town and surrounding area were under the influence of whatever those black-fatigued men were doing. He wished they could have gotten something off those computers before they went up in smoke.

Rogan was almost thrown from the back of the pickup as the vehicle came to an abrupt stop. He scrambled back to his feet. He scanned around the pickup, trying to determine why Troll had slammed home the brakes. He turned to look towards the front of the truck, and there, right at the edge of the headlight's range, stood a group of people milling around. Shouts and hollers came from the group as they stretched out from edge to edge of the gravel road into town.

"What do we do?" yelled Troll through the opening in the sliding back window.

"Can we go around?"

"Doesn't look like it," said Tanya as she motioned to the edge of the road at either side of the mob. "They have us at a choke point; we aren't going to be able to get around those big cedars."

"I'm going to fire a warning shot," said Rogan, steadying his shotgun against the roof of the pickup. He picked out the biggest, meanest looking one in the front line and pulled the trigger. The bean bag banged into the chest of the man; he fell back and howled. The shot had the opposite effect that Rogan was hoping for—instead of scattering, the group seemed enraged. The mob charged towards the truck. Rogan counted around twenty-five people in the mob.

"Okay, that didn't work," yelled Rogan.

Troll stepped on the gas. The pickup lurched backwards away from the mob. He only made it a few feet before a large pine tree came crashing down across the road. The back of the pickup rammed into the thick trunk, sending everyone pitching backward and then violently forward. Rogan flew against the front of the pickup box, smashing the back of his head into the metal. Angus ended up in a ball beside him. Tanya flew headfirst over the side to the ground.

Rogan fought away the pain ripping through his skull and jumped to his feet. He fired three rounds into the crowd approaching Tanya. She clambered back into the pickup bed as Rogan emptied the rest of the shotgun magazine into the crowd.

A loud bang came from the front of a pickup as another giant cedar slammed into the road. The crowd chortled their approval.

"It would appear they're getting smarter," said Troll, clutching his chest.

The pickup began rocking back and forth as the mob huddled around the big diesel. Rogan reloaded while Tanya and Angus fired down at the growing mob. It now looked like nearly fifty people had surrounded the vehicle. Rogan kicked a middle aged man in the face as he tried to climb into the pickup bed. He swung around and fired a shot into the chest of a blonde woman who was climbing over the hood of the pickup.

"You okay? asked McKenzie, tightening Lizzy's seatbelt. Lizzy nodded.

"I'll keep an eye on her," said Troll. "Go."

McKenzie nodded and crawled out through the sliding glass of the back window. Angus handed her his shotgun. He picked up a thick branch that had fallen into the back of the pickup when the big pine tree had fallen across the road. Angus jumped over the cab and onto the hood of the pickup, swinging the club at any members of the mob who tried to gain purchase. The pickup rocked more and more, side to side. Rogan could feel the wheels lifting off the ground. He fired on an older man with silver hair who was climbing in over the tailgate.

"We need an escape plan," said McKenzie, laying a round into another of the mob trying to climb the side of the pickup bed.

Rogan went to respond but as he opened his mouth he felt the pickup lift high into the air. The driver's side of the pickup was nearly vertical. Something banged into the underside of the pickup and it went over on its side, sending Angus, Tanya, McKenzie and Rogan sprawling out into the mob. Rogan came up firing laying out two men who were trying to hold him down. He was out of ammo. He swung the shotgun like a club, taking down three more men while working his way towards the others.

Angus was working his way around the crowd like a samurai carrying a wooden sword. Tanya was laid out a few feet from Rogan; he helped her to her feet. One of the mob leapt at her, she sent a bean bag into his forehead. Rogan couldn't see McKenzie. He spun around, trying to locate her. Then he saw five men in a circle, all pushing each other and trying to get at something on the ground. Rogan and Tanya ran towards the group. Tanya sent her last two rounds into the backs of two of the men. Rogan swung hard with the butt of the shotgun, sending another man flailing.

At the bottom of the pile, Rogan could see McKenzie curled up in a ball. He dove over her as the remaining two men tried to claw at her. He felt hot pain down his back as the claws tore through his shirt and into his skin. He looked up to see Tanya braining one of the men with her shotgun, and a beanbag flew into the face of the other, courtesy of Troll, who was standing on top of the tipped diesel.

"You okay?" asked Rogan.

"Yeah. Luckily they were too busy fighting over me to actually hurt me."

Rogan helped McKenzie to her feet. She pushed him down and shot a man in the face who was leaping, claws out, at Rogan's back.

"Thanks," said Rogan.

McKenzie nodded. They worked their way back towards the pickup. Troll stood on the cab, beating down the group that was trying to claw their way up to him with Lizzy's twenty-gauge shotgun. Rogan fought his way to the windshield of the rolled pickup. He could see Lizzy inside, her face buried into the passenger's seat. He took the butt of his shotgun and smashed in the glass.

"Lizzy! It's me, Rogan. Come on honey, we need to go, now!" Lizzy crawled out through the broken window and wrapped her arms around Rogan's neck. He stood up his full height and maneuvered her onto his back.

"Let's get the hell out of here!" Rogan yelled. The rest of the group fought their way to Rogan's position at the front of the pickup. They stood back to back in a circle facing the mob. There were at least twenty of the mob remaining. The group slowly climbed over the fallen tree, bashing in any of the mob that got close to them.

Angus stopped beyond the tree, while the rest of the group moved on. He swung his machine gun forward. Rogan took a step towards Angus trying to stop him. He was still convinced they did not need to kill these people. Before he could make his move, Angus pulled the trigger. Shards, bits, and chunks of wood flew off of the fallen tree as Angus mowed a line of bullets into it. Beyond the tree, the remaining group howled and wailed as they scattered into the woods.

"Maybe we should have led with that," said Rogan.

Angus turned around and smiled. Rogan slapped him on the shoulder. Wasting no more time, the team broke into a run towards town.

Minutes later, they'd covered the remaining distance to the town. Turning the last curve, they could see that the small town of Evergreen was a disaster area. The windows of all the small, quaint shops and businesses were broken out. Bodies were strewn about the street and sidewalks. Groaning, moaning, howling, and yelling echoed off the walls. The wild people of Evergreen lurked in the shadows, their eyes glowing in the faint light as the team ran for the sanctuary of the sheriff's office.

14.

As the next day dawned, Rogan stood on the roof of the sheriff's office, taking in the devastation. Here and there, one of the zombie-like citizens would amble out from the long morning shadows. He hadn't seen any of the violent ones in a while, which was fortunate; their defenses had stood through the night. Rogan glanced over at the sun as it split open the clouds and filled the main street with light.

With the violence and intelligence of the people of Evergreen increasing in equal measure, he wasn't sure they would last another night. Rogan also wondered what had happened to Clay. They'd tried to call him several times the night before, but got no answer. Tanya said it was like he had disappeared. It sounded like she had some experience in the woods with hunting and tracking, so if she said he left no trail, Rogan believed her.

The moans and howls continued on as the sun drifted upwards in the sky. It seemed like most of the chaos was happening around the town, in the woods and the small clusters of residences. Other than the occasional wanderer, the town proper was devoid of life.

McKenzie walked up the stairs and handed Rogan an orange and a bottle of water. She sighed as she looked out over the town.

"What are we going to do?" she asked.

"I don't know. I'm not sure we can take another night. Heck, I'm not sure this town can take another night."

"Angus has been up all night looking at those hard drives he got out of the bunker. Maybe he'll find us a lead."

"That would be good. I've got nothing else. I know it has something to do with that farm, and with those men in black fatigues. But what? What is this? I mean why this town? Why these people?"

Troll walked up the stairs. He was talking on the phone with someone. He looked serious.

"Okay, Marg, thanks," said Troll, hanging up the phone.

"Got something?" asked McKenzie.

"Well...that was Marg from the city lab..." said Troll.

"Awesome, did they find anything? Something to explain what the heck is going on here?" asked Rogan.

"No. They never got the samples."

"What? Clay said he sent them off right away," said McKenzie.

"Yes, very strange..." said Troll, cocking his eyebrow.

"Well based on our experience last night, it's possible the courier never got out," said Rogan.

"Maybe, but it seems odd. But now we're out of luck," said Troll as Tanya stepped off the stairs.

"Out of luck?" she asked, looking out over the city and shaking her head.

"Yeah. I sent some samples into the city lab. I was hoping to have them analyze the blood, see if there was anything odd to explain what was going on, or even better, how to stop it. They never got the samples, though."

"Could you do the analysis yourself?" asked Tanya.

"Sure, if I had a lab. Though at this point, I'd settle for a microscope."

"Well then...let's get going, big boy," said Tanya, turning to the group.

"You have a microscope?" asked Troll.

"Yeah, at my cabin. If you end up spending any time with me, it'll become pretty clear that I'm a bit of a work-a-holic. I converted the basement of the cabin into a small chemistry lab. I have a couple microscopes down there. I'd think one of them should work."

"Wow, that's awesome. Are you a chemist?"

"Yeah, I work for a big pharmaceutical company back in Queen. I head up one of their research teams."

"Okay...okay! Let's do this. We'll need to get a fresh sample on the way," said Troll.

"Shouldn't be a problem," said McKenzie, motioning towards the street below.

"I don't want to jinx it, but did we just get a break?" asked Rogan.

"Here's hoping," said Troll. "Okay, Tanya, take me to your place."

"That's a little forward, isn't it?" said Tanya, walking down the stairs.

Troll looked bewilderedly at Rogan, who just laughed. Rogan was starting to like Tanya more all the time. He was close to forgiving her for throttling him in her kitchen when they first met.

"Well...go get her, big guy. Bring us back some good news...but above all else—be careful."

"True. You did just meet her," said McKenzie, fighting back a laugh.

Troll rolled his eyes and disappeared down the stairs. McKenzie and Rogan laughed. They needed the momentary relief from the devastation that was littered everywhere around the sheriff's office. As the laughter settled, their gaze was drawn back out over the town. The dead bodies, broken windows, and bashed in doors were sobering. They sat in silence. Rogan hoped that the blood would lead to something. They needed *something*.

＊ ＊ ＊

Tanya and Troll drove towards her cabin in Clay's other pickup. This one was old and in ill-repair, with dents and scratches gouged in the brown paint. Troll hoped his own pickup was okay. They had left it at the cabin that he and Rogan had been staying at before all of this started—back when this was just a peaceful fishing trip. They bounced down the gravel road in silence. Troll always felt awkward around new people, especially women. He never knew what to say or how to start a conversation. Finally, Tanya broke the thick silence.

"So a medical examiner huh?" she said.

"Yeah. I'm really happy they took me on. Passed my boards, and now I'm all official."

"Is that what you always wanted to be?"

"More or less. I've always been fascinated with the human body. A couple times I thought about going into family practice, or some specialty—pediatrics maybe—but I don't know...just didn't suit me."

"How do you mean?"

"Can you imagine me walking into an examination room?"

"We'd have to get you a white coat, and maybe heal up those bruises some more, but I don't see why not."

Troll thought that was sweet, albeit misguided. He was glad she wasn't afraid of him. Though, based on what she had told them about her time leading up to their meeting, he wasn't sure she was scared of anything.

There was a time when Troll dreamed of being a pediatric surgeon. He'd imagined himself saving children. He'd switched his focus after shadowing a pediatric specialist. He was supposed to follow the doctor for a month, but he'd transferred to the medical examiner program a week in. The kids would scream and hide under their covers whenever Troll followed the doctor into the room. It had been the most devastating week of Troll's life. He had always been judged for his size and rough looks. He was used to woman crossing the street to avoid him. It didn't bother him when store clerks eyed him suspiciously. But having children be legitimately frightened by the very sight of him was all Troll could take. So he'd chosen to be a medical examiner. He figured corpses were already dead—there was nothing for them to be afraid of.

"It's just up there on the left, the brown one," said Tanya.

"Wow, nice place."

"Yeah, used to be nicer. This whole zombie apocalypse thing has really put a bad shine on the place."

"Oh, I don't know, once we figure this out, though. I mean lake access, huge yard, view of the pines."

"I'm just not sure the place is going to feel the same anymore," said Tanya, rubbing her arm.

Troll looked over at Tanya. She looked lost in thought as he pulled the old brown pickup to a stop in the driveway. She sighed and opened the pickup door. The two walked up to the front steps of the cabin. Troll searched for something to say. Tanya was obviously working through something, but he wasn't sure what and he wasn't sure how to ask. He chewed his lip and thought. He was thinking, or rather overthinking, what to say as he opened the door for Tanya and followed her in.

The cabin was a mess. The kitchen stunk of rotting meat. There were broken dishes and overturned furniture everywhere they looked. Tanya stepped over an overturned stool and opened the door at the end of the hall.

"What the hell happened in here?" asked Troll.

"Nothing good," said Tanya, disappearing down the steps.

Troll followed her down the stairs into the basement. It reminded him of the basement where he had gone toe to toe with a housewife and lost. The walls were the same cement block. There was a stack of pipes in the center and a washer and dryer pushed into one corner, and just like the other basement, Troll had to crouch over to keep from scraping his bald head on the ceiling. Tanya pulled back a curtain that ran from one wall to the other just past the stack of pipes. Behind it was a glass wall with an inset door.

"Wow," said Troll admiring the setup.

"Just a little something I threw together," said Tanya. Troll smiled as her eyes twinkled. She had beautiful eyes.

Troll looked through the glass wall to see a long black work bench. On the bench sat a centrifuge, various beakers and vials, and a decontamination hood. Towards the far end sat three microscopes. On one wall sat a floor-to-ceiling cabinet with glass doors. Troll could see canisters inside all marked and organized. Charts and monitors hung from the other walls. A series of vents ran along the ceiling as well as water sprayers and what he believed was a halon system, which would quickly remove all the oxygen from the room when triggered. The place reminded Troll of some of the labs he'd taken classes in during his undergrad—only this one was nicer and better stocked.

"This was a little more than I expected," said Troll.

"I had to take precautions. Some of the substances I work with are a little...temperamental, let's say. It's also contaminant free," said Tanya, pulling a white suit off the wall. "I'm sorry, I only bought them in my size. I didn't plan on having guests to my secret lab."

"Oh...yeah...no, that's fine. I can wait out here."

"Okay. I'm sorry, Troll. I'll swing the monitor over so you can see what I see and there's an intercom, too, so we can talk."

Troll nodded and found a stool sitting in the corner. He brought it over and sat down near the microscope side of the room and turned back towards Tanya, who was undressing. He caught himself following the curves of her legs as she pushed her camouflage pants to the floor. He felt his breathing increase as she stepped out of the pants. He could hear his heartbeat in his ears as his eyes wandered back up and across her tight stomach. He gulped as she pulled her long hair back in a tight ponytail, her chest heaved outward. He quickly averted his eyes when she glanced over at him. She smirked. His eyes thoroughly examined the ground.

"I'm sorry...I'm sorry...I'm sorry," mumbled Troll.

"It's okay, Troll, I pretty much wear the same thing to the beach. Well, less lace, I suppose," said Tanya, pulling on the white suit. "You might want to close your mouth."

Troll felt like such an idiot. What was he doing staring at her like that? She was amazingly attractive though, and smart...and funny. He noticed his heart wasn't slowing down.

Tanya stepped through the glass door. Troll hadn't noticed that there were actually two doors. Tanya stood between them in a clear box. Troll could hear the hum of fans as Tanya slowly turned in a circle. She looked like a fluffy marshmallow as the suit flapped up and down. When the fans died down, she opened the interior door and entered the lab. She walked over near the last microscope. On the wall hung a 32" monitor, attached by a moving arm. She pulled the monitor out and towards Troll. Then she walked over to the glass. All he could make out were her eyes behind her safety goggles and air respirator. She pressed a button on the wall.

"Testing, testing...Tanya to Troll."

"Five by five," said Troll.

"Good, okay. Let's see what these bastards have been doing to my people."

Tanya pulled out a slide and placed a drop of blood on it. She then slid it under the microscope. Troll immediately saw red on the monitor.

"Are you able to see?" asked Tanya.

"Yep, pretty blurry, though," said Troll.

"One sec."

Tanya fiddled with the dials on the large beige microscope. The image began to clear. Troll could make out cells now, the donut shaped red blood cells and puffball white blood cells. The image cleared more and more. Troll could make out platelets and then something foreign. A virus, maybe, or bacteria? No...nothing like that. Those were...

"Holy shit."

15.

Tanya and Troll got back to the sheriff's office around noon. Tanya couldn't believe what they had seen in the microscope. It didn't seem real, but after thorough analysis, there was no doubt. What they had seen in the sample of brain matter that Troll had procured was the most disturbing. Before they left the cabin, she had taken a sample of her own blood and looked at it under the microscope. Her blood was clean. She wondered why she had been spared.

While Tanya drove, she found herself stealing glances over at Troll. She stared at his cauliflower ears. For some reason, she thought they were cute. She fought the urge to run her finger along the ridge. She figured he would be a handsome man if it weren't for the bumps and bruises on his face. Tanya also couldn't explain why she had been so seductive back at the lab. She could easily have stepped behind the curtain to change, but a part of her wanted him to see her. There was just something about him and his big muscled arms.

At the cabin, they had swapped out Clay's old pickup for Tanya's Jeep. She wanted to be able to flee in her own vehicle if things got real bad. Troll didn't argue, which was nice. Tanya pulled the Jeep up behind the sheriff's office and found the team inside eating sandwiches and playing cards, all except Angus, who was staring at a computer screen. His eyes looked bloodshot. Tanya wondered if he had slept at all yet.

"Hey, our scientists have returned," said Rogan.

"Find anything useful?" asked McKenize.

"More like disturbing. Here check this out."

Troll took out his laptop and set it on the table on top of the card game. On the screen was a video Tanya had recorded off of her microscope. The video showed a blood sample with a foreign object floating amongst the other cells.

"What am I looking at?" asked Rogan.

"Blood sample that we analyzed. Okay, see those red blobs? Those are red blood cells, the white ones, white blood cells, now see those black cubes?"

"Yeah."

Troll shook his head and sat down next to Rogan at the table. "Those are something I've never seen before, something I thought was more science fiction than fact, to be honest. I mean, sure, I knew they existed, but these are really sophisticated. Here, watch this," said Troll, clicking on another video.

A small white cell passed the center of the image. The black squares surrounded it. After less than a second, the white cell emerged from the huddle of black squares and travelled off the slide.

"What was that?" asked McKenzie.

"That was a group of, I can't believe I'm about to say this... A group of nanobots."

"Nano what?"

"They are nanotechnology, microscopic machines programmed and built to carry out a set of functions. In this case, and again, this is crazy, but they just attached to a brain cell and altered the DNA."

"Little robots?" asked McKenzie.

"Basically. They could very well lead to a new medical frontier. Imagine if you could program a little robot to float around in your blood and attack cancer cells, or rebuild neurons and synapses in the brain, or repair a spinal cord. I mean it's amazing science, but in this case I think it isn't being used for good."

"So you think these people were injected or something with these nanobots and that the bots went in and reprogrammed these people's brains to make them what...ultraviolent?" asked Rogan.

"Something like that," said a barely-awake Angus as he slumped against the table. "There wasn't much usable data on those disks—their destruction protocols were real good—but I got snippets. All of it referred to something called Project Darwin. It talked about dulling the analytic parts of a human's mind and returning them to base programming."

"Base programming?" asked McKenzie.

"Fight or flight, survival of the strongest," said Rogan.

"Yep," said Angus.

"So they have the nanotech going in and modifying the brain to turn people back to their animal nature. Remove all the constraints of society and reason and just turn them into beings of instinct," said Troll.

Tanya handed a folder to Rogan. "I found this on the front seat of one of the 4 x 4s those guys had."

Rogan flipped through the file. "It has the name of every citizen of Evergreen," said Tanya. "With a number next to their name."

"We had talked about this being a staged thing, so I suppose the number is what stage they are in?" said McKenzie.

"Four levels," said Angus. "First, Darwin, as the notes on the computer refer to it, goes in and starts turning parts of the brain off, which leads to stage one, which we would call the wandering zombie phase. Also during that phase, it goes in and strengthens muscles and the nervous system to beyond human norm. Next, Darwin hyperactivates the parts of the brain that are responsible for aggression and survival, so they can use that new strength and speed."

"That would explain the enlarged hypothalamus and amygdala too," said Troll.

"Part three, Darwin removes all human reasoning and replaces it with pack mentality and predator intellect. Which, I would say, is what we saw last night."

"So they start to work together against a common threat, taking down common prey when it is useful to them, just like a pack of wolves," said Tanya.

"Yeah, except according to the computer notes, once there is no common goal, they will splinter off into smaller packs and start fighting for territory and resources."

"And part four?" asked Rogan.

"All damaged, but I'd bet a burrito we don't want to see it," said Angus.

"Why would anyone want to do this to a town?" asked McKenzie.

"Good question. I mean given these notes and what Angus found on the computer, this was a monitored experiment. All of this was done to these people on purpose," said Rogan.

"Tanya, did you see your marking in this file?" asked McKenzie, pointing to the file in Rogan's hands.

"Yeah, I'm a zero. Apparently it didn't take for me."

"Tanya Tucker displays no signs. She has been dosed multiple times, with no result. It is possible that she represents the one percent assumption," read Rogan.

"What does that mean?"

"I think it means I'm immune, and they assumed that one percent of the population would be."

"What about Clay? Is he out there getting his zombie on right now?" asked Angus.

"His name isn't on the list."

"That's weird."

"Could be a control," said Troll.

"Have to ask him, if we ever find him," said Rogan.

"How come only during the night?" asked McKenzie.

"Vitamin D," said Tanya. "It seems to be their energy source. When we were looking at the samples in my lab, we noticed that the nanos were not moving. We thought maybe they died when the host died, but then genius over there mentioned the night thing, so we dropped some liquefied vitamin D onto the slide and they woke right up and started attaching to brain cells."

"That's crazy! So what now?" asked McKenzie.

"I'd like to get back to the city, maybe see if I can find a way to neutralize these little bastards," said Troll.

"I'm going to take a nap, then plug away at these drives some more, see if there is any hint about who is actually behind all this."

"Let's send out a group to look for Clay. Keep working on what we have, and if we have nothing, we'll split up. Part of us will head towards the city, where Troll and Tanya can hopefully find a cure. The rest of us will try our best to keep the populace from killing each other to extinction," said Rogan.

"Is there a cure?" asked McKenzie, "I mean if those things are changing these people's DNA..."

"It depends on what exactly they are doing. All we could see in the microscope was that they would attach to a cell and then insert something into the cell. It also seemed like they were interacting with the cell's DNA. We are assuming that it's being modified, but it's equally likely that certain strands are being suppressed. We have a few experimental drugs we are working on right now that suppress the genes associated with heart disease, for example. The thing is, once you stop taking the drug, the genes stop being suppressed. If that's the case, we just need to get those nanos to stop. Otherwise, I don't know..." said Tanya.

"Either way, we'll do whatever we can," said Rogan. Everyone nodded at the computer screen as the nanobots attached to another set of cells.

Angus wondered off and collapsed onto one of the beds, while the others loaded up shotguns and gathered gear. Rogan sat staring at the computer screen. He couldn't believe what he was seeing. The idea that someone could have a tiny robot inside of them made no sense to him.

A loud banging echoed from the back door. Rogan jumped from the chair and pointed his shotgun at the door. Tanya, Troll, and McKenzie also had firearms up and aimed.

"Come on, open up, it's me, Clay. Please."

Rogan went to the door, nodding towards the others who kept their guns aimed on target. Rogan threw the deadbolt and leapt back, bringing the shotgun up to his shoulder. Clay stumbled in and collapsed on the floor. Rogan scanned the area past the door. All clear. He sunk the deadbolt and held the door tight while Troll and Tanya nailed up boards across the doorway.

Clay's brown shirt was torn. His hair was matted with dried blood. He had scrapes up and down his arms. His chest heaved in and out as he struggled for breath on his hands and knees. Troll pulled over a chair and helped Clay into it. He nodded his thanks and started to slow his breathing.

"Here drink this," said McKenzie, handing him a bottle of water.

"Thank you, McKenzie. Man, what a night. I thought I was dead about six dozen times," said Clay, addressing the group.

"What happened to you?" asked Rogan.

"So I ran out after that guy we saw in that bunker. Boy, he was a fast one. Knocked me out cold outside the barn. I came to and hid out in the chicken coop. Once I realized what had happened, I started heading back here to get help. Made the dumb choice of going through the woods, ran into a bunch of those violent ones. I was on the run all night, got lost a ton, those damn woods...finally made it back. Glad you're all okay. Sorry I couldn't get back sooner."

"Don't worry about that, Clay, we got out. Had a rough night ourselves, but other than some cuts, bumps, and bruises, we're all okay," Rogan said.

"Oh good. I was worrying something fierce. I just couldn't find my way. I'm not a woodsman, that's for sure, got turned around a bunch of times, almost fell in a couple of those darn bear traps. Tanya, is that you?"

"Hi, Sheriff."

Clay stood up and hugged Tanya. "It's mighty good to see you, Tanya."

"You too," said Tanya. "Here, sit down. You should eat something."

Rogan filled Clay in on the happenings of the night before while Tanya got him some food. Tanya filled him in on her experiences so far, leaving out the part where she'd killed Vick. The group also told him about Project Darwin, and the list of names that he was not on.

"Any idea why you wouldn't be on that list?" asked Rogan.

"No. I don't have any idea. Maybe they wanted to keep the law up and running for some reason? Oh, I almost forgot, I got into a tussle with one of those military-looking guys. I'm not ashamed to say it didn't go all that well, but I did manage to grab this before I ran off," said Clay, holding up a small green notebook.

The notebook was pocket sized; it had a fish printed on the cover. It looked like the type of fish you might draw if you were doing stick figure animals. Rogan opened the notebook up. Most of it was random scribbling and notes, mostly stuff they had already discovered. Near the middle was a folded piece of paper. Rogan pulled out the paper and unfolded it. On the top was written three numbers: 33, 03, and 60. Below the numbers, line after line of zeros and ones were printed across the page.

"What the heck is this?" asked Rogan staring at the long lines of numbers.

The group came over and looked at the odd sheet of paper. Angus smiled and yanked it out of Rogan's hand.

"Binary!" said Angus running over to his computer. The rest of the group exchanged confused looks as Angus began tapping away at his keyboard.

"It's a cipher. I'm running it through a bunch of decryption algorithms right now. Might take a minute."

McKenzie and Lizzy tended to Clay's various cuts and scrapes while Angus worked. Rogan stood behind him, staring impatiently at the screen. After ten minutes of Angus clicking, tapping and humming, a message visualized on the screen.

Field Tech Code Green Protocol

Step 1: Find and neutralize the impacted technician. Tranquilizer rifles can be found in   the nest storage room.

Step 2: At rally point HOME, locate the safe. It is behind the bookcase on the main   floor. Combination is at the top of this memo.

Step 3: Retrieve antidote and administer using the supplied instructions.

Step 4: Return the technician to Q lab Alpha.

"There's an antidote," said Rogan.

"Where?" asked Clay.

"It's vague, but my guess would be that old farmhouse," said Angus.

"Whole town is gone coon crazy, we need to go check that out, even if it's just a chance," said Clay, jumping to his feet.

"I agree. You sure you're up for that, though? You look a little rough, pal," said Rogan.

"Don't worry about me. Give me a minute to clean up and grab a clean shirt, and I'll be ready to go."

"Can we just take a minute?" said Troll.

Rogan turned towards Troll with a confused look. "For what?"

"Are you sure we should be rushing back out to that farm?"

"We need the antidote."

"Something doesn't add up though. An organization that can pull off something like this, keeps a loose leaf piece of paper in a random book with the location of an antidote? Come on, Rogan, you're a smart guy. This is clearly a trap."

"Even if it is, there might still be an antidote. We have to try," said Clay pulling on clean shirt.

Troll raised an eyebrow at the Texan and sat on the edge of the desk crossing his arms, "Something's off here, Rogan. You know it is."

Rogan nodded, "I know, but like Clay said, we have to try. This town isn't going to last much longer."

"There just has to be a better way than walking square into a bear trap..."

"Love to hear it, big guy. We got people tearing each other apart out there. If there is even a sliver of a chance, how can we not give it a go?" asked Clay.

"Tanya and I could work the samples. We might be able to figure out how those things tick, get them to stop. We'd just need some time."

Rogan stood up and faced Troll. He put a hand on each of the big man's shoulders.

"Listen buddy, we don't have time. These people don't have time. We'll be safe. I need you on board. I need you to watch our backs, because you're right there is chance this is a big horrible trap."

Troll sighed and stood up. He looked around the room, his eyes settling on Clay.

"Fine. We need to be careful though. Maybe we can see the trap before they spring it,"

"Okay, then let's do this. We can be out and back before it gets dark. Troll, how about you, me, and Clay head out there. Everyone else stay here and work through this notebook and anything else Angus finds."

"Sounds good to me, Rogan, but Tanya has some experience out there. Why don't we leave big muscles there to protect the office, and she can help us find our way around," Clay inserted.

Tanya looked over at Troll and smiled. He looked down at the floor and smiled back. He was so meek and mild for such a large man. She found it adorable. She was becoming more and more intrigued by the brilliant man with the bowling ball-sized shoulders. She imagined that he could pick her up like she weighed nothing.

"That's a good point. Might need you back here, Troll, to protect the place. We might be coming in hot from this run."

"Great, we'll take my diesel," said Clay.

"Yeah, about that..." said Rogan, following Clay out the door.

Tanya walked over and squeezed Troll's shoulder. She smiled at him as she hiked a shotgun over her shoulder.

"Be careful," said Troll.

"Don't worry about me. This isn't even my first trap of the week."

"I know, but I don't trust that cowboy."

"Clay? He's harmless."

"Just...keep him in front of you."

She leaned in and pecked Troll on the cheek and then walked out the door. Troll watched her leave, his face growing hot.

Even considering how close the group came to dying, Clay wouldn't stop giving Rogan the evil eye while they drove out to the farm in Tanya's Jeep. Rogan made sure to mention all the individual heroics—and detailed exactly how the pickup was paramount to their survival. No matter what he said, Clay just sat there in the backseat, glaring at Rogan in the rearview.

Tanya drove them out of town the opposite direction of the fallen pickup. They looped around the woods, towards the highway and the dormant farm. Rogan tried to stay alert to his surroundings, not wanting a repeat of last night. Once in a while he saw someone or something bolt in and out of the edge of the woods. Nothing approached the road.

They made it to the farm without incident. Angus's van sat silent at the end of the long driveway. Rogan noted that the tires had been slashed as they drove by. Tanya parked the Jeep on a small approach down from the farm. Then she led the two men through the deep weeds that came up to the back of the barn. The team slowly cleared each area as they went watching for any sign of a trap. The place seemed deserted.

Finally, the trio made it to the farmhouse. After peeking in all the windows around the old structure they met near the porch.

"Why don't you two go on ahead? I'll do a quick swing around and make sure no one came up behind," said Clay.

"Sounds good. We'll clear the house and locate the bookcase," said Rogan.

Clay nodded and went off around the side of the house. Rogan and Tanya stepped up onto the porch and went to either side of the door. Rogan threw the knob and strode inside, swinging his gun from left to right and cleared the entryway. Tanya waited by the old staircase to the second floor while Rogan cleared the small rooms on the main level. Running his gun from corner to corner in each room reminded Rogan of his former days as a police officer, when clearing a building was just another day on the job. He could feel his adrenaline pumping on high as he went into each room, waiting to spot movement or someone lurking in the shadows.

After the bottom floor was cleared, Rogan and Tanya worked their way upstairs, where there were two bedrooms and a small storage room. All three rooms were empty. One of the rooms had a set of bunk beds that looked much newer than the rest of the house. Below them they heard an engine. Rogan slowly eased down the stairs and turned towards the front door. The door opened.

"Freeze, hands up!" shouted Rogan.

"Woah, woah...just me," said Clay, holding his hands up.

"Clay, don't you remember anything from training? Announce before you enter."

"Oh, sorry, Rogan. Forgot all about that big city stuff. I brought the Jeep over in case we need to get out of here quick. Mind not pointing your steel at me?"

"Yeah, sorry. Anything outside?" asked Rogan, lowering his firearm.

"Nada. Place is totally cleared out. Those boys must have run out of town."

"Now let's hope they didn't take the antidote with them," said Rogan.

The group walked into what was likely the living room of the old house. A bookcase stood in the far corner. It was no more than three feet tall, with three shelves. The shelves each held dusty books of varying sizes. Clay walked over and grabbed the bookshelf and attempted to move it. His face turned red with effort before he relented.

"Old thing won't budge," said Clay.

Rogan studied the books, assuming that one of them was the trigger to open some sort of trap door. Or perhaps there was a hollowed out book with a vial of the antidote nestled inside.

One book, a small blue one with the same imprint of the stick figure fish that was on the notebook stood out; it had much less dust on it and there were minute scrapes at the edges, running perpendicular to the front of the shelf, like a track leading to the book. Rogan gripped the book and pulled. The book slid forward with a soft click. Rogan gripped both sides of the bookcase and pushed to the right, and the whole shelf easily slid to the side, revealing a cubby hole. The square hole was two feet by two feet. It looked to go back into the wall a couple feet as well, but Rogan could not determine if anything was in there through the dark shadows.

He went down to his belly and wiggled into the hole. Inside he could see a small safe. He grabbed the combination lock and put in the numbers from the binary sheet, 33, 03, 60. The lock clicked. Rogan opened the door reaching out with his hands, hoping to grab onto something inside the safe that might be the antidote. It was completely empty. He slid back out of the hole and up onto all fours.

"Thing's empt—" Rogan started. His face rebounded off the hardwood floor, sending shockwaves of pain through his body. He grabbed the back of his head. Something blunt had struck him hard.

He struggled to maintain consciousness. He tried to get up, but before he could move more than an inch, he felt a knee in his back holding him to the ground. Rogan struggled, but the boney knee dug harder into his spine. Someone pulled his hands behind his back and then Rogan felt the cold steel of handcuffs. His captor then reached into Rogan's back pocket and slid out his mobile phone.

Rogan rolled to his back and sat up. Clay stood in the center of the room. He had a gun pointed down at Tanya, who lay unconscious near the doorway. He threw Rogan's phone on the ground and stomped it with the heel of his boot.

"Clay? What the hell are you doing?"

"Me and the little lady here are going to take a drive. Seems we're interested in her."

"What are you talking about?" asked Rogan.

"You saw the notes. She's immune to Darwin. The boys back at the lab are going to tear her up and find out why."

"You work for them?"

"Yep, sure do. You seem surprised."

"How could you do this? Most of the people in your town were killed, and you're their fucking *sheriff.*"

"Come on, Rogan. This ain't my town. I've just been biding my time, waiting for the call. These people don't mean a thing to me. Well, except for a paycheck."

"So, you're sitting there in your little office, and one day some military-looking guys walk in and say, 'Hey guy. We want to kill everyone in your town, you okay with that? Oh here's a bag of money.'"

"Wow, you really don't know much, Rogan. Do you? I've worked for them for, what, six years now?"

"Six years? You would have been on the Queen City force then."

"Ding, ding."

Rogan's mind was reeling. The further down the road they got on this case, the stranger the puzzle became. He couldn't wrap his mind around the idea that Clay would have been working for this Project Darwin when he was an officer. He seemed like a dopey Texan, loping around the precinct like a lost puppy, not a pawn in some giant conspiracy. Rogan wanted to keep him talking, though. Assuming he lived through this ordeal, any information he could get might help him rescue Tanya and stop the bigger looming problem.

"Why you? Why cops?" asked Rogan.

"I don't know. I suppose they sensed I wasn't happy. Figured they could give me an out. Why cops? Wow, you Rogans are a delusional bunch. Queen cops? Filthy. All of 'em."

"That's not true," spat Rogan.

"Believe what you want, but what you saw the last few days was just a trial run. Wait until Darwin is let loose in Queen. Can you imagine that? Don't much matter to me, though, I'll be down in Texas by then. Buy myself a big ranch, be surrounded by cactus and cattle."

"Why are they doing this? What possible reason could there be to turn people into monsters?"

"They say they're going to cleanse the world. Make it safe again. As long as I'm still here when they're done and I have some land, don't much matter to me."

"This isn't you. What the hell happened to you?"

"Sometimes you just got to back the winning side, no need for questions. I was recruited about six months after I started the force. Did some small odds and ends around the city, then they shipped me up here. I hated it. I may not have fit in in Queen City, but I sure as shit was not made to sit around in the woods all day. Give me ranch land. If you can't see a mile in all directions it's too crowded for my likes. That's a point I agree on with these guys. Powerful people, Rogan. Don't mess with them. I know you're like a bulldog salivating on a bone, but you need to let this one lie, okay? They won't hesitate to take care of you and yours."

"If they think they are going to do to Queen City what they did here in Evergreen...you can let them know I'm coming for them and theirs," said Rogan, fire burning in his emerald eyes.

"Then you are a dead man, Richard Rogan."

Rogan attempted to check his emotions and get back to gathering as much information as he could and buy as much time as he could get.

"If you work for them...why did you ask me to help?"

"Because I know you, Rogan. If I wouldn't have asked you to help, you would have just done it anyway. Better to keep you close...keep an eye on you."

He wasn't wrong on that. Rogan had made up his mind that he was going to find the missing townspeople well before he stepped foot in that sheriff's office. He would have tracked down every lead and every possibility with or without Clay's support.

"Who recruited you?" asked Rogan.

"That's a point I can't much talk about," laughed Clay. "But let's just say you'd be surprised."

"What's that mean?"

"Mean's I've said too much. Me and Tanya here have a date to get to. I like you, Rogan, so I'm going to do you a favor and not shoot you right here and now, but if you try to come after me, I won't hesitate."

Clay threw Tanya over his shoulder like she was a light sack of potatoes and backed out of the room. He kept his pistol trained on Rogan the entire time.

"Wait, Clay, wait, what do you mean? Who are these people? You can't honestly think it's okay to let so many die!" shouted Rogan, but it was too late. Rocks shot in through the front door of the farm house as the tires on Tanya's Jeep spun in the gravel.

Rogan jumped to his feet and ran out the door. The Jeep turned onto the highway and shot off to the west. More than likely they were headed for the city, but the highway branched off several times before it meandered into the outskirts. Rogan's head was pounding. He stumbled as he ran towards Angus's van. It was the only vehicle on the property; he had to get back to town, round everyone up, and go after Clay.

He couldn't let Tanya get hurt, and he had to find out what was really going on here. He slammed hard into the driver's door, losing his balance on the ruts of the driveway. He turned around and grabbed at the handle with his bound hands, and after a couple attempts, he managed to press in the button and pull the latch. He crawled inside. Angus had taken the keys, which was just as well since all four tires were slashed. Rogan would have been willing to try and make it to town on the rims, though.

He searched around for a phone or some way to call back to the team. He found a lot of empty energy drink cans, but nothing of use. There were computers and equipment in the back of the van, but Rogan hadn't the slightest clue how to use any of it, especially since his hands were securely behind his back. Clay clearly remembered the handcuffing lessons from his days as an officer, even if he didn't remember anything else.

Rogan stood at the end of the driveway and looked both ways down the highway. No matter which way he went, he would have to go around the long forest. Even at a full run, he would be an hour away from town by road. By then, Tanya would be a lab rat in some secret lab. Rogan sighed and stared across the street. The woods seemed to loom in the distance like some monster waiting to pounce. The long shadows of the trees struck out into the grasslands, menacingly dancing along the tall, wind-brushed grasses.

Rogan looked down the highway one last time, hoping to see a vehicle coming his way, but the old highway was empty as far as the eye could see. With no time to waste, he took off jogging towards the woods. The ditch was filled with cockleburs, and he felt the spines on the tall weeds rip at his jeans as he powered through the deep ditch. He felt like he was walking through water in the thick, waving grassland. The ominous shadows came into view. He took a quick scan of the forest's edge, looking for movement. All seemed quiet; he hoped it wasn't too quiet.

A half dozen more long strides through the grasses brought Rogan into the woods. He felt like he was entering a haunted house. The temperature immediately dropped, and his vision was reduced as the canopy above blotted out the sunlight. He ran. He ran hard, looking in all directions for movement as he went. More than once a root found his foot, sending him face first into the forest floor.

He saw a hole up ahead. Almost too late, he skidded to a halt, his left foot travelling over the edge of the pit. He threw his weight backwards, landing hard on his rear. He looked down to see a dead man wearing black fatigues.

Rogan stood up and ran around the hole, and he started scanning the ground in front of him as he ran, not wanting to end up like the man in the pit. The deeper he got into the woods, the darker it got. Only slants of sunlight found their way through, giving the area an almost mystical appearance. The shimmering rays were barely enough to allow Rogan to see what was coming up ahead. As he ran, he began to hear noises. Groans came from all around him. Screams and yells echoed through the tree branches. The further he ran, the louder the noises became.

Suddenly Rogan found himself in a clearing. He remembered Tanya talking about a clearing that was nearly dead center in the woods. He was only halfway. He felt like he had been running for hours. He stopped in the middle of the clearing to catch his breath. The sun shining down through the opening in the thick canopy helped to warm his chilled limbs. Giant pines surrounded the perimeter of the clearing. Short grasses and bushes covered the floor. Rogan knelt down for a moment, trying to rest his tired legs. His wound was throbbing. He wished he was flexible enough to pull his legs through his arms so he could have his hands in front of his body.

From behind him, Rogan heard a stick crack, and then another. He jumped to his feet and turned towards the noise. He stood frozen, listening as hard as he could. To his left he heard pine branches striking together. He turned again, but saw nothing. Behind him, he heard something scraping across the ground. He had heard enough.

Rogan decided the best course of action would be to not be in the clearing when whatever was making those noises came out of the shadows. He ran hard towards the edge of the clearing, away from the noises and towards town. He was a mere six paces from the edge when three men stepped out from the shadows in front of him. Rogan came to a halt, falling backwards. He scrambled away from the men. All three were bare chested, tall, and muscular. Two of them were wearing jeans in various states of destruction. The middle man wore plaid shorts. None of them wore shoes. All three men had dried blood around their mouths. Long, sharp fingernails projected from their wide, stretched hands.

Rogan got to his feet, looking for an escape route. His six o' clock had been filled in by more of the wild people. As had his three o'clock and nine o'clock. Rogan backed away from the three big men in front of him as they stomped heavily forward. His mind raced, trying to find a way to get out of this snare.

Rogan found himself standing back in the center of the clearing, completely surrounded. He spun around, doing a quick head count. He came up with twenty people, all various ages, some men, some woman. All looked strong, violent. The group slowly and methodically closed in on him like the jaws on a trap.

Rogan looked for a weak link in the chain. His best bet seemed to be off to his right where two women stood together as part of the closing ring. Both were short, no more than five feet. As he looked, he saw more people emerging from the woods. Another ten for sure. He had no time to waste.

Rogan ran straight at the two women, springing off his good back leg when he got close enough. He took to the air, his front leg forward, his back leg curled up behind, like a hurdler going for gold. One of the women saw it coming. She leapt into the air, matching Rogan's height easily. The woman kicked out with her feet, landing them both into Rogan's chest. Rogan flew backwards, landing hard on his back. He crab walked backwards as best he could. His chest pounded with pain from the blow.

The crowd hooted and hollered their approval of the violence. The group continued forward until Rogan was crouching in the middle of a five-foot circle. *This is it,* he thought. *I'm going to die here, in the middle of these damn woods.* He shook his head. *No, not like this, I'm a Rogan, we fight to the end.* He stood up to his full height and turned in a slow circle, waiting for the first attack. He had only his legs, but he would fight to his last.

Rogan felt the breeze increase in speed while he waited. It whistled through the needles and leaves surrounding the clearing. The first strike came from a young man that probably wasn't old enough to buy cigarettes. Rogan kicked out and knocked the young man's hand away. Rogan felt thick arms wrap around him. He kicked out, sending another man flying out into the crowd. The momentum of the kick caused the man holding him to fall backwards to the ground and lose his grip. Rogan rolled away as two more people grabbed him. Rogan broke free and fought with everything he had. He kicked and head-butted, but he was taking much more damage than he was dishing out. He took a vicious shot to the stomach and then another across the jaw. He stumbled away, bent over, and spat blood.

"That all you got?" he yelled at the mob.

The wind picked up more. It seemed to be swirling up from around Rogan's feet. The mob began to whoop and holler; almost in unison, they all took a stumbling step back from Rogan. The wild ones closest to him clawed at him, but they too kept their distance.

Leaves and fallen pine needles spun up into the air. Soon Rogan could barely see through the spinning debris. It was as if a tornado were forming on the spot. The spinning vortex picked up speed. The mob yelled out in panicked calls. They began running into each other. All of them turned from the wild wind, stumbling over one another to get clear of the whipping vortex.

Then Rogan felt the presence. A warm light bathed over him, and he suddenly felt calm and peace. His ghost was here. Was his ghost producing these gale force winds of dirt and fallen leaves?

The misty apparition formed in front of him, dancing just above the ground. She was more defined, no longer a clinging ball of mist, but person-like. He could make out curves where her hips might be. The wispy mist near the top looked like strands of long hair gently responding to a breeze. The mist raised what would be her arms. The tornado shot out into the clearing. It picked up the mob, sending them spinning through the vortex like Dorothy on her way to Oz. In a matter of seconds, the entire group was swept up into the thundering flow, their arms and legs flailing. Rogan stood in the eye of the storm with his ghost and waited.

A clap of thunder sounded, and the vortex was gone. The tornado vanished as suddenly as it had come. Rogan watched as people were flung out into the woods in all directions. He heard moans and the cracking of branches—and likely bones.

Rogan stood in the center of the clearing on a patch of short grass five feet in diameter. Black dirt lead out from the perfect circle of grass to the edge of the tall pines. It was as if the tornado tore up and then exploded everything between Rogan and the tree line. Rogan looked at his ghost, staring where he thought her eyes would be. She bobbed slightly up and down, floating above the black dirt.

"Thank you," Rogan said. The ghost continued to bob. "Who are…" Before he could say you, the ghost vanished in a blink.

Rogan fell to his knees and looked around, taking in deep breaths. Did that really just happen? Maybe all the shots to the head were getting to him. Maybe the people, the ghost, all of it was just a hallucination. Either way, he couldn't think about it now; he had to keep moving.

Tanya was counting on him.

16:

The historic gravel main street of Evergreen was overrun with living zombies. Rogan stood behind the diner, looking out at the roiling sea of infected townspeople. The sheriff's office was completely surrounded. With his hands cuffed behind his back, he could not see how he could get through the mob without getting torn to shreds. He wondered if maybe his ghost would show up again and part the sea. He waited a couple minutes, but the ghost was a no show. The wolves and zombies were busy banging their fists and claws against the office building, leaving the rest of the town unoccupied.

The back window to the diner had been shattered. Rogan carefully stepped through the opening, avoiding the shards of glass still sticking to the window sill. He wished he could bring his hands up to cover his nose and mouth. An army of flies buzzed around the diner, hovering and landing on bodies lying on the floor, over the counter, and on the booths. Rogan looked around, trying not to gag. There were several more corpses than the last time he was in the diner scavenging for food.

Rogan worked his way through the decaying bodies to behind the counter, where an olive-colored phone hung on the wall. Using his mouth, he pulled the receiver off the wall and set it on the prep station just under the phone. He put his ear to the receiver, there was a dial tone. Rogan stared at the phone in a state close to disbelief. *A rotary phone?* he thought. *They still have those?*

A cup of pencils lay overturned on the prep bench. Rogan worked a long yellow number two out of the cup with his mouth. He took a good grip on the pencil with his teeth and dialed McKenzie's cell phone number. It took him three attempts, but finally he heard the phone dialing.

"Hello? Rogan?"

"Hey Mac."

"Oh thank god. We thought maybe you guys got caught or something."

"We kind of did. I'll explain later. I'm across the street in the diner of death."

"So you see our situation then?"

"Yeah, I'm trying to figure out how to get to you through that mess."

"Maybe you can get a vehicle and we could do a roof jump?"

"That's a good idea, except I have a little problem...my hands are cuffed tightly behind my back."

"What?"

"Long story, but it's going to make driving a little interesting."

"Why don't you just pick the cuffs, find a paper clip or something."

"That only works in the movies."

"No, that's a real thing."

"No way."

"Really? We have time for this?"

"Maybe you guys could lay down some cover fire and I could just run for it?"

"We're pretty low on ammo, at least the non-lethal stuff. A couple of the crazies have managed to climb onto the roof. We've had a couple close calls. Plus, getting you here just makes one more person trapped."

"Okay. So our best bet is for me to somehow get a vehicle and ram through that crowd. I guess I drive with my knees after I hit a drive thru, how different could it be?"

"That's the spirit, sparky. Now find something with a sturdy roof. We'll get packed up and ready to leap."

Rogan hung up and headed back out the rear window. He went to the western edge of the town near the bed and breakfast where he had his first standoff with one of the alpha wolves. That seemed like a long time ago. He weaved through the shadows of the buildings, looking for a vehicle that would have the force to get through the crowd and the height to keep his team safe once he got there. He found it in the middle of the road outside the bed and breakfast. A black Suburban sat diagonally on the road with its hazard lights blinking. The driver's door was open.

Rogan rounded the rear of the vehicle, checking to make sure the crowd was still occupied. He came around to the driver's side and skidded to a halt. A girl no more than ten years old, wearing a polka dot sun dress, had her jaws clamped onto the neck of a man who was hanging out of the driver's door. She turned towards Rogan; blood soaked her braided pigtails. Dried and fresh blood surrounded her mouth, like she had gone crazy with her mom's red lipstick. She crouched low, holding her small hands out wide. Suddenly she leaped at him, claws first. Rogan stumbled back, brought his leg up, and kicked the girl in the chest. She rolled away, her arms and legs twisted up around her body.

"I'm sorry," said Rogan.

With his back to the man, Rogan grabbed onto the man's collar and pulled him from the running vehicle. The man was wearing black fatigues.

"Serves you right," said Rogan, climbing into the driver's seat.

He compressed the brake, and using a combination of his mouth and forehead, moved the shifter to drive. He pulled his left leg back, bringing his knee to the bottom of the wheel. He pressed the gas and shot off down the road. He quickly jerked his knee right, sending the Suburban lumbering to the left through the lawn of the bed and breakfast. He turned again and lined up on the alley that led behind the office.

The rear of the building was just as overrun as the front. The crowd was ten deep in spots, all of them milling around, trying to get to the building. Rogan saw McKenzie, Angus, Troll, and Lizzy standing on the top of the building. He let out a long blow of breath, made sure the wheel was straight and slammed down the gas. The front of the vehicle came up as the rear wheels dug into the dirt alley.

Rogan made adjustments with his knee, trying to keep the vehicle as straight as possible. He hoped that the raging crowd had enough intelligence to run. They didn't. Rogan slammed on the brakes and listened to the horrifying sound of thumps and crunches as the heavy vehicle ran into and over people. He put his head to his chest as the big Suburban came to a stop. *How has it gotten this bad?* he thought. Someone pounded on the roof, snapping him back. He put the pedal down again and drove out of the alley to another round of thumps. The vehicle bounced over what Rogan wished was speed bumps as he tore out of town. He didn't stop until they were well away from the carnage.

"You okay?" asked McKenzie, opening the driver's door.

Rogan felt numb. He didn't know how many people he had just killed, but it had to be several. He knew that he didn't have a choice, and that they would not have hesitated to kill him and his team, but he still felt terrible about the loss of life, especially since it was at his hand—or rather, his knee.

"Come on, Rogan. Let's get you out of those cuffs."

Rogan slid out of the seat. McKenzie came up behind him, and in seconds, the cuffs fell to the ground. Rogan brought his hands around, rubbing his wrists. His wrists ached, as did his shoulders. McKenzie placed a twisted paperclip in his hand and smirked. Rogan rolled his eyes and turned to the group.

"Everyone okay?" asked Rogan.

"We're alive," said Troll, helping Lizzy down from the roof of the Suburban.

"Good. Everyone load up. We've got work to do."

✵ ✵ ✵

Rogan sped off towards the highway. He figured that the city would be the most likely destination for Clay. While he drove he filled in the team in on the recent events. He left out the part about the ghost tornado.

"Clay's a bad guy?" asked McKenzie.

"I did not see that coming," said Angus.

"How are we going to find him?" asked Troll. "Queen City is a big place, if that's even where he's headed."

"I don't know. I know they're in Tanya's Jeep, and I memorized the license plate number when they drove off, but it's still going to be a haystack situation."

"You have her license plate number?" asked Angus.

"Yeah?"

"Okay, stop at the farm. I need to get my van."

"Bad news about that, man. Someone slashed your tires."

"Oh come on! Okay...well, that's okay. I have satellite in there."

"What are you thinking?"

"If you have the plate number, I can...uncover her VIN number, and with that, find out if she has an antitheft device, and if she does, I can track it."

"Nice..." said Troll.

"You should call Sam too, and put out an APB or whatever," said McKenzie handing him her phone.

"All Points Bulletin...good idea, Mac."

Rogan pulled into the driveway of the farm. Angus jumped out and ran over to his van, disappearing inside. The team sat waiting to see if he could deliver. While they waited, Rogan called Sam Stone, one of Queen City's finest detectives. She and Rogan also had a history. They had been a hot item back when he was on the force, back before all the death in his family drove him away from the thin blue line. When he left, he'd left her too, choosing to go the route of not talking to her instead of actually breaking off the relationship. Deservedly, she was not one of Rogan's biggest fans. After he'd coerced her into working with him on a recent case involving murdered prostitutes and organ thieves, Sam and Rogan were back to speaking terms, though the arrangement was tenuous at best. Rogan listened to the phone dial hoping that the call would go through now that the phone blocking equipment was destroyed. He smiled as he heard Sam's unmistakable voice.

"Thought you were fishing or something," said Sam, answering the call.

"Plans changed. There is some bad stuff going on in Evergreen."

"Hah, good one, Rogan. What, did you get sunburned?"

"I'm serious, Sam. It's a long story, but the important point right now is that a woman was kidnapped. I believe the perp is bringing her into Queen. I'm hoping you can put out an APB for the vehicle."

"Run it down."

"Blue Jeep, license plate 145, Echo, David, Charlie. Woman is Tanya Tucker, mid-twenties, brunette, around five foot six inches."

"Got it, and the guy?"

"You're not going to believe this one..."

"Try me."

"Remember Clay Stevens, that lanky Texan with the drawl?"

"Yeah, jumped out of his snakeskin boots at pretty much any loud noise?"

"Yep, he's the guy."

"Okay, so you are pulling my leg...? Come on, Rogan. I know Clay is working up in Evergreen, suppose you two think you're real damn funny. I have better things to do."

"Sam, Wait...wait... I'm serious. I wish I were joking, but Clay...he went to the wrong side. Claims he's been there since he was in Queen. Says there is dirt on the force."

The line went silent for a moment. Rogan knew better than to speak. He needed to let Sam work through the situation.

"Okay. I believe you, barely. I'll put out the All Points. Call you if I hear anything."

"Thanks, Sam."

Angus ran to the driver's door and pounded on the glass. He looked like an excited puppy jumping up against the car. Rogan rolled down the window.

"I got it, I got it, bro. I'm going to have to stay here though; the satellite uplink is not mobile. Jump out a sec."

Rogan stepped out of the Suburban. Angus ducked under the steering wheel and pulled down a bunch of wires. After quickly sorting through them he clamped a module onto one of them. Angus exited the Suburban and handed Rogan two small pieces of plastic that looked like hearing aids. Rogan looked over at Angus.

"Earpieces, so I can guide you outside the Suburban. I only have two, though. What are you waiting for? Go save the girl!"

Rogan nodded and tore out of the driveway. He headed down the highway towards Queen City. While he did, he pushed the small ear bud into his left ear. He handed the other to McKenzie, who was sitting in the front seat.

"Testing, testing. Can you hear me, bud?"

"Loud and clear, Angus. What's the range on these?"

"World."

"What?"

"It's a little complicated, but they work off a bunch of signal sources, primarily a military satellite that, let's just say I have access to, as well as the cellular network, wireless internet connections, pretty much anything that can carry a signal."

"Angus..."

"Yeah, Rogan."

"I didn't understand much of that, but I'm real glad you're on our side."

"Aww shucks... Hey, tune the radio to 97.3 for me."

McKenzie pushed the tune button to 97.3 FM. Rogan focused on the road. He wondered how much more complicated this could get.

"Check...check...this is Angus FM, all awesome, all the time, coming to you live from a van on an abandoned farm. We play all the hits, all...the...hits," said Angus, in his best radio DJ voice.

"Unbelievable," said Rogan, listening to Angus's voice come out of the Suburban's speakers.

"Rogan, what about Evergreen, should we call the National Guard or something now that the phones are back?" asked McKenzie.

A vision of tanks rolling into Evergreen materialized in Rogan's mind. How could they convince soldiers that the wild people of Evergreen were real people? At the same time, what if the wolves decided to migrate to new territory? He wanted time. He and his team could handle this. If they could catch Clay,

Rogan felt sure that they would have the antidote and be able to save more people than might be dispatched if the armed forces took over.

"Let's wait on that for now. I want to see if we can get that antidote before we send machine guns in," said Rogan gripping the wheel tighter, already questioning his decision.

"What's this thing?" asked Lizzy from the back seat. She held up a gray block that had a folding antenna on the side.

McKenzie took it and turned it over in her hands. "It's some kind of phone, I think."

"Big round antenna?" asked Angus.

"Yeah."

"Satellite phone."

"Let's see who black fatigue guy has on his frequent callers list." McKenzie flipped open the cover on the phone. The screen lit up, showing a number of options. She pressed the recent calls button.

"Okay, no incoming calls, only outgoing, all to the same number."

"Let's see who answers," said Rogan.

McKenzie dialed the number and set the phone to speaker. After one ring, someone picked up on the other end. "Darwin's," said a male voice.

"Who is this?" asked Rogan. The other end disconnected the call.

"You probably needed to have a pass phrase or something," said Troll.

"Hey McKenzie, turn that phone off and take out the battery, okay? If they have anyone with skills, they might be able to track you by that," said Angus through the earbud. McKenzie powered off the phone.

Completely ignoring the speed limit, the Suburban entered the outskirts of Queen City. According to Angus, the Jeep was heading towards the Basin, which was the old downtown, now derelict. Rogan tore down the streets in the long, black Suburban. McKenzie called Sam to let her know where the Jeep was heading. According to Angus, they were closing in on the Jeep's location.

Rogan turned the corner onto 15th Avenue. At the very edge of his vision, he could make out the Jeep. He put down the accelerator. The Suburban's big engine responded. The vehicle shot down the street towards the Jeep. Rogan dodged the light traffic as he went. He focused completely on the back of the Jeep. The Jeep turned a corner. His eyes narrowed. He gave the engine a little more gas, coaxing a few more horses out of the engine. He wouldn't lose it. He was going to catch Clay.

"Rogan, it stopped," said Angus.

"Come again?"

"The Jeep. It stopped. Take your next right, and you should see it on your left."

"10-4."

The Suburban's tires squealed as Rogan spun around the corner. He felt the back end fishtail. He turned the wheel hard into the fishtail to bring the big rig straight once more. A block up on the left, he saw the Jeep in front of an abandoned auto garage. The single story building stood alone in the center of the block, surrounded by much taller brick buildings. Grass and weeds crept up through the cracked cement of the parking lot. The front of the building had two large garage doors that were barely hanging on their hinges. The main door was completely gone. Rogan slammed the brakes down, coming to a rough stop in front of the garage. The Jeep sat diagonally across the aged lot.

"Christ, Rogan... For a second there, I thought Angus was driving," said Troll.

"Hey!" said Angus.

"Sorry for the rough ride. We have to catch Clay."

"I get that, but let's make sure we all live through it, m'kay?" said McKenzie.

"Noted," said Rogan, jumping out of the Suburban.

Rogan drew his Smith and Wesson pistol and approached the Jeep. It was empty. A second later, he heard another set of tires skid to a stop behind him. He turned, gun up. It was a black unmarked police cruiser. Inside he saw a scowl and a blonde ponytail. Sam.

"What in the *hell* have you gotten into this time, Rogan?" asked Sam.

"Oh you know, the usual. People killing each other, kidnapping, secret evil organization..."

"I see you brought the whole gang," said Sam, waving at the Suburban.

"Of course. So...wanna raid a rundown auto shop with me?" asked Rogan, waggling his eyebrows.

"Sounds lovely," said Sam, pulling her pistol.

"Troll, you stay here. Make sure Mac and Lizzy stay safe. Sam and I are going to go flush out that bastard. He comes out this way, pop him with every bean bag you got."

Troll nodded and took up his position in front of the Suburban. Sam and Rogan approached the open main door of the auto shop. One to each side of the garage door, they listened to the gloom inside. Rogan looked down at the dirt just inside the building. There were two sets of tracks: the first set short shuffling steps backwards, the second a set of feet being dragged. Rogan motioned towards Sam and pointed towards the tracks. She nodded, mouthed "cover me," and went into the building. Rogan raised his pistol and scanned the immediate area as he listened to the soft tap of Sam's stiletto heels on the concrete floor.

Sam stood with her back against the wall, peering around a corner towards the back of the building. She nodded at Rogan. He ran low and fast to her location. Rogan scanned the area while Sam ran to a rusting barrel deeper into the shop. Then Rogan leap frogged to an overturned oil tank. The tracks continued on into the darkness. The further back the tracks got, the harder they were to see in the dusty darkness.

Sam made her next move to a set of stacked worn out tires. Rogan was about to head towards the next piece of cover when he heard an engine start up. It was deafening in the long, narrow space. Next he heard the spinning of tires on concrete. He ran for Sam.

Out of the corner of his eye, he saw a set of headlights emerge from the darkness like a train from a tunnel. It was coming fast. Rogan grabbed Sam around the waist and together they rolled towards the far wall. Rogan felt a whoosh of air on his back as the vehicle slammed through the stack of tires.

Sam got up on a knee and fired rounds at the vehicle. Rogan did the same, aiming for tires, but it was going too fast and it was too dark. The vehicle blasted out through one of the decrepit garage doors and slammed into the front end of the Jeep, sending it spiraling 180 degrees. The nose of the Jeep smacked into the side of the Suburban, missing Troll by inches. Sam and Rogan ran out the new big opening in the building just in time to see a black Suburban just like the one Rogan and the team had procured heading down the street.

"Everyone okay?" yelled Sam, running towards the stationary Suburban.

"Yeah, yeah, we're fine," said Troll, staring at the Jeep that was inches from his leg.

"See anything?" asked Rogan.

"Yeah, Clay was in the passenger seat and one of those men with black camo was driving," said Lizzy, leaning out of the window.

"New team member?" asked Sam, eyebrow raised towards Rogan.

"Extremely long story," said Rogan. "Angus, are you able to follow that Suburban?"

"Trying my best. Using traffic cams and whatever else I can crack, but I'm not going to be able to keep with them for long. Not many cameras down in this older part of town. I'd say they are heading towards the Basin. They turned back onto 15th and haven't changed course yet."

Sam was already back in her vehicle, backing up. She swung the black car around the back of the Suburban and took off down the street. Troll got into the passenger seat. Rogan watched Sam turn down 15th and then jumped into the Suburban.

"Okay...here we go again," said Rogan, backing up the Suburban.

McKenzie settled into the back seat, and tightened Lizzy's seatbelt. Rogan winked into the rearview mirror and slammed down the gas. He took the Suburban around the corner onto 15th Avenue, trying to be more considerate of his passengers. He could see Sam up ahead; she was already right on the tail of Clay's Suburban. Rogan always admired Sam's driving ability and her relentlessness. She would chase after that Suburban until she either ran it off the road or it ran out of gas.

"Wonder why the switch," asked Troll.

"They figured out we were tracking the Jeep," said Angus. "I noticed someone poking around. I shut them down, but they saw what I was doing before I got them completely out."

"Must be pretty good to get one past you," said Rogan, swerving around an old woman crossing the road pushing a walker.

"Yeah...and well-funded, I'd say. The gear they'd need to even get the glimpse they got would be *mucho dinero.*"

Rogan managed to catch up to Sam. She was about two car lengths behind the Suburban. The Suburban seemed to be making no effort to outrun her or lose her. Rogan settled in a couple car lengths behind Sam. He considered running down a side street to see if he could get in front of the bad guys. The Suburban passed the next intersection, and Rogan decided that would be the one he would attempt to turn down to flank the other Suburban.

Just as the nose of Sam's cruiser passed through the intersection, a black panel van came flying through the intersection. It slammed into the front quarterpanel of Sam's cruiser. Rogan slammed on the brakes. He watched as Sam's car spun 360 degrees and then flipped side over side down the street. The van continued on through the intersection and down the cross street. As he watched Sam's car flip one more time, he almost missed the two men on motorcycles following the van. The men wore black, skintight masks. They both had machine guns.

"Down!" yelled Rogan, ducking his long frame down as low as he could.

A spray of bullets made contact with their car. The windshield shattered, along with the rear and side windows. The bullets contacting the shell of the Suburban sounded like two men playing steel drums. After the cacophony of shattered glass and penetrated steel stopped, Rogan rolled out of the Suburban. The two men pulled in their weapons and turned their attention towards escaping with the van.

Rogan ran to the intersection, planted both feet, and pulled his pistol. He took careful aim on the man riding to the left, who was drifting back from the other rider. He pulled the trigger. The bullet flew through the air, making contact with the man's left shoulder. The motorcycle careened off course as the man flew forward into the handlebars and then off the back of the motorcycle. The motorcycle flipped end over end, catching the other motorcycle's rear tire. The second rider lost control. The rider and motorcycle slid on their side into a parked car with a crunch.

As the rest of the team got out of the Suburban, Sam's car decided which way to fall, landing hard on its roof. Rogan ran over and fell to his knees, looking in through the windows. Inside, he saw a blonde ponytail hanging down.

"Hang on, Sam!" yelled Rogan.

Rogan tried the driver's door. He yanked at the handle with all his strength, but the door wouldn't budge. He ran around to the passenger side; it also was locked. Troll came over carrying a shotgun. Using the butt of the gun, he smashed in the passenger window. Rogan reached in, releasing the lock. Together he and Troll pulled the door open, its frame digging into the asphalt street. Rogan crawled inside. He could smell gas, and he knew he needed to get her out right away before anything sparked. She had her seatbelt on, her body pressed against the restraints, a trickle of blood dripped from her forehead, pooling on the ceiling panel. Her arms stretched out limply, her hands lying to either side of the blood pool.

"Sam? Sam, are you with me?" Rogan got no response. He reached in, feeling her neck. He couldn't be sure it wasn't broken, but he did know for sure this car was going to go up in flames any minute. He wedged himself under her, reached around and pressed the seatbelt release. It didn't want to give. Rogan smelled something hot. He was running out of time.

"Rogan, turn her face," Troll shouted.

Rogan put his hands over Sam's eyes and turned her face away from the driver's window. The sound of smashing glass echoed through the interior of the cruiser.

"Okay, Rogan. You lift up on her, get some weight off the restraints. I'll push the button. They won't let go with that much pressure on the latch."

Rogan maneuvered his large frame the best he could to support Sam's neck and back. He wanted to make sure that when she was released her head didn't smash into the ground. He pressed up with his hips, feeling her move upwards. Then he heard a click. He lowered himself back down and with Troll's help, he and Sam slid out of the passenger door. Rogan carefully picked up Sam and ran away from the now-smoking car.

McKenzie was in the driver's seat of the Suburban. She pulled away just as the car exploded into flames. Rogan felt the heat on his back as he ran. He didn't stop running for nearly a block.

Sam was unconscious, but alive. He heard sirens in the distance, heading their way. He slumped against a brick wall, laying Sam gently across his legs. He was wiping up the blood on her forehead when the rest of the group ran over.

"Is she okay?" asked Lizzy.

"I think she will be, but she's out right now," said Rogan. "I hope there is an ambulance in that group of sirens."

"What about Tanya?" asked Troll.

"Once we get Sam taken care of, we'll head after her."

The sirens were growing closer. Rogan pushed the blonde hairs out of Sam's face, pushing them gently behind her ear. He wished he could take back what happened between them—not the relationship, but how it ended. He wondered how different his life would be if he wouldn't have fallen so deep into his own silent depression. If he would have just let her in, would they still be together, would he be happier?

Rogan said a silent thank you when he saw an ambulance pull up. There was also a fire truck and two police cars. Rogan was happy to see all of them except one man. Out of the driver's seat of one of the police cars slithered Detective Rodríguez. He and Rogan did not see eye to eye on anything. Rogan blamed him for his sister Sarah's death. It had been Rodríguez's call that they went into that warehouse without backup. Rodríguez ran towards Rogan, or rather, Sam. He tugged off his mirrored aviator sunglasses as he knelt down beside her.

"What the hell, Rogan? What did you drag Sam into this time? Fuck, is she all right?"

"I think she'll be okay. Car accident," said Rogan.

"She'd better be."

Rogan glared at Rodríguez. He was wearing his usual blue jeans and tweed jacket. He looked like a certified jackass to Rogan. He knew that Sam was an officer of the law, but he still felt guilt as he watched two paramedics lay Sam down on a stretcher and start checking her vitals.

"She going to be okay?" asked Rogan, pleading.

"She seems okay. She's knocked out, but pulse and breathing are strong," said one of the paramedics.

Rogan nodded. Rodríguez let out a sigh of relief and stood back up, looking around at the mess.

"Woah...what the heck are you into?" said Rodríguez, looking down the street towards the wrecked motorcycles.

Rogan frowned as he looked at the wreckage. Neither of the motorcycle riders were moving. Rogan gave him a quick rundown of the situation. He didn't mention much about Evergreen, but made sure it was clear that Clay Stevens had kidnapped a woman from the small town and was at this moment getting away. Much to Rogan's surprise, Rodríguez didn't quip or make any smart-ass comments. Instead, he got on his radio and called out an APB on the Suburban and asked that all units in the area descend on the Basin to look for it.

"You're in some shit, Rogan. You have any idea who those two guys lying on the pavement down there are?"

"No. I assumed they were working with whoever Clay is working for."

"You don't remember those masks? Skintight, black, tiny little slits for the eyes?"

Rogan furrowed his brow and shook his head.

"Those two are members of The Black."

"That gang in Chinatown? What the heck would they have to do with this?"

"I don't know, but they aren't to be messed with. They've gotten ten times stronger since your cop days," said Rodríguez.

"Well...that's a place to start anyway," said Rogan, moving to head towards the bullet-ridden Suburban.

Rodríguez grabbed his arm and pulled him in close.

"Listen, I know you and I have our problems, but you need to stay out of this, okay? Let us handle this one. You go down to Chinatown halfcocked, and you'll end up dead. The Black run that whole place now, and they don't mess around."

Rogan tore his arm free and silently walked away. He found Troll, McKenzie, and Lizzy standing by the ambulance. The paramedics hoisted Sam up into the back of the ambulance and climbed inside. Rogan wanted to go with her. He needed to make sure she was safe.

"Rogan," said McKenzie, squeezing his arm, "she's going to be okay."

Rogan nodded and stared into the ambulance. Troll patted him on the back. Lizzy stared into the ambulance, mesmerized by all of the gadgets and gauges.

"I need to go with her, make sure she's okay," said Rogan.

McKenzie reached up and grabbed him by the chin, pulling him down to her level. She stared into his green eyes. Her face was hard, cold. It was a look Rogan was not used to. Even when she was angry or being particularly sarcastic, there was always a softness in her eyes. Not today. Today she looked like angry ice.

"Lizzy and I are going to go with Sam. We will make sure she's taken care of. You go find that son of a bitch and make him pay."

Rogan stood up to his full height. McKenzie was right. This wasn't over. He had a score to settle.

"So...we out of this fight?" asked Troll.

"Far from it," said Rogan.

17.

Angus felt sick. He could barely count the number of times he had been a part of a convoy bust. They always did it the same. Two men in a heavy van with a reinforced front end rammed the lead vehicle, while two men on sport bikes trailed behind with automatic weapons. The tactic was extremely effective.

As soon as he had realized what was going on, Angus grabbed his laptop and ran down the road from the farm. He remembered seeing another farmhouse two miles down the highway when they were heading towards the farm. He ran as fast as he could and found an old white Ford pickup sitting on the side of the house. From what he could tell, no one was home. *Probably out prowling for necks to bite,* he thought as he jumped behind the wheel.

Much to his surprise, the keys were in the ignition. He started up the old pickup and headed for Queen City as fast as the Ford would go. He hoped he could get to Chinatown before Rogan and Troll made their way down there. He also wanted to make sure his brother was okay. Assuming this was an important job, Ken-shin would have been a part of the bust team. Angus hoped that his brother was smart enough to ride in the van.

✳ ✳ ✳

Rogan used to patrol Chinatown. It always seemed to have some sort of action, which he was hungry for in his early days as a cop. He would spend his nights, on his own time, walking the narrow streets, looking for trouble. Most nights he found it. He had tussled with The Black on a few occasions. They were ruthless, well-organized, and careful. Rogan had them pegged for a dozen or more unsolved murders when he and his sister had started working cold cases together after their parents died. He couldn't prove a single one of his accusations. The leader of The Black was a mystery. Speculation was that he was an older man, but no one had ever seen him.

Rogan knew that the heavy hitters hung out in a few of the dark alleys near the end of their turf, which by the looks of it had gotten much larger since the last time he had been down to Chinatown. He pointed to an alley a half block away. On the corner was drawn a small circle with two horizontal lines in the center.

"Okay...these guys are serious, Troll. You sure you want to go with me? You could wait here, get in a good spot, and watch my back from a distance."

"I won't be benched for this one. This is our only lead to figure out where that jackass is taking Tanya. I'm in."

Rogan nodded, and he grabbed Troll's shoulders, looking up into his dark eyes. "Listen, keep your head, okay? I know you're mad, raging bull mad, but charging down that alley looking for a fight is not the smart play. It's not going to get us what we want...it's just going to get us dead."

"I'm good. I'll just follow your lead."

"Perfect... Let's go."

Rogan knew the game. He saw a noodle stand just outside the alley. An old woman stood behind a giant concaved wok, stirring noodles. Rogan walked over and pulled up a stool to the cart. Troll did the same, glancing over at Rogan. The woman ignored them and continued to stir and flip the long, thin noodles around the bowl.

"Two house specials, please," said Rogan.

The woman jerked her head up and looked Rogan in the eyes. Her almond eyes were intense, staring at him. Rogan did his best to hold her gaze. She whistled and placed three bowls of noodles on the bar attached to the cart. Rogan grabbed a pair of chopsticks and ate the noodles. He motioned for Troll to do the same.

A few minutes later, a young man walked out of the alley. He was clearly Japanese. He was wearing black pants, a black T-shirt, and a black leather jacket. His hair was kept long and cut jaggedly around the sides of his face, much of it covering his eyes. He was smoking a cigarette. Rogan couldn't see him being older than nineteen. The young man sat down next to Rogan, poured some sauce over his noodles, and tapped out his cigarette.

"You have ten seconds," he said, slurping up a mouthful of noodles.

"All I want to know is who hired you. Where are they?"

"Don't know what you're talking about," said the young man, glancing over at Rogan.

The kid sat eating noodles. He was cold, stone faced. Rogan felt his temper rise. After everything that had happened, his patience was long absent.

"I know you were the ones that crashed our party earlier."

"Don't know what you're talking about."

"Sure you do. I shot one of you pieces of shit in the back."

That got a response. The man dropped his chopsticks, his chest heaved. He stared at Rogan through his hair. His brow furrowed. Rogan prepared to be attacked. Then, as quickly as his anger rose, it fell away and blankness once again covered the young man's face. He took up another round of noodles.

"Said I don't know nothing about that."

"Look kid, I'm not asking for a lot here. Think of me like a missile, an atomic warhead. Right now, I'm pointed at you, and believe me, I will rain down hell. All you have to do is point me in another direction."

The young man chewed on his noodles, staring at Rogan. Then he scoffed and dropped his chopsticks into his half eaten bowl of noodles. He stood up and without a word disappeared back down the alley.

"That went well," said Troll.

"Better than you think. I know they were involved. I also know that they are working for someone. Now we just need to find out who."

"Raging bull time?"

"Yup," said Rogan, heading for the alley.

* * *

Angus pulled the Ford into a dark alley and got out, pulling his hood low over his head. He quickly walked down the alley and into Chinatown. He jogged through the shadows towards the alley he knew Ken-shin would be monitoring. He saw the noodle cart. They were open for business. Angus was surprised to see that they were open after having just lost two soldiers.

Angus peered around the corner into the alley. He could barely make out a group of men milling around behind a dumpster. Ken-shin would be further into the alley. Angus slowly snuck into the alley against the wall and crept towards the dumpster. He knelt down on the opposite side from the men and counted feet. Six pairs. Not ideal. He decided shock and awe might be the best approach. He stepped back from the dumpster and launched a spinning back kick into it. The dumpster lurched forward, smashing into the group of surprised men. Before they could react, Angus leapt off the wall, and in a tornado of kicks and punches, he dropped each of the men to the alley floor.

He walked down the alley and found Ken-shin sitting in a doorway. Completely unaware of what had just happened. He stared at the doorjamb, lost in thought.

"Hurts, doesn't it," said Angus.

Ken-shin jerked to his feet. "What the hell!"

"Sorry to drop in again," said Angus.

"What do you want?"

"I wanted to make sure you were alive. I heard you had a little run-in with some friends of mine."

"I was in the van," said Ken-shin.

"Smart."

"Not really. Can't ride a motorcycle. Never learned how."

Angus smirked. He remembered trying to teach Ken-shin how to ride a bike. The poor kid looked purple by the end. Angus was amazed that Ken-shin could stand on one leg with his other pointed at the ceiling for minutes at a time and walk across a wire suspended between two buildings but not grasp the balance to ride a bike.

"Want to talk about it?"

"Not really..."

"Fine, but I need you to help me out. Did Father order the bust?"

"Why should I tell you?"

"Because you want to," said Angus, staring intensely into Ken-shin's eyes.

"Yeah, he ordered it, but only after he received a call. We were playing chess. He got a call. He walked away from the table so I couldn't hear, but I could tell that he was getting more and more agitated. He came back mumbling something about white devils and told me to get a crew together."

"So he's working for someone else? He didn't call the strike?"

"I don't know, but that's the way it sounded."

Angus let out a sigh. He had been worried that his father had been the originator of what happened in Evergreen, but now it sounded like he was just a pawn in a bigger game. It made Angus both pleased and worried.

"Do you have any idea who?"

"No."

"Father meet with anyone recently? Face to face? Think, Ken-shin, this is important."

"Yeah, actually. I've driven him down to this big warehouse building on the other side of the river a couple times. He goes in for a couple hours, comes out, always seems to be in a good mood. Always carrying a bag. Money I think."

"Anyone else, anywhere else?"

"Nope, just there."

"Has to be it..."

Angus pulled out his laptop and pulled up a map of the city. He had Ken-shin point out the location of the warehouse. Angus placed a mark on the map and pushed the laptop back into his messenger bag.

"Thanks, Ken-shin. You may have just saved a lot of lives."

Ken-shin smirked and shook his head. "I have no idea why I told you any of that."

"I do...and you'll figure it out eventually. You okay, though?"

"Yeah. Van, like I said."

"No...I mean. You lost two soldiers today."

Kenshin looked away and closed his eyes. Angus gave him a moment.

"I'm fine. It's the job," Kenshin managed.

"Ken-shin, this path you're on. It only ends in blood. Your people, your friends...eventually you. Even if you outlive father and take over, there will always be blood spilt, and it will always be on your hands."

"We talked about this already. I'm not leaving. I can't."

"I know. But when you're ready...I'll be here."

Angus then did something he had never done. He reached out and hugged his brother. Ken-shin stiffened in shock and then dropped his head into Angus's shoulder and cried. Angus said nothing; he just held his brother. He regretted leaving. He regretted it all, but if he would have stayed, Ken-shin would be crying over Angus's grave by now. Angus would do what he could. He would get his brother out from under their Father's grip yet.

Ken-shin pulled away and wiped his face. He looked discombobulated, unsure of what to do. Angus punched him in the shoulder.

"Stop crying, baby," said Angus, smirking.

"You're such a dick," said Ken-shin smiling.

"One last thing...where are my friends?"

✳ ✳ ✳

Rogan woke to someone shaking him. His head throbbed. His vision was fuzzy as he peeled open his lids. He felt a little like he was drunk. Troll stared down at him. Rogan reached up and touched his face, making sure it was real. He felt like he was floating.

"Where am I?" asked Rogan groggily.

"A place we don't want to be," said Troll.

Rogan continued to stare up at Troll, his brow showing lines of confusion. He lightly slapped Troll on the cheek a few times.

"It's okay, buddy. We'll just float here awhile and then go get ice cream," said Rogan.

"Aww...crap," said Troll.

Rogan sat up and rubbed his head. He was in a cement block room. The room was only about eight feet by eight feet. There was a solid steel door in one wall. Something red splattered the walls. Rogan began to laugh.

"We're in a kill room, Troll... Look at all that blood," said Rogan, still laughing.

"And that is funny why?"

"Look....look...buddy, we're alive, right? So, there you go," said Rogan, slumping against the wall.

Troll sighed and stood up. He yanked on the handle of the steel door, but it wouldn't budge. He pounded on the steel with his fist and screamed out in frustration.

"Dude, just chill. We're good," said Rogan.

"Damn it, Rogan, snap out of it. Don't you remember anything? We need to get out of here. We need to help Tanya."

"She's real pretty, Troll...I seriously think you should go after that."

Troll made it over to Rogan in two steps, grabbed him by the collar, and lifted him off the ground. Rogan patted him on the head.

"Listen...I need you to focus. We went down that alley. Then...something happened. Shadows moved and then I felt pain in my neck, then I woke up here. Now we need to get the hell out of here before they come back and splatter us on those walls. You think you can maybe get it together?"

"Right, right...of course, you're right, Troll," said Rogan. Then he broke out laughing again. "So serious all the time, big guy. You need to lighten up. Enjoy the ride a little, you know? What you need is a woman. Seriously, we need to get out of here and rescue Tanya. Because...damn. You and her...? Nice..."

"I'm going to knock you out just so I don't have to listen to your drugged ass in my last few minutes."

"Why are you so worried? We can leave whenever we want..."

"Oh, really. Did you recently acquire the power to walk through steel?"

"No, but I can walk through that door," said Rogan, pointing to the steel door.

Troll stared at the door, not believing what he was seeing. Maybe the drugs weren't completely out of his system either. The door stood wide open and a guard lay unconscious across the threshold.

Troll picked up Rogan and threw him over his shoulder. Carrying Rogan like a sandbag, Troll walked to the door.

"Yaaah! Yah, big horse," chuckled Rogan, smacking Troll hard on the ass.

Troll gritted his teeth and carefully stepped over the guard and out into the hallway. He looked down the hallway and saw three more men lying unconscious. He decided to follow the trial of limp bodies. After a turn, he came to a set of steps. At the base of the steps was a bench. On the bench sat his wallet and his phone. Rogan's pistol and wallet sat right beside, along with the keys to the Suburban. Troll scooped up their stuff and walked up the stairs.

At the top was a flat door like on a storm shelter. Smirking, he used Rogan's backside to open the door. Rogan let out an oomph as Troll looked out into the dark alley. Two more men were laid out by the entrance to the stairwell. Troll wondered who'd provided their escape route, but he was ready to get out of Chinatown.

He broke into a quick jog back towards where they had parked the Suburban, trying to keep to the darkness. Rogan sang, "Ride Em' Cowboy" the entire way, making it nearly impossible to get away unnoticed. The big man carrying a big man got a lot of stares as he trundled down the narrow streets and out of the area.

✳ ✳ ✳

Angus watched from the rooftops as Troll carried Rogan over his shoulder. Based on what Ken-shin had told him about the short fight, Rogan had to be feeling pretty groggy. Angus jumped from roof to roof, keeping pace with Troll. He wanted to make sure that they made it back to their vehicle safely. He had risked a lot setting them free. He hoped that none of the guards got a good look at him. That last thing he needed was for his father to know that he was meddling in the family business.

Angus felt a pang of guilt and wished he could have spent more time with Ken-shin. Perhaps he could have gotten more information out of him, but it seemed like their father was keeping his connection to the Evergreen disaster close to chest.

After watching Troll flop Rogan into the backseat of the black Suburban, he climbed down a drainpipe and returned to the old white Ford. He considered driving back to Evergreen, but his apartment was closer and had more equipment.

Angus stashed the white pickup in the parking lot of a convenience store a couple blocks from his studio apartment. He waved at the doorman and ran through the door and up the six flights of stairs to his apartment. He pressed his hand to a blank piece of metal to the right of the door and then input a six-digit code into a keypad above the doorknob—a few security precautions to protect his domain. Angus was fairly sure that no one, not even the members of P.I.T, knew where he lived. He preferred it that way.

Angus walked over to a bank of computers set against the far wall and logged into his system. He immediately started trying to find a way into the security system of the warehouse that would be Troll and Rogan's next destination. His brow furred as he stared at the lines of code on the screen. Whatever was hiding in that building was being carefully protected. He cracked his knuckles and sighed. This was going to take some work.

✳ ✳ ✳

Troll drove up and down the streets in the Basin, looking for black Suburbans. He was not having much luck. Rogan snored in the backseat as he drove aimlessly down the streets. He needed to figure out where Tanya was. He had to save her.

Troll drove twenty more minutes while trying to come up with a plan when he heard a crackle in his ear from the bud he had taken from McKenzie, hours ago.

"Angus to world, anyone out there?"

"Angus! Are you okay?"

"Me? I'm fine. What about you guys? I lost you after the crash. Thought maybe you guys got hurt or something. Everyone okay?"

"Yeah, Sam got hurt, but paramedics said she'll be okay. We had an interesting time in Chinatown..."

"Oh, that place is bad news..."

"No kidding. I'll have to tell you all about it after this is over. Rogan is knocked out. I can't find a trail..."

"I have good news for you, then."

"I could really use some, Angus," said Troll.

"I found Clay, or at least I think I did."

"Where?"

"I managed to catch a glimpse of the Suburban on a security cam and then followed it on the network and stuff into the warehouse district. It pulled up to a big white warehouse across the river. I'll guide you there."

Troll followed Angus's directions. He drove the Suburban through the Basin and then over a bridge into the warehouse district. Troll's jaw was tightly set as he stared out at the big buildings on either side of the street. The buildings were all tall, some with multiple floors, others with what looked to be a big empty space. Trucks were backed up to the loading docks of several as they drove by.

Troll felt his muscles clenching and unclenching. He was grinding his teeth. He felt anger like he hadn't felt in a long time. He'd always worked himself up before a match in his days as a collegiate wrestler. He always imagined that the man he was about to fight had done something terrible to someone. He worked the story in his head, adding more and more details about the heinousness of this man, until he felt his skin crawl with the need to tear the other man's head off. This was different, though. Now he felt real anger. True anger. He wanted to literally tear Clay's head off. He wanted to hunt down every one of those bastards in black fatigues and make them pay for every life they'd destroyed in Evergreen.

Angus's voice in his ear broke him from his thoughts. "Troll, you're close. Take the next left, and then it's a mile or so down on the right."

"Got it. Thanks, Angus."

"No problem. I've been looking over the building plans for the warehouse you're headed to. It's big. There is a large open cargo type area, and then three floors of offices. Though it's not in the official plans, I'd bet a fair amount of Washingtons that there is at least one basement level."

"Can you tell what they have for security?" asked Troll.

"Plans say nothing. I'm trying to weasel my way in though. There is a giant computer core in that building, and their firewalls are pretty intense, like Maui waves in winter intense."

"Where are we?" asked Rogan, sitting up in the backseat and rubbing his head.

"Well...morning, sunshine," said Angus.

"You okay, Rogan?" asked Troll.

"Fine, why?"

"Because about forty-five minutes ago you were three shades of drunken sailor," said Troll.

"What are you talking about? I don't....hmm...I don't remember anything after we went down that alley."

"We got poisoned or something. A bunch of guys in black masks came out of nowhere and shot us with blow darts."

"Why are you okay?" asked Rogan, rubbing his temples. He looked like he was going to be sick.

"Well, two reasons I'd say. First, I'm bigger than you. Second, I went down right away because they got me in the neck. Whereas you started throwing haymakers. I saw you take probably six shots before you went down."

"That does sound like me," said Rogan. "What are we doing in the warehouse district?"

"Huntin' Texans..."

"Excellent."

Rogan crawled up to the front seat. He reached back and grabbed two assault shotguns that were sitting on the floor. He opened the breach of each shotgun; they were both empty. He grabbed a red box that read non-lethal. There were only four rounds.

"How are we on ammo?" asked Troll.

"Not great, only four bean bags left."

Rogan put two of the non-lethal rounds into each gun. Then he started thumbing in lethal rounds after, to fill the magazine.

"Lethal? Are you sure?" asked Troll, looking over at Rogan.

"We have no idea what we're about to walk into, Troll. I don't want to get caught with our pants down."

Troll nodded. Rogan continued thumbing rounds into the shotguns. Rogan focused on Clay while he pushed each shell into the magazine. He felt his jaw clenching, and his right eye twitching. The tight jaw and twitchy eye were his telltale signs that he had crossed the threshold into anger. It was a rare feeling. He got mad on occasion, but Rogan had a very long fuse. This organization, whatever it was, and Clay Stevens had burned through the last of it.

Rogan considered snapping out the non-lethal rounds from the shotguns, but thought better of it. He also grabbed his Smith and Wesson 686+ from the backseat and placed it into his shoulder holster. He chose the 686 because he preferred the feel of a revolver, especially a custom-tuned .357 magnum. The 686 had the extra advantage of holding seven shots instead of the standard six of most revolvers. He liked having the steel there, ready, just in case, though he preferred to not use it. Rogan wasn't sure he could follow his father's mantra—that killing a criminal is the easy way out—today. The twitch in his eye told him he was out for blood.

18.

Troll took a left on River Road Boulevard. Rogan was very familiar with this run of warehouses. More than one of them had been used as an import site for drugs into Queen City. He had been on countless raids in this district. He didn't remember a warehouse with a basement, though. The Boulevard curved slightly right, following the gentle curve of the river. Troll drove past the first building on the right, a disheveled tin building. Its large doors stood open, weeds growing up through the concrete inside.

"There," Troll said, pointing to the next building's loading dock. Backed up near the personnel door by the loading dock was a black Suburban. There were no other vehicles in the large surface lot in front of the immense building. This warehouse was made of concrete, and thick square pillars ran skyward on each corner, with tan concrete walls stretched between.

One half of the building sported three long rows of windows, the other half had a single row of narrow windows near the top. There were six large rolling doors at the bottom, each outlined by black and yellow padding, for trucks to back up to. Troll brought the Suburban to a stop in front of the black SUV. He got out and walked around, making sure no one was inside. It was empty.

Rogan tossed him a shotgun and the pair walked to the personnel door set into the concrete wall next to the first loading bay door.

"You don't have to do this, Troll. There's a good chance we're going to get shot at in here. I'm not asking you to risk your life."

"We're a team," said Troll as he dropped a half dozen extra rounds into Rogan's hand. "We stick together. We see this through."

Rogan smiled and kicked in the door. He rushed through, shotgun up. They were in the storage area of the warehouse. The room was gigantic, with steel girders spanning the steel ceiling and running down near the concrete outer walls. Lines of desks ran down the center of the room. In the far corner, there was an elevated office, roughly twelve feet square. Other than the desks and some random boxes, the area was empty. Rogan looked at the floor. He saw drag marks leading off towards a single door set into the wall between the main floor and the office area. They followed the drag marks. Troll stood next to the door where the tracks stopped.

Rogan turned to take one last look out on the huge open space to make sure no one was lurking. Just in front of him was a large steel desk that had been turned on its side. A memory crept into Rogan's mind. He'd been here before.

He ran around the desk to look at the top. It was riddled with bullet spray. His mind raced back in time. This room had been dark then, except for a few overhead lights above the desks. There had been people there, counting money. He had hidden behind this desk. Rogan ran to the large vertical steel column to the left. The side away from the office area door was marred by bullet pocks. Rogan felt his heart racing; he couldn't control his breathing. Rogan fell to his knees while staring up at the elevated office with the catwalk balcony. He couldn't believe it. Of all the warehouses, why were they in this one?

"Rogan," Troll whispered, crouching beside him, "what's wrong?"

"Sarah."

"Your sister? What are you talking about?"

"This is the warehouse where Sarah was shot. A sniper, on that balcony," said Rogan, pointing, "shot my sister while we ran down that wall by the rolling doors."

Troll opened his mouth to speak, but said nothing. Instead, he put his hand on Rogan's shoulder. Rogan fought back tears. He had pushed that night from his mind, but now it came rushing back. Rodríguez, their commanding officer at the time, had sent them down to check out the warehouse. They were after a serial rapist, but they had stumbled across something else.

Rogan and Sarah had gone in through the office area, down a hallway of doors. Some open, some closed. They found their rapist dead, lying across a conference table in the second to the last room on the right. The two were about to call in a bus for the dead man when they heard something coming from the main floor. From what they knew, the building was supposed to be empty.

They opened the office door and saw money being counted, and both of them instantly knew that they had stumbled across another drug import business. Gunfire rang out almost immediately. Rogan dove behind the overturned desk, Sarah behind the column. The people counting money ran out of the building.

The lights went out. Rogan and Sarah returned fire, not knowing if they were on target. A couple cries of pain told them they were. The twins raced down the outside wall, ducking from pillar to pillar as they went dodging shots. With the exit door in sight, Rogan saw a muzzle flash from the balcony. Then his sister sprawled to the ground. He dragged her outside, where she died in his arms.

"Why would Clay bring Tanya here? There are dozens of empty warehouses in this area. Is he playing a game with me?" asked Rogan, shaking.

"It could just be a crazy coincidence. Maybe Darwin set up shop here. I mean of the warehouses in the district, this one does seem to be the most intact."

"Maybe, but I don't like it. This whole thing is starting to feel even less right than it did before."

Rogan collected himself the best he could. Waves of confusion washed over him as he stared out over the giant room. This could not be a coincidence. He had to put it away for now, though. He had a job to do, but maybe he could find some answers about his sister along the way. Troll led the way back to the office door. Rogan stood back, ready to kick it in.

"Ready?" asked Rogan. "Be ready. If they have cameras hidden, they might see us coming." Troll raised his shotgun towards the door. Rogan pulled his leg up and shot it out towards the door.

"Wait!" yelled Angus in his ear. Rogan pulled his kick at the last second, sending the bottom of his converse shoe into the wall next to the door.

"What, Angus?" asked Rogan, hopping around on one leg. "And it better be good, because that freaking hurt."

"Sorry, man. That door is secured. Kick it in and off go the alarms."

"How do you know that?"

"First off, I'm awesome. Second, because I have access to their security system. I see you right now, as a matter of fact."

"You do?"

"Yep, wave up and to your right."

Troll and Rogan looked above the door and to the right. There in the corner, hidden by the shadows, was a small camera. It waggled back and forth as they looked up at it.

"So if you see us, do they see us?" asked Troll.

"Remember that awesome part? Right before you two stormed the castle, I got access. I've basically blinded their viewing stations, so if they look out this camera; they just see an empty floor. You're invisible, as long as you don't trip any alarms."

"Wow...you terrify me," said Rogan.

"You're welcome. Now give me thirty seconds and I'll pop that door for you."

Angus delivered less than twenty seconds later. Rogan and Troll stood ready by the door. It popped open with a soft buzz. Troll grabbed the handle and pushed open the door. Rogan entered the familiar hallway.

"Angus, what are you seeing?"

"No cameras in the rooms. The hallway to the lobby is clear."

Rogan and Troll worked their way down the hallway, checking each room as they went. Rogan paused for a second, staring at the oak conference table where the serial rapist that he and his sister were after had bled out. No one had found out how or discovered who had killed him. The entire building had been swept after Rogan had dragged Sarah out. By the time the building had been flushed, everything was gone. The police found no trace of money or drugs, and no people. It was as if the whole thing had been a dream, the only evidence was the pockmarks in the walls and floors from the various caliber assault weapons that had been fired at Rogan and Sarah.

Rogan turned away from the desk and continued following Troll down the hall. The two cleared the rest of the rooms and then entered the lobby.

"Okay. If it were me, boys, I'd head down. There are no cameras on the floors above, which leads me to believe that the real action is below."

"How do we get down?" asked Rogan, scanning the empty lobby.

"Okay, take a left, then go down a bit and you should see an alcove with two elevators in it."

Troll and Angus worked their way left and down the back wall of the lobby, ending in the alcove, where there were two elevators as promised. Rogan found the button for the elevators. It was not lit. He pressed the button. Nothing happened.

"That's odd," said Angus.

"Odd how?" asked Troll.

"I don't think there's any power to these elevators, Angus," said Rogan.

"Hold on, something's off here. This doesn't... Oh, those tricky bastards."

"What is it?"

"These plans say there should be three elevators. Look to your right—what do you see?"

"A wall."

"Stellar...walk through it."

"Come again?"

"Walk through it."

"Pardon?"

Angus sighed loudly. "It's holographic. Very high tech; these guys got some cool tools. Just trust me on this. Damn, that's cool."

"Now really isn't the time for envy, Angus," said Rogan.

Rogan walked to the wall and gingerly put his hand out towards the wall. His hand went right through like the wall wasn't even there. He shrugged back at Troll and walked through the wall. On the other side, there was an elevator. This one had a down button, and it was lit up. Rogan looked back the way he had come. He could not see the wall. Instead he saw what looked like a small movie projector mounted in the ceiling. It sent out streams of light towards the alcove. Rogan watched as Troll cautiously stepped through the illusion.

"Wow, that is really cool," said Troll.

"See, told you," said Angus.

Rogan shook his head and pressed the down button. "Angus, what are we going to find when we get down there?"

"You'll be going down a ways by the looks of it. Then you'll enter sub 1. It's a square area, with a lab in the middle and a bunch of offices and rooms. I haven't seen Clay or Tanya yet, so they must be in one of the rooms without cameras, or they are down on sub 2. There is another elevator that takes you down there, on the exact opposite wall of where you'll be coming out on sub 1."

"Bad guys?"

"Yes, lots. None in the hallway at the moment, but I've seen about a dozen of those black fatigued boys, and a few people in lab coats."

The elevator doors opened. Troll and Rogan stepped inside. Rogan looked at the floor; there were a couple red drops on the low pile carpet. He knelt down and touched them. Still wet, fresh blood.

"Someone's bleeding," said Rogan.

"Here's hoping it's someone wearing a cowboy hat," said Troll.

Rogan felt another round of hot rage burn through his body. His anger had been subdued by the confusion he'd felt by being back in the place where his sister had been killed, but then he thought about Tanya, bleeding in this elevator, while Clay Stevens delivered her to these Darwin psychos. The blood also reminded him of the slow trickle that had been gently meandering down Sam's forehead. He felt his eye twitching again.

"Okay guys, you're going to have company as soon as you step off the elevator. Two guys are out patrolling, they must have heard the elevator. They are standing just past the door, pistols drawn.

"10-4," said Rogan.

Rogan pulled Troll to the ground. They laid prone, weapons pointing towards the door. The elevator stopped, announcing its arrival with a soft ding. The doors slid apart. Before they had opened fully, Rogan laid out two rounds, each bean bag smacking the guards in the face. The guards fell back.

Rogan stood and charged out of the elevator, looking for more contacts. The hallway was empty. Troll knelt down and inspected the downed guards. Both were unconscious but breathing, their noses broken. Rogan dug through their pockets, and he found six long, plastic ties. He rolled the two men over and restrained their hands using the ties.

After replacing the two spent rounds in his shotgun, he and Troll cleared the two rooms nearest the elevator. The room to the left was a basic-looking office with a desk, computer, and books. The other was a janitor's closest. Troll dragged the two men into the closet while Rogan stood guard.

"Give us a heads up if you see any more coming okay?" said Rogan.

"You got it," said Angus.

The hallway came to an intersection after four more sets of doors, all of which had been unoccupied offices. To the right, down a short hallway, was a set of double swinging doors. A red sign hanging above the door announced that contamination protocol was strictly enforced in the area. A biohazard symbol was etched into each of the swinging doors.

"Past those doors is a small area, like a locker room, then past that the big central lab. There are a bunch of people in white lab coats in there."

"Thanks, Angus. So not that way then," said Troll.

They continued down the hallway, checking rooms as they went. In the last room before the corner, Rogan burst through the door to find a woman mid-bite into a turkey sandwich. She tried to scream, but fortunately her mouth was full of bread.

"On the floor, now," said Rogan.

The woman complied. Rogan tied her hands behind her back, looping the tie around the pipe of a small heating unit that sat in the back of the room. Rogan joined Troll back in the hallway. Rogan rounded the corner. Troll grabbed him by the collar and pulled him back, putting his finger to his lips. Just down the hall, two men wearing white coats and carrying clipboards walked out of one of the rooms. They continued away from Rogan and Troll, finally turning down what was likely another short hallway to the lab.

"Close one," said Rogan.

Troll nodded. They headed out into the hallway. Finding nothing in the rooms, all of which were offices, they turned down the last hallway. At the end of the hall, they saw the elevator that would lead them further down, along with several more doors.

This wing contained what looked like smaller labs. All but two of them had been empty. Troll and Rogan easily restrained the two scared scientists that had been working in the two occupied mini labs. The last door stood next to the elevator. Rogan opened the door and ran in, shotgun up, expecting to see another set of beakers and test tubes. Instead, he saw a pop machine, a couple round tables, and six surprised guards eating lunch. For a moment, time stopped, everyone staring, the six men watching Rogan.

"Gentleman," said Rogan.

The man furthest to the left started drawing his pistol. Rogan sent a shot into his chest. Rogan hoped that would be enough to gain cooperation, but the other guards were just as dedicated as the first. Each jumped to their feet, drawing their weapons. Rogan emptied the magazine. Each round sent a spray of shotgun pellets out into the room. At the close range, all six guards died instantly, the pellets ripping through flesh and finding vital organs.

In the aftermath, soda hissed from punctured pop cans. Smoke and the smell of gunpowder hung in the air. Rogan stood panting, transfixed by the scene. He had reacted, no thought, just action. He wondered if this was how the wolves felt.

The six men lay sprawled out across the room. Two men lay over tables, three others on the floor, the last had fallen back into the shattered front of the pop machine. Rogan backed out of the room, still aiming his empty shotgun. Troll reached over and pulled the door shut.

The elevator door opened, and a man in a white lab coat stepped out. Rogan turned on the man and pulled the trigger, hearing a click. Troll smashed the shocked man's head with the butt of his shotgun. Rogan fell to his knees, his shotgun rolling to the ground. Troll tied up the unconscious scientist and put him in a nearby office. Rogan sat on his knees, jaw open, staring at the break room door.

"You didn't have a choice," said Troll, kneeling down next to him.

"Didn't I?" asked Rogan, his voice barely above a whisper.

"No, you didn't. They were armed, and we know full well these people don't mind killing people."

Rogan nodded. He knew that was true, but he also knew that he could have fired shots into the tables and near the guards. Enough to ricochet pellets into them, but giving them a chance to live. Rogan felt paralyzed. He couldn't move.

Troll reached over and grabbed Rogan's chin, pulling it around to stare him in the face.

"Game time, Rogan. We count our fouls afterwards, but right now, it's us or them. I don't like it either, but we need you right now. Tanya needs you. Get it together, and snap the heck out of it. Remember Evergreen, those people, those kids? Those black-fatigued assholes studying them, watching them die? They don't deserve your remorse."

Rogan didn't feel right about what he did, but Troll was right. He didn't have time to deal with it right now. He pushed his discomfort to the back of his mind and focused on Clay and Tanya. Rogan put his hand on Troll's shoulder.

"You should have been a coach."

"I was. Coached varsity wrestling at Queen Central while I was in college. You back on the right page? If not, I'm willing to slap you until you are."

"I'm good," said Rogan, standing up.

Troll and Rogan stepped onto the elevator. Rogan reached into his pocket and refilled the shotgun.

"Okay, Angus. Next floor?" asked Rogan, still pushing the bloody scene from his mind.

"Okay, you're....square...smaller...then—"

"What? Angus, come again?"

"Clay....seven....right.........dead."

"We must be getting too low underground for Angus's miracle buds."

"Yeah, all I hear is... Ouch!" said Troll and yanked the earbud from his ear. Rogan did the same as a high pitch whine entered his ear.

"Well there that goes," said Rogan pocketing the earbud.

Troll nodded, and then he took a knee and aimed at the elevator door. Rogan joined him. This time they wouldn't have the advantage of knowing what was coming. The elevator came to a stop and dinged. The doors slid open. Rogan and Troll scanned the hallway. It was empty. The hallway was wider than the floor above and not nearly as long. Rogan counted six doors before the corner, and no intersections along the way.

"How are you on ammo?" asked Rogan.

"Down one bean bag, that's it. You?"

"Five left."

"Here," said Troll, handing Rogan three more rounds. "Let's make sure we're both locked and stocked."

"Thanks."

"Going to miss Angus in my ear," said Troll.

"I guess we end this the way it started," said Rogan, loading the rounds.

"What do you mean?"

"Just you and me....fishing."

Troll laughed. Rogan snapped the rounds in and approached the first door on the right. A clipboard hung outside the door. A small door was inset at roughly eye level. Rogan cautiously opened the inset door. It covered a glass window that was crisscrossed with thin wire mesh. The room beyond was small, with a slab attached to the wall with a thin mattress on it and a toilet in the far corner. A woman stood in the room, slowly turning in circles, her arms held out parallel to the ground. Troll grabbed the clipboard.

"Test subjects. This one, average female, no resistance, day one suspend, whatever that means."

"What are these people up to?" asked Rogan, moving to the next door. The door across from the circling woman held a man who was bumping repeatedly into the door. The second set of doors also held a man and a woman. Both of them moved faster, but they were still bumping into everything in the room. Rogan peeked in the next door on the right while Troll checked around the corner. This one held a woman; she had to be in her late fifties. She was shredding her bed with her fingernails, screaming, though through the thick door, her screams were barely audible.

They rounded the corner to find three more sets of doors and another right turn at the end. The first door had a man who was jumping up and down on the bed slab, tearing at his chest with his fingernails. He was completely naked; his skin looked stretched over his hard musculature.

"These have to be the stages of the Darwin virus," said Troll. "We saw the same thing in Evergreen."

"Which means I don't know if I want to see what's in the rest of these rooms."

The next set of doors were like the last: a woman on the right, a man on the left. Rogan peeked in on the woman. She was naked and in her late thirties, by his guess. She looked over at Rogan, fire in her eyes. Before he could react, she yanked the toilet off the floor like it was a beach ball and flung it into the door. The glass cracked, but it did not give. Rogan stumbled back and slammed the viewing door closed.

Rogan and Troll looked at each other after seeing the last set of doors before the corner. The doors were steel like all the others, but these had six-inch square steel girder sections welded to the center of the door and into a steel plate bolted into the floor. Rogan could hear thuds coming from the door on the left.

He considered not looking in on what he assumed was the final stage, but he had to see it. Inside, a man stood near the center of the room. He had pulled his bed apart and braided the strips into a rope, which he had tied around the bottom of the toilet. He spun the toilet above his head like a lasso and hurled it towards the door. It banged against the door, sending shockwaves through the steel. The man was in his middle twenties, six feet tall. His fingernails could no longer be called nails. Instead, they were claws, almost three inches in length. The man had torn off his clothes but had opted to keep on his underwear, a pair of green boxers with dogs printed on them.

Rogan looked at the back wall, where there were short, vertical scratches. He counted 47. It reminded him of a prisoner counting the days. Could this man, who seemed barely human, have the ability to count and conceptualize time? The man looked to have no fat on him at all. His thick muscles stretched his skin and large veins ran down his limbs. He ran towards the door and pounded on the glass with one hand, attempting to turn the knob with the other. Then he screamed out and sent a kick into the door. Rogan fell backwards over the steel door brace. He looked back to see a dent in the steel door. He took one last look into the window; the man inside seemed to be uninjured by the heavy kick into solid steel. He went back to the tied toilet and began spinning it once more above his head.

"Wow..." said Rogan, slamming the viewing window closed.

"Yeah, steel or not, it's only a matter of time before she gets out," said Troll, staring at the door opposite the one Rogan had been looking through.

Rogan rounded the next corner, gun raised, ready for anything. The hallway was shorter and wider, with only four doors. Two doors stood on the left and looking just like the holding cells Rogan and Troll had just gone past, though these were not reinforced. A single door was cut in halfway down the right wall, with a final set of doors at the end of the hall. The hum of machinery came from the double doors. Rogan peeked in the first door while Troll stood in the corner, watching both directions. The room was empty.

He moved onto the next door. Rogan opened the view window and saw a brown haired woman curled up on a bed slab. She was wearing a hospital gown. Though her back was to the window, Rogan felt confident it was Tanya. He pounded on the door, but she did not move. He pulled on the door knob, but it was locked. He wished McKenzie were with them; she could probably take care of the heavy deadbolt lock with a toothpick.

"She's in there," said Rogan.

Troll scanned the ceiling. In the corner was a small security camera. He waved his arms at it. It moved in his direction. Then he pointed towards the door Rogan was standing by. The camera moved up and down.

"Come on Angus..." said Troll staring at the door.

After a few more moments, Rogan looked back at the camera. It moved back and forth from left to right.

"Shit. No luck. We need to find a key, get her, and get the heck out of here."

"I couldn't agree more. This place is getting freakier and freakier."

Rogan moved across the hall and opened the door. The room was empty. In the center of the room was a chair with a reclining back. Restraints hung from the arm and foot rests. Two big circular lights hung from the ceiling on pivoting arms. A table with a number of surgical-looking instruments sat next to the chair. A bank of machines with dials, buttons, switches, and various screens ran along the back wall. Rogan wondered what sort of horrible things these people did in this room. He wondered if this was were all those people who were suffering in the holding cells were infected. He also wondered what they had done to Tanya, or what they were planning to do.

He rummaged around the drawers and cabinets looking for a key, but there was nothing but medical instruments and tools. Rogan backed out of the room. He heard the boom of a gun and rolled to the floor. Troll stood at the corner, the end of his shotgun barrel smoking.

"Okay?" asked Rogan.

"Yeah. Guard," said Troll. "Watch the corner a sec."

Troll grabbed the guard under the shoulders and dragged him into the surgical room while Rogan stood watch. That left one way unexplored.

"Let's check that last room down there. If there isn't a key in there, we'll have to double back and check the offices upstairs."

Troll nodded and walked towards the double doors at the end of the hall. Rogan followed, walking backwards and keeping his eyes on the corner. A small window was cut into each door. Rogan and Troll ducked down in front of the door and listened; they could not hear anything through the heavy doors except for the sound of machinery moving. Rogan rose up high enough to peek through the glass. The room beyond looked like some sort of cargo area. Rows of boxes, two or three high, ran in long rows along the floor. The room was long and narrow, the length running away from the set of doors, ending with what looked like a cargo elevator in the far wall. Rogan could see men roaming around the room, some carrying automatic weapons, others using palate movers to move the boxes towards the center, where men on forklifts picked up the pallets and carried them towards the elevator. Quick math put the fight at ten bad guys versus two good guys, though Rogan couldn't see what was to the far left of the room because a series of boxes blocked his view.

"What's the plan?"

"Well, we've been through every room of this place except for the main lab up above and this room right here. I doubt old Clay is hanging around in a lab, so chances are he's either in this room, or gone already. I'm thinking we try to get in there and check things out. There's a lot of cover. If we can make it through the door and head to the right, there is a stack of boxes in the corner we can hide behind and survey the situation."

"All right then. Ready?" asked Troll, taking a grip on the handle. Rogan nodded, preparing to roll hard to the right once the door was open enough. Troll tugged on the door, but it would not budge.

"Shit, locked," said Troll.

Just then, a soft buzz came from the locking mechanism on the door. Rogan looked around and mouthed thank you at the camera hanging overhead. Troll opened the door, and Rogan rolled into the opening, coming up behind one of the crates. He had not been detected. He waited until the backs of the nearest workers and guards were away from him and motioned for Troll to follow. They ran, crouched, to the corner of the room and stopped behind two three-tall stacks of crates in the corner.

Rogan looked at the crates in front of him. All six boxes had Darwin printed on the side. From their vantage point, Rogan could see a total of twelve men in black fatigues. Four of them carried compact automatic rifles and walked around the stacks. The rest stacked and moved the crates, placing eight crates on a pallet. They would then plastic wrap the pallet and move it to the center. While that was interesting, what caught Rogan's attention was the scene to the left of the entrance doors. There, in the corner, sat a large oak desk. Behind the desk sat a man wearing a white lab coat. He had on black horn-rimmed glasses that were a sharp contrast to his snow-white hair. He was talking with someone, occasionally laughing. The man slid a silver briefcase across the desk to the person he was talking to. Rogan could not see the person—there was a box in the way— but he did know who it was. His heart started to pound. Two cowboy boots were crossed on the corner of the desk, leading to a pair of faded blue jeans.

"Target acquired," whispered Rogan.

"Pretty hard to miss those boots. What do we do?"

"We won't last in a shootout with this many guys. I think we should probably assume that those guys moving crates are armed as well, though the real problem is the four guys with autos. It looks like they are walking a circuit. We might be able to take out a few of them before we're noticed. I'm thinking I go through the stacks, get to the other side of the room and try to take those two out, you stay on this side, try to take the two over here out. Then we at least have the others surrounded even if we are way outnumbered. Give me two minutes to get across, and then go to work. This is going to get ugly."

"Good thing they call me Troll."

Troll smiled and moved off to the right. Rogan went stack to stack, nearly running into workers twice. He made it to the far left of the room and crouched in the shadows near the corner. A few seconds later, one of the auto-carrying men walked past. Rogan came up behind the man and put a tight choke hold around his neck, dragging him back into the corner. After a few moments of kicking and thrashing, the man went limp.

Rogan took the automatic and threw the strap over his shoulder. He snuck over to the next row, where the second guard was patrolling. He came up behind him and was about to lay in the choke when he heard automatic fire from across the room.

The guard turned towards the sound, bringing up the compact rifle. Rogan kicked his leg up in the air, bringing it down hard on the top of the gun. The force pulled the man forward. Rogan followed up with a haymaker to the man's chin.

He went down hard. Rogan followed him down, staying low behind the crates.

The men who had been working on the pallets immediately drew pistols. Rogan hoped he could maintain his current ninja tactics, but Troll wasn't making it easy. He saw flashes of the big man through the far stacks, swinging away and smashing anything and everyone near him. He looked like Godzilla gone mad on a box city.

"The crates, careful with the crates, you idiots!" shouted the white-haired man who was now cowering under his desk. With their attention on the marauding Troll, Rogan came to his feet and shot three men in the legs with his recently acquired automatic, and then emptied the magazine into the nearby crates for good measure.

Troll came smashing through the center aisle with his fists clutched around the collar of a muscular man wearing black fatigues. The man was almost as big as Troll. They wrestled on the ground, fighting for purchase. Rogan saw another worker sneaking around the end of the last stack, trying to aim on Troll. Rogan popped him in the shoulder with a blast from his shotgun. Out of the corner of his eye, he saw the white haired man running full out for the main entrance. Rogan took a shot at his legs, but missed. He wanted that man alive. After arriving at the door, the man jerked on the handles, but they didn't budge. Rogan smiled and said a silent thank you to Angus.

Rogan felt the hairs on the back of his neck stand up; it was a feeling he got either when his ghost was around, or his instincts told him someone or something was nearby trying to catch him off guard. He heard the soft crinkle of a foot breaking a wood splinter from one of the crates. Without looking, Rogan launched a back kick straight back, catching Clay right in the stomach. He flew backwards, taking a stack of crates with him.

In the meantime, the white-haired man was running down the line of crates towards the freight elevator. Rogan pulled out his 686 and shot the controls just as the man's hand was about to push the button. The white haired man grabbed a pistol from the hand of the nearest fallen worker. Before he lifted it, Rogan shot him in the foot. The man fell to the floor, screaming in pain. Then, with cold running through his veins, he turned to deal with Clay.

Clay was just getting to his feet when Rogan turned his intense gaze on him. Clay stumbled backwards, raising his revolver towards Rogan. Rogan shot it out of his hand. Clay clutched his wounded hand and dove behind the nearest stack. Rogan holstered the 686 and swung up the shotgun. He blasted away the crate, sending shrapnel flying in every direction. Clay rolled to another set of boxes, which Rogan again decimated with pellets.

"Rogan! Come on, man. We can talk about this."

"Talk? Go ahead, talk," said Rogan, destroying Clay's hiding spot.

"Shit, stop shooting at me."

"Give me a good reason."

"Come on. I know stuff, and I can help you fight these guys."

"These guys? You ARE these guys."

Rogan kept his eyes on the box he knew Clay was crouched behind. To his right, he saw Troll lift his muscular opponent above his head and toss him through a tower of crates. It was like a battle of Titans; the other man got up like he hadn't felt a thing.

"I just wanted the money, Rogan. And the respect. You know I didn't get none of either."

"And that excuses you letting an entire town kill itself?"

"I feel bad about that, Rogan, I do, but these guys, they get to talking, and what they say kind of makes sense. Come on. We used to be friends."

Rogan could just see the top of Clay's tall tan cowboy hat sticking up above the crates. He dropped his empty shotgun and shot the hat off of Clay's head with his 686.

"Christ! Okay, okay, money? How about that? You can have every penny they gave me."

"How much?"

"Two million bucks, Rogan. Think about that. You let me walk out of here, I promise I'll never come back, head south, work on a ranch or something. You take it all, you'd be set up for life."

"Where is it?"

"Half of it's in that briefcase on the desk, the rest is hidden under my desk in Evergreen. There's a loose floorboard. I had hoped to grab it before I got out of dodge, but that didn't work out. Come on, we have a deal?"

"You're going to stand up right now. I may or may not shoot you. You'll turn around, put your hands behind your head, and drop to your knees. I'm going to restrain you. We walk out of here together, and once we're out of the building, I give you a thirty-minute head start."

"But I'm giving you the money."

"And that buys you thirty minutes..."

"Fine, Rogan. That's fine. I'm standing up now."

Clay stood up with his back to Rogan. Rogan fought the urge to shoot him. Clay dropped to his knees and put his hands behind his head. Rogan walked up behind him and put the barrel of his .357 to the back of Clay's head. He felt his hand shaking with an overwhelming animal urge to pull the trigger. It was all he could do to keep himself from applying the couple pounds of pressure it would take for the hammer to strike the cap and end Clay's miserable life. Rogan had no intention of taking the money or letting Clay get away, but he wasn't an executioner. Rogan pulled out a set of plastic restraints and tied Clay's arms tightly behind his back and knocked him out with the butt of his pistol.

Troll stood up, his chest heaving, blood running from his nose. He looked at Rogan. His face was a mix of sadness and confusion.

"You okay, big guy?"

Troll nodded yes and looked around the room. Rogan walked over to the white-haired man who was still rolling on the ground. Rogan aimed down on him with the 686. The man froze, staring up at the barrel of the gun.

"Name?" asked Rogan.

"Johnson. Frank Johnson."

"What's in these crates, Frank?"

"Darwin virus."

"Going where?"

"Test sites around the country. We're perfecting the programming, need a few more mass tests."

"A few more?" asked Rogan, looking around at the vast number of crates.

"Well, comparatively a few."

"What do you do here, Frank?"

"I'm the project manager for this facility, and that is all you are getting out of me."

"I doubt that."

"I'm not afraid to die. I believe in what we are doing."

"Who said anything about dying?"

Rogan kicked the man hard in the ribs. He curled up on his side. Rogan removed all the bullets from his pistol. He showed them to Frank, and then he put one back in the cylinder and gave it a spin. He pushed the pistol down onto Frank's knee.

"A key. I need a key to the holding cells out in that hallway. One bullet in this gun. Every time I pull this trigger, it might go off, it might not. Neither of us will know until it happens. A little game I learned from the Russians. Give me the key and the game stops," said Rogan, squeezing the trigger. Frank stared at Rogan. Rogan pulled the trigger all the way. *Click.* Frank flinched. Rogan began squeezing the trigger again. He stared into Frank's eyes with deadly intent.

"Wait! Wait! In my desk, top drawer, big key, yellow top. You can't let them out. You have no idea what they are capable of."

"Unfortunately, I do, Frank. We've just come from Evergreen, one of your so-called test sites. Watched a lot of innocent people die the last couple days at the hands of those monsters you're making."

"It's necessary."

"Got the key," said Troll, standing behind the oak desk and holding up a yellow key.

"Is there an antidote?"

Frank spit up at Rogan. Rogan rolled his eyes, picked Frank up by the collar and slammed him into the wall. He never understood why bad guys spit. He held Frank off the ground by the collar, staring into his eyes.

"Here's how this is going to go. Tell me where the antidote is, or, I throw you in with one of your science experiments down the hall."

Frank stared at Rogan with cold eyes. Rogan dropped him to the ground.

"Fine," said Rogan. He grabbed Frank by the back of the coat and dragged him across the floor. Frank kicked and flailed, trying to break free, but Rogan's grip was too tight.

"Wait," said Troll, who was staring down into an opened crate.

"What?" asked Rogan in a tone more frustrated than he intended.

"I found it. There's a briefcase in each of these marked antidote."

"Well done... Grab as many as you can manage."

"Got it. What's this?" asked Troll, holding up a blue binder with the stick figure fish emblem on it.

"Frank?"

"Go to hell."

"This is getting old, Frank," said Rogan as he laid another brutal kick into Frank's side.

"Directions..." wheezed Frank.

"That sounds useful. I'll take a few with us," said Troll.

"Everyone else in this complex as dedicated as you, Frank?" asked Rogan, planting a foot on Frank's chest.

"We are true in our belief. You may not see it, but we are doing this for the betterment of the world. You don't stand a chance; everyone here believes in what we are doing, and we're all willing to die for the cause. You aren't making it out of here alive."

"I think we'll be just fine. What is this grand plan?"

"To save humanity. Now kill me, I'll say nothing more."

"Save people by killing people? That's a new one..."

"Someday you'll understand. Now just kill me."

"If you guys believe this is going to save the world, why bother with an antidote?" asked Troll.

"It's for our soldiers and researchers. We can't risk them getting the virus while they are researching its effects," volunteered Frank.

"What does my sister have anything to do with this?"

"I don't know your sister."

"Come on. Your evil lab was in the basement of the building she was shot in after a bum lead. What's the connection?" asked Rogan, pressing his pistol into Frank's shoulder.

Frank turned his head away from Rogan and closed his eyes. Rogan pulled the trigger. *Click.* Frank kept looking away. *Click.*

"Stop. Stop...okay? I'm sorry, I don't know anything about that. Really, you have to believe me. Just shoot me and get this over with."

"No. Troll, tie him up, gag him. We're going to have another conversation when we get back to Evergreen. I want you to see what you've done."

While Troll restrained Frank, Rogan used the fork lift to move all the remaining boxes to the center of the room. He then went around and picked up the automatic rifles that had ammo left and unloaded them all into the pile of crates. A strange green liquid oozed out of the bullet holes and onto the floor.

"Let's do a quick search, see if there is anything else useful, then we're out of here," said Rogan.

Troll nodded and started working his way around the room. Rogan walked to the desk and rummaged through the drawers. He found basic office supplies and a shipping manifest. It showed fifteen locations where loads of Darwin were meant to go. According to the manifest, none of the product had left yet. Behind the desk, a door opened to a supply closet. It contained more guns, ammo, and blocks of plastic explosives with timed triggers. Rogan smiled and pulled out twelve blocks of the explosive. He placed four of the charges around the pile of crates and one in the elevator.

"What are we doing with them?" asked Troll, motioning towards Clay and Frank Johnson.

"I've got some ideas. Load them up on that jack," said Rogan, putting a fresh set of rounds into his 686.

Troll loaded Clay and Frank up on the pallet jack along with several of the cases marked antidote and pulled it towards the main doors, which buzzed when he approached. He pushed through the heavy doors and out into the hallway. Rogan set the timers on the explosives, grabbed the silver case of money off of the desk, and followed. They stopped in front of Tanya's cell. Troll inserted the key, and the lock clicked open. He went inside and picked up Tanya, placing her gently on the dolly.

"Help me with him," said Rogan, picking up Clay by one shoulder. Troll grabbed the other and they dragged him into the cell. Rogan took out his pocket knife and cut his restraints. He was still out cold. Troll looked at him with a question on his face.

"Justice." Rogan walked out of the room. He placed a brick of explosive on each of the locks of the reinforced doors holding the Darwin patients at the highest level and another brick on the hinges of each door. Frank screamed through his restraints, pleading eyes stared up at Troll and Rogan.

Troll pulled the dolly carrying Tanya and Frank. Rogan led the way, revolver in hand. They reached the elevator and went up to the next floor. The two walked down the long narrow hallways, the dolly barely fitting. Troll worked the dolly into the elevator to the surface. Rogan pressed the up button moments later a buzzer dinged and the door opened out into the elevator alcove. Troll rolled the dolly out into the lobby. Rogan dropped a brick of explosive on the floor of the elevator, pressed in the trigger, and then pressed the down button.

Rogan led the way down the hallway towards the cargo area. He clipped more rounds into his pistol as he scanned the area. Troll followed close behind with the cases of antidote, their prisoner, and Tanya rolling behind him on the dolly. Rogan stopped with his hand on the door to the cargo area. He could hear a beeping.

"You hear that?" asked Rogan.

Troll nodded and pulled his earbud out of his pocket. Rogan reached in his pocket and pulled out the small plastic bud. It was indeed beeping. He put it in his ear.

"Angus?" said Rogan as he pushed open the cargo room door.

"Trap!" screamed Angus. "Can you hear me? It's a trap!"

Rogan immediately registered the men with automatic weapons. He grabbed Troll by the arm and yanked him behind the overturned metal desk that he had hid behind years before. Bullets slammed into the old, solid desk.

"How many?" asked Rogan.

"It's hard to see, low light, but I'd say ten give or take," said Angus.

Rogan peered around the edge of the desk. The men were hiding behind pillars and other obstructions. From his vantage point, he could only see three men. He worked his arm around the desk and fired a round at the nearest man. He managed to hit him in the kneecap. The man hollered and fell backwards, a spray of automatic fire arching towards the ceiling. Rogan heard another holler following a blast from Troll's shotgun. Rogan rolled out and laid down a few more shots; one connected. He sat with his back to the desk and reloaded his revolver while Troll laid out a series of shots.

Troll crouched back down and thumbed a few more rounds into the shotgun. Rogan noticed the dolly sitting near the open door to the office area. The cases were riddled with bullets. He could see blue ooze coming from several of them. He could see Frank wiggling around behind the cases. It appeared that the cases were stopping the bullets. Tanya was tucked up tightly behind the cases. She appeared to be safe for now. Rogan saw one case that had fallen to the ground next to the dolly. It looked to be unharmed. He needed to get that case before the men with machine guns managed to hit it.

"How are you on rounds?" asked Rogan.

"Good."

"Me too. I figure there are eight left out there. I need to get that case before one of them shoots it," said Rogan over the report of bullets contacting the desk and wall.

Troll nodded. "I got you."

Rogan crouched like a sprinter and stared at the case. As Troll rose up from behind the desk and blasted away, Rogan ran as fast as he could for the case. He grasped it and rolled behind the pillar that Sarah had hid behind as bullets whizzed over his back. He crouched behind the pillar and cracked open the case. Inside was a series of vials. They were undamaged.

Rogan glanced around the pillar and took a head count. It looked like Troll had taken down a couple more while he was covering Rogan's dive. He looked over at the dolly. Tanya seemed to be free of bullets, but it didn't look like the metal cases were going to hold up much longer.

Frank wriggled off of the dolly and began crawling towards the remaining gunmen. Rogan aimed his pistol at Frank, who just kept crawling. He considered firing on the restrained man, but he couldn't bring himself to do it. Rogan watched out of the corner of his eye as Frank managed to crawl past the pillar and the desk. Just then, Rogan noticed a flash of light from the balcony at the far end of the cargo area. Frank's head exploded against the concrete floor. Rogan yanked his head back behind the pillar as another shot from the sniper slammed into the back wall, intended for him.

Another splay of bullets slammed into the desk as Troll fired off two more rounds; both connected. Rogan jumped to his feet and fired all six rounds he had left at far balcony. He cursed as he realized he'd just wasted bullets on an unlikely target. He let his emotions get the better of him. He couldn't believe he was having another shootout in the same warehouse where his sister was shot, and that there was a sniper shooting from the exact same spot. Rogan snapped rounds into his empty pistol and tried to think as another flock of shells flew past him. He patted his pocket and remembered the plastic explosive.

Rogan smiled and then dove back behind the desk. Troll was desperately slamming rounds into his shotgun.

"Nice standoff we have here," said Troll.

"Yeah and we need to end it. At some point they are going to get people around the other side to flank us. Then we're toast. We need to get Tanya and the antidote and get the heck out of here."

"Plan?"

"Cover your ears and duck," said Rogan, pressing the trigger into his last block of explosive. Rogan tossed the brick over the desk and out to where he suspected the gunmen to be. He ducked down behind the desk and covered his ears. The ground thundered as hot fire burst around the top and sides of the desk. The intense explosion slid the desk towards the dolly, taking Rogan and Troll with it.

As the dust settled, Rogan cautiously got to his feet. No bullets flew in his direction. Without thought, he ran towards the far end of the cargo area. On his way through the room, he saw that his bomb had worked. Several men in black fatigues were spread out across the floor, several in pieces. He ran up the stairs to the balcony where the sniper had been. There was no sign that anyone had been up there, not even a bullet casing or a footprint.

Troll stood up and looked around at the carnage. Then he spun around and pushed over the stack of cases. He smiled as he saw Tanya curled up on the base of the dolly, completely free of bullets. He scooped her up in his arms, grabbed the briefcase Rogan had managed to save, and headed for the outside door.

Rogan searched every inch of the balcony and the small empty office attached to the platform. He hoped he would find blood, but he found nothing. He wanted to stay and search more. He was convinced that all of this was somehow connected with what happened to his sister. He didn't have time, though— as much as he wanted to find out what really happened those many years ago, people were counting on him, and he had to get that antidote back to Evergreen. Rogan ran back through the cargo area, scooped up the case of money he had recovered from Clay, and ran after Troll.

✳ ✳ ✳

The explosion shook the hallway. The cloud of debris from the loading area blasted out through the double doors and flew down the hall, pelting every surface with hunks of wood. Clay Stevens fell to the floor. He was groggy, disoriented. His ears buzzed and his head ached. He stood up, using the nearest wall for support. *What happened?* he thought, trying to stop the world from tumbling around like a cactus weed. *I tangled with Richard Rogan*, he thought, *that's what happened. Just my luck him and that behemoth were up in that shit hole during the experiment. I should be down in Texas already, picking up some girls in my new dually Ford.*

Clay stumbled out in the hallway. He couldn't believe Rogan had actually left him alive. He looked around at the debris caking the walls and the floor. Thick dust hung in the air, making it hard to see. *Hope the elevators are okay,* he thought, turning the corner.

He stopped cold. Standing in front of him, facing away, stood a man and a woman. The man wore green boxer shorts with dogs printed on them. The woman had on a white sports bra and a pair of yellow underwear that read "Party Girl" across the rear in bright pink letters.

Clay took a slow step backwards, hoping the couple hadn't seen him. His cowboy boot crunched in the debris. He froze. The man and woman turned their heads back at him. When they saw Clay standing there, they looked into each other's eyes and grinned.

"Oh shit," said Clay.

* * *

The black Suburban hummed down the road towards Evergreen. Rogan drove while Troll sat in the front passenger seat. Tanya lay unconscious in the backseat. Rogan hadn't said a word since walking away from the exploding complex. He felt himself starting to calm down. He knew he'd let his anger take it too far. He couldn't stop thinking about Sarah. Somehow all of this madness was related, but he couldn't make the puzzle pieces stick together.

"Rogan, you okay, buddy?"

"Yeah, Troll. I'm fine."

"That was crazy back there. I learned a lot about myself, and I'm not sure I like some of it."

"I know what you mean, man."

"Does it get easier?"

"What?"

"Killing people."

"No, not even a little bit. I'm sorry you were involved in that, Troll."

Troll nodded slightly and looked out the window.

"I also wouldn't have wanted anyone else watching my back," continued Rogan.

"Thanks, Rogan."

The hum of the tires sung along the asphalt of the highway leading from Queen City to Evergreen. Troll continued staring out the window. Rogan patted him on the shoulder. He knew exactly what the big man was going through.

"You're going to have nightmares. You'll see their faces. Sometimes normal, other times twisted, obscured, like Picasso went to work on them. You're probably going to get sick at random times. Other times something will trigger a memory and you'll sit and shake—your teeth chattering. Taking life takes a big toll. It's a weight you'll carry forever."

Troll stared at his hands, opening them and closing them.

"Don't even feel like yours, do they?" asked Rogan.

Troll shook his head.

"It gets better. Eventually your subconscious will stop tormenting you so much, I promise," continued Rogan.

"If we went back in time and went down there again, I'd do exactly what I did all over again, but I just feel so..."

"Empty?"

"Yeah."

"It'll get better, big guy. Truth though, it'll always be with you, lurking around. You have to know, though, that there wasn't a choice. Those guys in the fatigues wouldn't have thought twice."

"My problem is that I didn't think twice either," said Troll solemnly.

They drove in silence for the next couple miles, Troll watching the scenery and Rogan trying to compartmentalize what he had just done. He pictured a prison cell. He pushed all his thoughts and the images of what had happened back in the basement of the factory into the cell. Then he envisioned a key, locking the door up tight. He knew he had to deal with it. He couldn't throw out that key, but for today, there was more work to do, more lives on the line.

"Where the hell am I?"

"Tanya!"

"Troll? What am I wearing?"

"You don't remember anything?" asked Rogan.

"I remember that asshole Clay smacking me across the back of head in the farmhouse and then nothing."

"You were in some sort of lab. I noticed some needle marks on your arms. I think they ran some tests on you, though I couldn't begin to guess what," said Troll.

"Why?"

"Because you didn't respond to the virus. I'm sure they want to know why," said Rogan.

"You guys rescued me?"

"We sure did," said Troll, beaming.

"Thanks. So where are we now?"

"Heading back to Evergreen. We found the antidote, so we are going to try to save as many as we can," said Rogan.

"How is it administered? Won't be easy if we have to give them a shot in the arm or something."

"I'm not sure yet. I took a quick look in the case, but I'm not sure what to do with the vials. No needles in there though."

"Can I see it?"

"Sure," said Troll, handing Tanya the case.

Tanya opened the case and took out one of the vials. The vial was clear and cylindrical, about three inches long and two inches in diameter. The thick liquid in the vial was bright blue. Tanya felt around the lid of the case and found a Velcro pocket. She pulled out a laminated sheet that showed a chemical formula. She stared at the formula for a few minutes, tapping her fingers on the lid of the case.

"It's absorbed through the skin," said Tanya, matter-of-factly.

"How did you get that from that?" asked Troll, pointing at the formula.

"The liquid is charged. It hits the skin and is transferred through the pores based on electrical charge difference. You can see that here," said Tanya as she pointed to a section of the page.

"Wow, you are impressive," said Troll.

"It's actually an ingenious compound. Dissolved in water, it works its way rapidly into the blood stream once administered, and then it hitches a ride through the lymphatic system where it finds and tears apart those little nano-bastards," said Tanya, her cheeks turning rosy.

"Looks like Chinese to me," said Rogan, trying to look at the page in the rearview mirror.

"It's not much clearer to me, to be honest," said Troll.

"Don't feel bad. Chemist, remember? This is kind of in my wheelhouse."

"Finally, something goes our way," said Rogan.

"Those stupid misters!" yelled Troll.

"What?"

"In Evergreen, the entire main street is lined with misters that shoot mist out over the road. If we can get the infected to stand on Main Street and we put that stuff in the misters, we should be able to hit loads of them at once."

"Would that work?" asked Rogan, looking in the rearview.

"Don't see why not. We just have to find a way to get this blue goo in the water supply for those misters."

"Okay. Here's the plan, then. We get to Evergreen. If there are still a bunch of people mulling about, we find the water source, dump the goo, and fire. If not, you two find the source, and I go hunt up some crazies. Get them to chase me back," said Rogan.

"Sounds good. Then we just have to hunt down the stragglers. How fast will it take effect?"

"According to the documentation it should be within seconds, thirty at most."

Rogan pulled the Suburban onto the main street of Evergreen. A handful of infected people roamed around near the diner. Other than that, the town looked like death. Bodies scattered the street. Almost all the windows of the small shops were broken, and several had a body lying over the window sill. Rogan drove cautiously, trying to avoid the fallen townspeople.

"Looks like I get to play bait," said Rogan, pulling up behind the sheriff's office. "Find the source, get that goo going, and I'll round 'em up."

Troll and Tanya got out of the vehicle and ran into the sheriff's office. Rogan slammed on the gas. The Suburban blasted down the alley behind the buildings.

Rogan laid on the horn, honking it repeatedly while he drove. He circled the town, heading out by the lake, through the winding residential roads, and finally along the edge of the woods. As he drove, groups of people came out. Most of them started chasing the black SUV immediately. Rogan fishtailed back onto Main Street, where a crowd was starting to form. He felt like the pied piper leading zombies to a feast.

Rogan slammed on the brakes, skidding to halt behind the sheriff's office. Rogan jumped out of the SUV and ran through the back door of the sheriff's office. Troll and Tanya were nowhere to be seen. Rogan locked the door and ran up to the roof.

A large crowd had formed in front of the office. The crowd grew rapidly as Rogan started to hoot and holler from the roof. A couple men with torn shirts and ripped muscles leapt to the roof's edge and started pulling themselves up. Rogan stomped at their hands and heads. One of the men let go and fell back into the crowd as the misters turned on. Rogan stumbled backwards.

The remaining man hanging from the roof managed to clamber on top of it. He stared at Rogan with deadly intent. Rogan reached for his pistol, but then he remembered that it was empty. He backed across the roof line as the man walked towards him. Suddenly the man let out a guttural yell and tackled Rogan to the roof.

Rogan felt the shingles digging into his back as he and the wild man slid backwards down the roof. Rogan tried to wrestle the man off, but the wild man was too strong. Their momentum sent them over the edge of the roof and onto the ground behind the sheriff's office. Rogan felt the air rush from his lungs as the muscled man landed on top of him.

The man screamed into the air and slammed both fists down at Rogan. Rogan turned hard to his side, glancing away most of the massive blow. He threw his elbow as hard as he could into the temple of the wild man. The wild man rolled backwards and got to his feet. Rogan struggled to his feet. The man acted as if a small mosquito had bit his forehead and nothing more.

"Come on big boy, let's do this," taunted Rogan.

The wild man howled, spreading his clawed hands wide. Rogan could barely stand. The abuse his body had taken over the last few days was taking its toll. He wobbled back and forth, doing his best to look foreboding. The wild man reared back, ready to leap. Just then, Troll and Tanya rounded the corner.

"Hey, over here!" yelled Troll, running around the back of the sheriff's office.

Rogan looked over to see Troll and Tanya running towards him with what looked like green cannons in their hands. The wild man barred his teeth and leapt towards them. While he was in air, both Tanya and Troll pulled back the triggers on their green guns. Streams of water burst from the end, spraying the man. He landed on the ground and rolled around in pain, pawing at himself like he had just rolled over a fire ant hill. Then, after a few more seconds, he simply stood up and walked away.

"Nice work," said Rogan.

"Thank you," said Troll, smiling.

"Squirt guns?" asked Rogan.

"Yeah. The hardware store down the street always had a bunch of them," said Tanya.

"Awesome. You were just in time," said Rogan, getting to his feet.

"Looks like it worked. I wonder where they're wandering off to," said Tanya.

"The first day we noticed the wanderings, the zombie-like ones that just bumped into stuff, they went home in the morning. Maybe the same deal here?" asked Rogan, rubbing his sore chest.

"Could be," said Troll.

"We'll need to clear the woods yet and see if any of them are hiding out in the buildings or down by the lake," said Tanya.

"There's antidote left?"

"Yeah, our chem wiz here figured out the exact dilution amount for the misters on the run over there. We have several vials left. Should be plenty to hit the rest of the town."

"Once people start coming around, I'll get a group together and round everyone up."

"And somehow drive them back here? They are still going to be dangerous in smaller numbers, maybe more so," said Rogan.

"Thus the squirt guns," said Tanya, smiling.

"Nice. Let's get me one of those cannons and go hunting, then," said Rogan.

"Mind if we get me some pants first?" asked Tanya.

The three stared at each other for one unsure moment. Then Tanya smirked, and the three laughed together.

19.

The smell of pancakes searing on the griddle made Rogan smile; he had missed his diner. For almost a week he had neglected his morning ritual of going to the diner for pancakes with blueberry syrup. It was something he had done every single day since his father had died. He sat in the same booth every morning, staring at the bench across the table. The old green booth seat had a large indentation where "Big Mike" Rogan used to sit and eat breakfast with his son every morning.

After the deaths of his immediate family "Little Richie" Rogan had bought the diner, which was simply called The Diner. He couldn't allow the small, cramped diner to close. Rogan's dad and his dad's brothers in blue used to call Rogan "Little Richie" when he was younger. When Rogan grew into his 6'2" height and 240 pound body, his dad was the only one he allowed to continue using the name. Though, in later years, even his dad had dropped the little part. He would never admit it to anyone but himself, but the real reason Rogan had bought The Diner and ate at it religiously at the same time every day was because he believed in ghosts. Rogan hoped that, if he tried long enough, his dad would come back and eat with him one more time.

Edna, the ever-silent waitress, slid Rogan's high stack in front of him with a compliment of butter and blueberry syrup. She sauntered away as McKenzie walked through the door. She waved to Delores, the crafter of the lightest, fluffiest pancakes on this edge of the world, as she walked by. Edna and Delores had been with The Diner since the day it opened, over forty years ago.

"Imagine that! You're here," said McKenzie, sliding into the booth beside Rogan. She knew better than to try to sit in the spot reserved for Rogan's dad.

"Of course. Celebrating."

"Chalk up another one for the good guys."

"Not without causality, but yes. Heard from Troll this morning. Sounds like they've flushed out all the leftover Darwin cases, and he's coming back tonight."

"That was nice of him to stay back and help."

"Yeah, also odd how he sent me and Angus packing as soon as we got new tires on the van."

"Oh that's cute. Trolly has a girlfriend."

"I could see it. She likes fishing and hunting and all that, and they're both super nerdy."

"It's a pittance, but that two million bucks from Clay should give them a start on rebuilding their town."

"I hope so. I just wish we could have stopped the infection before so many died."

Edna walked over and placed a cup of green tea, scrambled eggs, and white toast down on the table, smiled at McKenzie, and walked away.

"How come she smiles at you? I get no love," said Rogan.

"Maybe 'cause I'm nice to her."

"I'm nice."

"Oh really? You come in here, slam down in your booth, and stare like a crazy person. Have you even so much as grunted your order in the last few years?"

"Okay, you may have a point, but it's a weak one," said Rogan, pointing his fork at McKenzie. "How's Sam?"

"She's good. No major injuries, fortunately. Broken arm, scrapes, bruises. They are going to let her go tonight. Super mad at you by the way."

"Par for the course."

"She did point out that you were such a prick that you hadn't even tried to stop by yet, which is good because she would probably beat you with her cast. Which in your twisted way of talking to each other, I think it means she'd like to see you."

"Well, that's something. And Lizzy?"

"She's good. One tough cookie. I have some friends with child protection. I'm going to make sure she gets the star treatment," said McKenzie.

Rogan hoped she would be okay. She'd been so brave. Not only had she lost her parents, but she'd found herself in the middle of possibly one of the craziest situations that one could find themselves in. Other than a few hours of staring blankly at a wall, Lizzy had taken it all in stride. Rogan decided he would do whatever was necessary to make sure she had a bright future.

"So what's next?" McKenzie asked, after a short silence.

"I don't know. We just keep getting more questions. I think we're grabbing onto the edge of something big with this Darwin thing. I mean, they sniped one of their own guys. The lab was well-funded. I don't know who these people are, but I think we are on a path to tussle with them."

"Well, you know we're in. I don't think any of us would turn away from finding and stopping whoever was behind what happened back in Evergreen."

"It's going to get more dangerous. These guys aren't afraid to kill people, obviously."

"Speaking of, how's Troll? How are you?"

"He'll get by. Fortunately, he's distracted right now. Me? I'll get through too. I regret what I did because it was from a place of anger. I completely lost control of myself. Once I saw where their compound was, it was like another person took over."

"That was a very odd coincidence..."

"There's no way that was a coincidence. The way Clay talked, if he can be believed, that is, these people pull the strings on the police force. I'm guessing they have roots spread out in lots of places, and I know they had something to do with my sister's death. "

McKenzie put a hand on Rogan's wrist. Rogan stared at his pancakes. He could feel his anger rising again. He closed his eyes and breathed out slowly.

"What about that book Troll found in the crates?" asked McKenzie, trying to change the subject.

"Tanya says that there are directions on how to deploy the virus. She thinks it is given as a shot."

"Really? How did they manage that?"

"Community flu shots a few weeks ago."

"Wow... Conspiracy theorists are going to love that one. So they get a shot and then go cuckoo?"

"No. First those little robot things multiply in the body, and then they are triggered."

"Triggered?"

"Yeah, it was hard to tell with all the bullet holes through the binder, but Tanya thinks the robots are turned on remotely by satellite."

"Then why the antidote? Why not just shut them off?"

"No idea. Like I said, everything we find just leads to more questions. I do know that these people have to be stopped. We can't let them do this to another town."

McKenzie and Rogan sat silently for a moment, each remembering the hell that had descended upon the small town of Evergreen. Rogan twirled his fork through his syrup and stared again at the depression his dad used to fill in the booth bench across from him. He wished more than anything that his dad would be there. He always had the answers. He would just give a big smile, slap Rogan on the back, and tell him what to do.

Rogan knew one thing, though. Even without his dad's guidance, he would do whatever he could to stop the people who did this to Evergreen. He would stop them, and he would find out how they were involved with his sister's death. Rogan felt his jaw tighten. His mind was made up.

"So what do we do?" asked McKenzie.

"We find them."

The End

About the Author:

Keith Allen lives in South Dakota with his fantastically supportive wife Becky and his best friend/dog, Callie.

Would you like to be the first to hear about New Releases from Keith Allen, including Medium, the sequel to Evergreen?

Sign up for his New Release Mailinglist:
http://www.KeithAllenAuthor.com/mailinglist

Other ways to communicate with Keith Allen:
Website: http://www.KeithAllenAuthor.com
Twitter: http://www.twitter.com/KeithAllenBooks

www.ingramcontent.com/pod-product-compliance
Lightning Source LLC
Chambersburg PA
CBHW051329250626
47155CB00007B/2508